He speaks to Miranda in her dreams . . .
but lingers even when she's wide awake.

"Help me," Nathan said to her. The soldier in gray, the young man with the helpless, haunted face. *"You're the only one."*

And his pale, outstretched hand . . . a short length of twine, woven, knotted . . . only *this* time her fingers brushed over it, this time her fingers closed around it.

Miranda touched his hand. His skin was ice cold; her fingers passed right through.

"Take it . . ."

Jerking upright, she saw the figure beside her bed.

The figure veiled in shadows, just beyond reach of the moonlight through her windows.

She tried to cry out, but couldn't; her heart leapt into her throat and stuck there as she gasped for breath.

"No!" Miranda choked.

She closed her eyes, willing him away. When she opened them again, he was gone.

Yet Miranda wasn't comforted. Tears ran down her cheeks; her covers were damp with sweat. She reached for the lamp on her nightstand, then suddenly froze.

She was holding something. Something clutched tightly in her hand.

Puzzled, she spread her fingers and looked closer. In the room's pale glow, she could see the small, familiar object nestled there against her palm.

"Oh my God . . ." she whispered.

It was a piece of braided twine.

Walk of the Spirits

Richie Tankersley Cusick

speak
An Imprint of Penguin Group (USA) Inc.

SPEAK
Published by the Penguin Group
Penguin Group (USA) Inc., 345 Hudson Street, New York, New York 10014, U.S.A.
Penguin Group (Canada), 90 Eglinton Avenue East, Suite 700, Toronto, Ontario, Canada M4P 2Y3 (a division of Pearson Penguin Canada Inc.)
Penguin Books Ltd, 80 Strand, London WC2R 0RL, England
Penguin Ireland, 25 St Stephen's Green, Dublin 2, Ireland (a division of Penguin Books Ltd)
Penguin Group (Australia), 250 Camberwell Road, Camberwell, Victoria 3124, Australia (a division of Pearson Australia Group Pty Ltd)
Penguin Books India Pvt Ltd, 11 Community Centre, Panchsheel Park, New Delhi - 110 017, India
Penguin Group (NZ), 67 Apollo Drive, Rosedale, North Shore 0632, New Zealand (a division of Pearson New Zealand Ltd.)
Penguin Books (South Africa) (Pty) Ltd, 24 Sturdee Avenue, Rosebank, Johannesburg 2196, South Africa

Registered Offices: Penguin Books Ltd, 80 Strand, London WC2R 0RL, England

Published by Speak, an imprint of Penguin Group (USA) Inc., 2008

1 2 3 4 5 6 7 8 9 10

LIBRARY OF CONGRESS CATALOGING-IN-PUBLICATION DATA:
Cusick, Richie Tankersley.
Walk of the spirits / by Richie Tankersley Cusick.
p. cm.
Summary: After losing everything in a Florida hurricane, seventeen-year-old Miranda and her mother move to her grandfather's home in Louisiana, where she falls in with an interesting group of students, and discovers that she can communicate with spirits like her grandfather did.
ISBN 978-0-14-241050-9 (pbk. : alk. paper)
[1. Ghosts—Fiction. 2. Space and time—Fiction. 3. Louisiana—Fiction. 4. Mystery and detective stories.] I. Title.

PZ7.C9646Wal 2008
[Fic]—dc22
2007036073

Speak ISBN 978-0-14-241050-9

Printed in the United States of America

For Aunt Deanie and Uncle Jim—because your love, support, and laughter through the years have inspired me more than you could ever know. I love you.

Walk of the Spirits

1

SHE WAS TIRED TODAY BECAUSE OF THE SCREAMING.

That horrible screaming that had woken her up last night, just like it had the night before. Screams out of the darkness that cut into her heart like razor blades; distant, muffled screams that trapped her and dangled her precariously between consciousness and full-blown nightmares.

"Miranda?"

At first she'd thought it was the hurricane all over again. Shrieking wind, screeches and groans of the roof and walls splitting and exploding around her. Or maybe her mother's cries of terror. Or her own hysterical weeping . . .

But then, of course, she'd realized where she was. In a different bed, in a different house—far from Florida, far from the home where she'd slept and felt safe. And those screams were so *real.* Much more real than *any* dream could ever be.

She hadn't had a decent night's sleep since they'd moved here to St. Yvette.

Naturally, Mom didn't believe her about the screams; Mom just kept telling her she was imagining it. And the harder Miranda tried to sleep, and the harder Mom tried to rationalize, the worse everything got. Miranda's energy was sapped. Her thoughts strayed down a hundred dark paths. It was impossible for her to concentrate on anything anymore.

"Miranda Barnes?"

"Huh?" Snapping back to attention, Miranda saw Miss Dupree paused beside the chalkboard, fixing her with a benevolent gaze. The whole class turned in Miranda's direction.

For a split second, Miranda wondered what they saw. A slight, not-very-tall girl with short brown hair pushed nervously behind her ears? A nice-enough girl with hazel eyes and a heart-shaped face and a light sprinkling of freckles across her nose?

Or the silent girl, the sullen girl, who, in her three days at St. Yvette High School, had yet to meet their eyes when they passed her in the hall? Who never spoke, never smiled, never bothered to be friendly?

They couldn't see the fear—that much she was sure of. The shock, the anguish, the grief, the emotions that choked her every time she let her guard down.

So she *wouldn't* let her guard down. Not with these kids, not in this school, not in this town. Not now. Not ever.

"Oh. Yes. I'm here," she mumbled. As her cheeks flushed, Miranda's hands clenched tightly in her lap.

"I know you're here, dear," Miss Dupree went on sweetly. "I was just explaining this little assignment we're all going to be working on."

"*Little* assignment?" a voice complained from the front row. "Come on, Miss Dupree, it counts for half our grade!"

"I'm well aware of that, Parker. And just think how much it would count for if it were a *big* assignment!"

The room erupted in laughter while the young man lounged back in his desk and grinned. *Parker Wilmington,* Miranda was already familiar with *that* name. She was sure she'd heard it uttered longingly from the lips of every girl in St. Yvette High, from giggly freshmen all the way up through her senior class. Tall and blond, sea-green eyes, those gorgeous, unruly strands of hair framing his handsome face, no matter how many times he shook them back. Star quarterback, not a single game lost last season. Self-confident swagger, cocky smile, and . . . taken. *Very and most definitely taken.* By the beautiful girl who was sitting next to Miranda at this very minute.

Miranda glanced quickly across the aisle. *Ashley.* Ashley . . . something, she couldn't remember. Ashley Something-or-Other with the long golden hair and the petite figure and the sexy little cheerleader uniform she was wearing today. One of those picture-perfect girls who would always be drooled over and sought after and passionately admired. *So of course she's with Parker Wilmington. Who else?*

Miranda didn't realize she was staring. Not until Ashley turned and beamed her a perfect white smile.

"Miss Dupree's broken us up into study groups," Ashley leaned toward her and whispered. "I asked her if you could be in ours."

It caught Miranda completely off guard. Study group? Oh, God, the *last* thing she wanted to do was be trapped in a group of strangers, especially curious ones. She'd felt the stares in the hallways, in the classrooms, across campus. She was all too aware of her novelty status here at St. Yvette High School as the Girl Who Lost Everything in the Hurricane. And soon, she knew, the questions would come—questions she couldn't handle, traumatic memories she didn't want to relive. So she'd tried her best to keep a low profile. Kept to herself and stayed invisible. Better that way, she'd decided, much better that way. She wasn't ready for socializing yet—not of any kind. She wanted to be alone—*needed* to be alone—to process all that had happened in the last few weeks, to sort everything out. What she didn't want or need right now were people feeling sorry for her or asking those painful questions or trying to butt into her life—

"I'm Ashley."

Again Miranda jolted back to the present. She was getting used to everyone's southern accents, but Ashley's still managed to fascinate her. Extra thick, extra rich, like warm, melted honey. She saw now that Ashley's hand was taking her own and giving it a firm, friendly shake. Conjuring a tight smile, Miranda kept the handshake brief.

"All right, class!" Miss Dupree motioned for silence. "You've had several weeks now to come up with your topics. Just a reminder: I want these projects to be socially oriented. Something that will get you involved in this town. Something to help you learn more about your community and the neighbors you share it with. I want to see some original ideas, people. Something creative and—"

"Gage wants to know more about *his* neighbor, Miss Dupree." On Miranda's left, a girl in black clothes and heavy black eye makeup stretched languidly in her seat. "The one who keeps getting undressed at night with the curtains open and the lights on."

In mock horror, Parker swung around in his chair. "Hey! *You and Ashley* are Gage's neighbors!"

"I *meant* the house behind him," the girl said calmly.

Clutching his chest, Parker gasped. "Gage! You pervert! That's Mrs. Falconi—she's ninety-six years old!"

This time the laughter reached hysteria. Miranda saw the girl give a slow, catlike smile, while a boy near the window—Gage, she supposed—blushed furiously and shook his head.

"Roo, stop it!" Ashley hissed, but she couldn't quite hold back a delighted grin. "Why do you always have to embarrass him?"

The other girl shrugged, obviously pleased with herself. "Because it's so easy. And he's so cute when he's embarrassed."

"All right, people, all right!" Clearing her throat, Miss Dupree struggled to keep her own amusement in check. "Thank you, Roo, for that fascinating bit of information. And should any of us notice a pervert lurking outside our windows tonight, we can all rest easily now, knowing it's only Gage."

The class went wild. Poor Gage went redder.

"Time to break into your study groups." Miss Dupree moved to her desk, then gestured toward the back of the room. "Oh . . . Miranda?"

"I told her she's with us, Miss Dupree!" Ashley spoke up quickly, while Roo regarded Miranda with undisguised boredom.

Miss Dupree smiled. "Then she's in good hands."

As the rest of the kids reassembled themselves, Parker sauntered back and eased himself down beside Ashley, giving her a quick kiss on the lips. Roo pulled her desk in closer. And Gage, flashing Roo an I-can't-believe-you-did-that look, made his way across the room and promptly smacked her on the head with his notebook.

Roo was right, Miranda decided: Gage *was* cute, embarrassed or not. The same height as Parker, but more slender, his shoulders not as broad. Soft brown hair, a little shaggy, big brown eyes, long dark lashes, and sensitive features, despite the huge frown he was currently leveling at Roo.

Gracing each of them with her smile, Ashley picked up a blue sequined pen. "Well, we're all here, I guess. Except for Etienne. Is he working today—do any of y'all know?"

"An alligator probably ate him." Roo yawned.

Trying not to be obvious, Miranda cast her a sideways glance. She could see now that Roo was short—not much over five feet—with a solid body, more curvy than plump. The girl seemed entirely unself-conscious in her long black Victorian dress and black combat boots. A silver crescent moon hung from a narrow black ribbon around her neck; silvery moons and stars dangled from her multipierced ears. Her bangs were long and thick and partially obscured her brows. And she had purple streaks—the same shade of purple as the heavy gloss on her lips—in several strands of her overdyed black hair.

As Roo's dark eyes shifted toward her, Miranda looked away. There'd been a few kids like Roo in her own high school at home, but she'd never gotten to know them. Never even spoken to them, really. In fact, she and her friends had jokingly called them the Zombie Rejects and avoided them at all costs.

"We definitely need his input." Once more, Ashley's voice drew Miranda back. "Etienne always has good ideas." She sat up straighter, pen poised over paper. "Oh, and Miss Dupree said Miranda can be in our group, okay?"

There were nods all around and mumbles of agreement. Parker winked. Gage shot Miranda a quick glance, while Roo still seemed bored. As Ashley made introductions, Miranda did her best to sound polite, but offered no more than that.

"So!" Ashley began cheerfully. "Out of all those ideas we had last time, which one are we going to do for the project?"

Parker shrugged. "They all sucked, and you know it."

"No, they didn't." Gage's voice was soft, gentle, like his eyes, just as Miranda had expected it to be. "I think the Symbolism of Cemetery Art is pretty good—"

"Good why? 'Cause you thought of it?" Roo asked.

"Good because it's . . . you know . . . interesting."

"Yeah, if you're a maggot."

"Well, it's better than Southern Belle Rock Bands."

Roo looked mildly annoyed. "The Development and Liberation of Women Musicians During the Antebellum Era, excuse me very much."

Ashley waved her paper at them. "Come on, we don't have much time. Maybe Miranda has some ideas."

"What?" Instantly Miranda felt four pairs of eyes on her. "Um, no. Sorry."

The truth was, she hadn't been paying much attention these last few seconds. It was something she was beginning to get used to—this zoning in and out of memories when she least expected it, when she was least prepared—but that didn't make it any easier. It still managed to catch her by surprise. *Sad surprise, lonely surprise.* Like just now, when Gage had mentioned something about art and cemeteries, a picture had snapped into Miranda's mind. She and Marge and Joanie in New Orleans over summer vacation, traveling there for a week with Joanie's parents. Shopping; flirting with those cute bellmen at the hotel; sightseeing around town—old buildings, museums, mansions, graveyards. *Was that only two months ago?* It seemed like years. The last really fun thing they'd done together before everything changed—

"What's this?" Leaning over Miranda's shoulder, Gage pointed to some scribbles on the front of her notebook. "Ghost Walk?"

Miranda looked down at the words. Yes, definitely her own handwriting, though she didn't remember putting them down just now.

"What the hell's a Ghost Walk?" Parker asked. His grin widened as he nudged Ashley in the ribs, and Miranda quickly turned her notebook over.

"It's . . . nothing."

"No, really," Ashley urged her. "Really—what is it?"

Don't make me talk about this—I had so much fun then—now it hurts too much to remember . . .

"Miranda?"

"It's . . . like a tour." Miranda kept her eyes on her desk, wishing they'd all just go away and leave her alone. "A haunted tour. My friends and I went on one in New Orleans. A guide takes you around to all these different places and tells you about their history. Except each place has some scary story connected to it—like some horrible tragedy or unsolved mystery."

"I've heard of those," Roo mumbled, far from impressed.

"Of course you have, O Queen of Darkness," Parker shot back at her.

Gage, however, was intrigued. "Do all the places actually have ghosts?"

"Well . . ." *Oh great. How did I get myself into this?* Meeting their gazes now, Miranda stumbled on. "Well, I don't know if *all* of them do—"

"Then why do they call it a Ghost Walk?" Parker challenged, even as Ashley clapped a hand over his mouth.

Miranda couldn't help sounding defensive. "People *have* seen ghosts there. But there's also local legends and superstitions—all kinds of weird supernatural things that have happened in the city."

"So it really is historical, right?" Ashley was squirming excitedly in her seat. "Not just made up?"

"That's what the guide told us—that all the stories are documented. So yes, it's all historical—just more of a *dark* history."

"Miranda, that's *perfect*!" As Ashley squealed, the whole class turned to see what was happening. Ashley immediately told them to mind their own business, then lowered her voice while Parker wrestled her hand from his face. "Oh my God, that's so perfect! That's *the* most perfect idea for *the* most perfect project! You're a genius!"

"What project?" Looking confused, Parker bent toward them. "Our project?"

"Not one single person's had an idea as good as this. And it'll be fun, too! Miss Dupree is going to *love* it!"

One corner of Parker's mouth twitched. He shifted in his desk, stretching his long legs out in front of him. "A ghost tour. Here. In St. Yvette."

"It's socially oriented, right? It involves historical research . . . we'll have to learn more about the community . . ."

Gage nodded. "I like it." He glanced over at Roo, who merely shrugged. A shrug that could have been either pro or con, Miranda couldn't tell.

Ashley, however, was still bubbling over. "Miranda, this is so wonderful! You'll have to tell us more about it! How to get organized, what we need to do, where we need to start—"

"Whoa! Hold on!" Backing up a step, Gage lifted both hands. "Give her a chance to breathe, why don't you?"

"I'm sorry. I'm sorry, you're right. Miranda, do you want us to explain the project to you some more? I mean, maybe we haven't filled you in enough on the details? Or the schedule or how it's graded and stuff? Or maybe you have some questions?"

"I have a question," Roo announced, before Miranda could even open her mouth.

The girl draped herself over her desk. Frowning slightly, she fixed Miranda with a solemn, dark-ringed stare.

"So," Roo said. "How does it feel living with a lunatic?"

"WHAT?"

At first Miranda thought it was a joke. Some private, inside joke the group had decided to play on her, just to see how she'd react.

Except she didn't *get* the joke. She didn't *understand* the joke. And slowly it began to dawn on her that Roo's stare wasn't wavering, that Roo wasn't smiling. And that the others had gone silent, that they were watching Roo with strange expressions on their faces, and there was an undercurrent in the air, like cold electricity.

"What?" she managed to say again. "I don't understand."

She wanted to say more, but her voice stuck in her throat. She wanted to walk away from them, but her stomach had gone queasy.

"Roo," Ashley whispered.

"What's wrong?" Seemingly puzzled, Roo glanced at each of them in turn, then back again at Miranda. "You know," she said matter-of-factly, "Jonas Hayes—your *grandfather*. I mean . . . what's it like? Aren't you scared?"

Parker snorted a laugh. "Jesus, Roo."

Gage said nothing, only folded his arms across his chest. He leaned back against the wall and focused on something outside the classroom window.

"Scared?" Miranda's mind was whirling. Her head was beginning to pound. "What are you talking about?"

"Nothing!" Ashley broke in. Reaching for Miranda's hand, she gave it a quick squeeze. "Look, Roo gets everything mixed up. Don't pay any attention to her."

Miranda's head pounded harder. *Lunatic? My grandpa? Why are they all watching me like that? I can't stand it—*

"Miranda," Ashley sounded alarmed. "Are you okay?"

But Miranda couldn't answer. It was Roo's voice that answered instead, toneless, coming from some far-off place. "I thought she knew about her grandfather. I thought she knew, or I wouldn't have said anything."

"You're so pale." Ashley's hands were on Miranda's shoulders now, patting gently. "Do you want some water?"

"Maybe she's going to pass out," Parker said. "Maybe you should slap her or something."

"Oh, for heaven's sake, Parker!"

"Well, I didn't mean hit her hard—"

"This isn't the football field. Nobody's going to hit anybody."

"I'm fine." Miranda nodded. "Honest. I'm fine." But her stomach was churning, dry heaves almost, at the back of her throat. She should have had something for lunch, should have eaten breakfast like Mom told her to do. "*What* about my grandfather?"

But it was as if she hadn't spoken.

"She *is* pale," Gage insisted. "Do you think she's gonna be sick?"

Parker was instantly on his feet. "Turn her the other way!"

"I told you I'm fine," Miranda snapped back at him, at all of them. Why couldn't they just mind their own business? Wasn't she already going through enough without adding more people and problems to her train wreck of a life?

The classroom, the study group, everything blurred in a hot rush of anger. She wanted to escape, but she couldn't see the door.

And if only it were that easy, Miranda thought. *If only there were some magical door I could just escape through, and be happy again . . .*

Not enough that the hurricane had struck. Everything lost, everything gone.

No house anymore, no possessions. Mom's business completely wiped out. Old friends, dear friends, never-seen-again friends. Some hopefully relocated to places unknown. Others left behind, helpless victims and heartbreaking fatalities of the storm.

"We'll go home again someday," Mom had promised her, trying to sound both brave and comforting. "This is a temporary situation, Miranda."

Miranda had wanted so much to believe her. But deep down, she'd wondered if Mom really believed it herself.

"Just till we get back on our feet," Mom kept insisting. "Just till then. It's not like we'll have to live in St. Yvette forever."

St. Yvette. St. Yvette, Louisiana. To Miranda, who'd spent her whole life on the sparkling white beaches of Florida, they might just as well have been moving to the darkest end of the earth.

"So why can't we just get our own place?" she'd begged her mother. "Why do we have to live with relatives I don't even know?"

"Because." And for just a heartbeat, she'd seen true panic in her mother's expression, a look so foreign that it scared her. "Because," Mom had repeated as the look vanished and her voice calmed. "We don't have anywhere else to go."

Just hearing Mom say it made Miranda want to cry—and she hadn't let herself do that since the disaster. Not since the brutal hurricane had ravaged the Florida coastline and their warm, sunny beach house and the only world she'd ever known. Not since they'd been forced to leave everything—and everyone—behind.

She'd felt sick as they'd driven the rented car into St. Yvette five days ago. The sticky heat choking her breath away, squeezing sweat from every single pore. They'd had to stop at a drawbridge, where she'd caught a glimpse of shrimp boats in the murky water. And on the opposite shore, an old Catholic cemetery, its aboveground tombs rotting away between moss-draped trees. The air so thick and heavy, like being wrapped in wet gauze. The stench of dirty water. A cloying sweetness of flowers. An undercurrent of fresh oil and sweat, raw meat and fish guts.

ST. YVETTE WELCOMES YOU.

She'd stared at the weathered sign on the side of the road.

She'd clenched her arms around her chest to keep from getting hysterical.

I've survived everything else. But I'll never survive this. Never. Not in a million years.

"Well," Mom had said cheerfully. *Way* too cheerfully, Miranda had been quick to note. "So here we are, huh? At last. And actually, it doesn't seem that different from when I left."

That was a million years ago, and do I even care? Miranda's shrug was equally grim. "How old is this place, anyway?"

"It predates the Civil War. There's a lot of history in this area."

"So where are all the plantations and stuff?"

"There're a few nearby. We'll go see them, I promise—"

"And what's that weird smoke?"

Mom had frowned at her, sniffed the air, frowned again. "I don't smell any smoke. You mean, like an actual fire?"

"No, never mind. It's gone now."

The truth was, it had vanished almost as soon as she'd noticed it—more like a thought, really, than an actual smell. And not like a cigarette either, or charcoal, or burning leaves, or any other smoke Miranda was familiar with. Pungent and faint and at the same time . . . acrid and damp . . .

"Don't recognize it?" Mom had pressed her.

"No." *But I* should *recognize it,* Miranda had thought uneasily, without knowing why. *I* should *recognize that smell . . .*

"Hey." Mom was talking again. "Don't be fooled by this side of town. The rest of it's really beautiful."

"You don't know that."

"Well . . . I remember that."

"Things change."

It was like an accusation hanging between them. Mom had been quick to try to dispel it.

"But some things don't. Like mystery. And romance. History and legends and old, old secrets—"

"What secrets?"

"I wasn't being specific, honey. I just meant that *all* small towns have secrets. That's part of their charm."

Miranda had watched more scenery go past the car window. Old neighborhoods. Old houses. Gardens. Civil War statues. Antique shops. Old churches. An elementary school. Another cemetery. An old train depot. A park. An old fountain. Another cemetery.

"Charm's not exactly the word I'd use," she'd muttered. "Try dead. God, it can't get any worse than this."

"Yes," Mom answered quietly. "Yes, it can always get worse."

"Oh. Thank you, Mom. I really needed that positive outlook."

"I *am* being positive, honey. I'm just trying to show you how lucky we are. It could be worse. For lots of people, it's worse. We didn't have to be separated, you and I. We didn't have to go into a shelter. We have each other. We have a home to go to."

"You call this a home?"

"We have family here."

"But you don't even love Grandpa."

"No, Miranda, that's not true—"

"The two of you haven't seen each other or talked to each other in . . . how long? My whole life?"

"It has nothing to do with you. It's—"

"I know, I know. Complicated. Why won't you ever tell me?"

Mom's hands had gripped the steering wheel. "It's nothing for you to worry about. Nothing for you to even think about. This is between Grandpa and me, okay?"

"Fine, Mom. Just fine."

And then the long pause. That long anger-hurt pause before Mom finally spoke again.

"Honey . . . for what it's worth . . . our lives really will be happy again."

"It's not worth much. And how can you even believe that?" Miranda shot back, then instantly felt bad at the flinch of pain on her mother's face.

"I have to believe that, honey," her mother whispered. "I have to . . ."

"—have to hand in your project ideas before you leave," Miss Dupree was saying. "And I expect a rough outline on Monday."

Miranda snapped back to attention How long had she been zoned out just now? Seconds? Minutes? Noting the four intense stares aimed in her direction, she remembered her rude little outburst and felt her cheeks go hot.

"Miranda, are you really, truly okay?" Ashley fretted.

"Of course I am." Trying to avoid Ashley's gaze, Miranda focused on the front of the classroom.

"You scared me," Ashley went on. "I thought for a minute we might have to take you to the nurse."

"It's nothing. I'm just—" As Miranda's brain scrambled, she heard the sound of the bell, Miss Dupree shouting last-minute reminders, the chaos of students spilling out into the halls. Thank God it was last period. Thank God it was the weekend. Thank God she wouldn't have to deal with any more people or conversations for a few days.

Grabbing her things, she bolted for the door. She kept her head down, pushing her way along the noisy corridor, but Roo's words echoed even louder in her mind.

"How does it feel living with a lunatic?"

So what haven't you told me, Mom? And what haven't you been *telling me all these years?*

"Miranda, wait up!"

Miranda walked faster. As a group of kids jostled her to one side, a hand closed around her elbow, steering her over to the wall and away from the Friday-afternoon stampede.

"You passed your locker," a voice said, and she found herself looking up into kind, brown eyes. Gage pointed in the opposite direction from where she'd been going. "Or . . . maybe you knew that."

"Look," Miranda answered irritably. "I just want to get home, okay?" Then, as Gage quickly stepped back, she took a deep breath and started over. "I'm sorry. And I'm sorry for how I acted before. I'm having a terrible life right now."

"I understand. I've had a terrible life myself more than once."

"Yeah, well . . . you've probably never felt like throwing up in the middle of class."

Gage considered this a moment. "No . . . but Roo threw up on *me* once in second grade."

She noticed his dimples now, as he smiled. A totally melt-your-heart smile, shy but sincere.

"—didn't mean it," he was saying, and Miranda focused back on their discussion.

"Didn't mean what?"

"Roo." He sounded apologetic. "What she said back there. About your grandfather."

"Look, I don't know anything about my grandfather, okay? If you want to know something about him, I'm the *last* person you should ask."

"I'm not asking."

"We're living in his garage apartment, but—thanks to my mom—I'm not allowed to meet him." Miranda didn't know why she was telling Gage all this. She certainly didn't want to, but there was something so unthreatening about him that her words kept tumbling out. "I've never talked to my grandfather. I've been here in town five whole days, and I still haven't seen him. Now I guess I know why."

Slowly, Gage shook his head. "I don't understand."

"Well, that makes us even."

Gage didn't seem to mind her bad mood. "The thing is, Roo doesn't mean to hurt anybody. She's just . . . honest."

"That's a tactful way of putting it."

"She says things out loud before she thinks them through."

"Well, she obviously knows more about my family than I do. So what's the story? Why don't *you* tell me?"

Hesitating, he lowered his eyes. "I don't think it's my place—"

"Here's the deal. I was ten years old before I even *knew* I had a grandfather. Alive, I mean. I always thought all my grandparents were dead, because that's what my parents told me. Then one day I was going through my mom's closet, and I accidentally knocked this box off a shelf. And this picture fell out—some man I didn't recognize, with his arm around my aunt Teeta."

"Everyone around here loves your aunt." Gage's soft eyes lifted again to Miranda's face. "In fact, she's about the best person I've ever known."

"I've always loved her, too. I've talked to her on the phone since I was little; she's never forgotten my birthday or Christmas. But the date on that picture I found? It was taken just two weeks before, and Aunt Teeta had written on the back: 'Love from your family.'"

"Wow. What'd you do?"

"I confronted my mother, and that's when she admitted I really *did* have a grandfather. Not only that, but I'd *always* had a grandfather, and not only that, but he *lives* with *Aunt Teeta*."

"And?"

"And nothing. She said they'd been out of each other's lives for years, and that's the way it would always be, and I should let it go."

"You never talked about your grandfather again?"

"I tried to. But Mom just wouldn't."

"What about your dad?"

Miranda's heart clenched. "My dad died before I could ask him. In fact, his funeral was that day—the day I found my grandfather's picture."

"I'm . . . sorry—"

"Don't be. You didn't know."

"So what about now?" Shifting his books, Gage leaned one shoulder against the wall. "Maybe your aunt Teeta could help you meet your grandfather. I bet she wouldn't tell your mom."

"I've almost asked her a couple times."

"But . . . ?"

But what if I finally meet Grandpa, and it all turns out wrong? She couldn't tell Gage what her biggest wish had been since she was ten years old, what she'd hoped and prayed for so desperately. That someday, somehow, maybe she really *could* get to know her grandfather. That maybe Mom and Grandpa would settle their differences, whatever they were. *And that maybe having Grandpa in my life could be like having a dad again . . .*

But before she could answer, voices shouted at the end of the corridor, and Parker, Ashley, and Roo came walking toward them.

"They're calling you," Gage warned her.

Flustered, Miranda started backing away. "Look, I don't know what got into me just now. I never do things like this, I never act like this, I swear. So if you could forget it ever happened—"

"Don't worry." Though his lips showed a trace of amusement, his eyes were warm and sympathetic. "Don't be so hard on yourself. And if it helps any—that stuff about your grandfather is just town gossip."

She wished she knew what he meant. Wished he'd say more, elaborate, explain. But the others were here now—Ashley chattering, Parker arguing, Roo watching Miranda and Gage with sly curiosity.

Squealing, Ashley threw her arms around Miranda, while Gage ducked swiftly out of the way.

"You'll get used to her, Miranda," Parker sighed, pulling Ashley back.

But Ashley broke free at once. "Miss Dupree loved your idea! She can't wait to see how we put it all together. She says it's the most original and creative topic in the whole class!"

"Make that the most ridiculous," Parker muttered.

Miranda tried valiantly to resist Ashley's hug. "Hey. It *wasn't* my idea—"

"Don't be so modest! Of course it was!" Giving Miranda one last squeeze, Ashley got down to business. "Okay. So we'll all meet at the library later and start our planning. You can come, can't you, Miranda?"

"Well, I—"

Parker's loud groan cut her off. "Oh please, not the library. All that whispering gives me a headache."

"You *are* a headache." Roo yawned.

"Let's just go to The Tavern. I need background music."

"Too crowded. Too noisy." Shaking his head, Gage leaned in toward Miranda. "It's a restaurant," he explained. "Not much to look at, but the food's great. Everybody hangs out there."

Roo did a thumbs-down. "Two no votes for The Tavern. It won't get dark for a while—why don't we just go to the Falls?"

Looks passed from one to another, followed by nods all around.

"Have you seen the bayou yet, Miranda?" Gage asked, while she fumbled for an excuse.

"Not exactly. I mean, sort of, from a distance. But really, I don't think I can—"

"Then this'll be a first for you!" Ashley was delighted. "We'll be right *on* the bayou."

Parker nodded, deadpan. "Alligators and water moccasins, up close and personal."

"Oh, Parker, for heaven's sake. Don't listen to him, Miranda. I've never seen any nasty things around there."

"Except for Roo," Parker added. "She can be pretty nasty."

Roo pointedly ignored him. The boys grinned, and Ashley chattered on.

"It's pretty at the Falls, but it has atmosphere, too—kind of spooky. Anyway, the *perfect* place to plan your Ghost Walk."

"It's not *my* Ghost Walk," Miranda said again, frustrated. "And I hadn't planned on going—"

"We'll pick you up at your grandpa's in a couple hours."

"Y'all are serious." As the reality of their project seemed to hit him at last, Parker burst out laughing. "A Ghost Walk in St. Yvette? There's not even twelve hundred people in this stupid town, and most of them are boring as hell. How much—what did you call it . . . dark history?—can there be?"

"Oh, stop whining." Losing patience, Ashley glared at him. "There's bound to be lots of old secrets buried around here."

Secrets, Miranda thought wryly. And what was it Mom had told her that day? *All small towns have secrets . . . that's part of their charm . . .*

She realized Gage was looking at her. She deliberately turned away.

Yes, you're so right, Ashley. There must *be lots of old secrets buried around here.*

Especially the ones in my own family.

3

"WHAT'S GOING ON, MOM?"

Miranda stopped in the doorway and glared at her mother, who was standing in the middle of the room, rummaging frantically through her purse. The upstairs garage apartment was small and stuffy—way too cramped for the two twin beds and antique sofa, the table and chairs, and the oversize armoire that had been brought over from the main house.

Oh, God, how depressing.

Her eyes made a quick sweep of the room, taking in the corner kitchen space with its tiny stove, microwave, mini-refrigerator, and narrow pantry; the old-fashioned lace curtains at the windows; the framed sepia-toned photographs on the pale pink walls. A vase of red carnations sat on the lemon-oiled coffee table, and though Aunt Teeta had done her best to make the place homey and comfortable, even those loving touches couldn't disguise the faint odor of age and mildew, or the relentless heat.

"Hi, honey, how was school?" Still digging in her purse, Mom didn't bother to look up. "Can you believe I have a job interview in about five minutes, and I can't find the keys to Teeta's car?"

"Mom—"

"I know, I know—the heat's terrible. Of all the days for the air conditioner to go out, but I think she's already called someone to fix it, and I've got this little fan running, so—"

"How *could* you, Mom?"

Loose change and crumpled tissues spilled from the purse onto the floor. Miranda's mother gave a cry of frustration and bent to retrieve them.

"How could I *what,* honey? Let the air conditioner break? Since when have I known the first thing about air conditioners? Okay, be honest—do you think this blouse is okay? Professional enough? I had to borrow it from Teeta, so it's a little big and—Oh, I almost forgot. She picked up a few things for you on her lunch hour today . . . wasn't that nice? Some shorts and T-shirts she thought you'd like—"

"How could you not have told me?"

"About the clothes? Because she wanted it to be a surprise!"

"I'm not talking about Aunt Teeta! I'm talking about how you lied to me!"

"Lied?" Mom was all attention now. Straightening, she fixed Miranda with a puzzled frown. "When? About what?"

"You know what. *Grandpa.*"

The change was immediate on her mother's face. A pretty face, Miranda had always thought—and still so incredibly young-looking, despite the lines of both laughter and pain around those wide, violet eyes; in spite of the gray highlights accenting that dark, shoulder-length hair. But as Miranda continued to stare, her mother's lips tightened, and those beautiful eyes sparked with anger.

"What *about* your grandpa?" Mom's voice had gone cold, yet Miranda pushed on.

"Everyone in school knows about him! Everyone in *town* knows about him! Everyone but me! How could you? How could you have kept—"

"Miranda, calm down. I just . . ." Taking a deep breath, Mom glanced at the clock beside the kitchen sink. "Look, I don't have time to talk about this right now. Your aunt Teeta went to a lot of trouble to get me this job interview, and I have to go."

"This is important!"

"Well, at the moment, *this* is *more* important. We need money so we can pay our own way. Get our own place."

"How can a stupid job interview—or a new house—be more important than my grandfather being a *mental case*?"

Miranda was shouting now, but her mother's tone was emotionless. "I'm sorry you had to hear those rumors. And I'm sure you . . . probably have questions—"

"Gosh, Mom, do you *think*?"

"But I can't go into it now. There's a lot to be said, and we'll need time. Maybe when I get back—"

"I don't know if I'll be here. I have a big school project. I have to meet some kids to study."

"Tomorrow, then. Another day won't make any difference."

"Of course not. I mean, what's one more day compared to seventeen years?"

She watched her mother's lips open, then close again.

Watched as her mother walked toward her and reached out, even though Miranda immediately jerked away.

"I didn't mean for you to find out like this—" Mom began, but Miranda cut her off.

"How *else* was I going to find out?"

There was a long pause. Then Mom said firmly, "I don't want you discussing this with anyone. No matter what people ask you, no matter what people say. This is a private family matter, and it's no one else's business. Understand?"

Miranda didn't answer. The lump in her throat was like dry cotton, and she closed her eyes against a furious sting of tears. Even when the screen door banged shut, she refused to turn around—not till Mom had driven completely away.

I'll never trust her again. Never, as long as I live.

She latched the screen door, then sank slowly onto the couch. She could hear the soft whir of the fan, but not a single breeze stirred the air around her. She felt trapped, her heart broken. When something wet trickled down her cheek, she couldn't be sure if it was sweat or tears or both.

There's no way I can stay here. I'll die if I have to stay here.

Here, with all the lies and shame and questions and secrets surrounding her. Here, with everyone pointing and whispering and gossiping behind her back. Bad enough to be the new kid in town, the hurricane refugee, the outsider—but the granddaughter of the town crazy, too?

I'm more than a freak. I'm a total alien.

Back home, before the hurricane, she'd had so many friends—Marge and Joanie, especially. The three of them had been invincible and totally inseparable. They'd been popular and smart—all of them honor roll students. They'd joined the same clubs, volunteered on the same committees, won awards for the yearbook and school paper, even triple-dated whenever they could. They'd studied together, shopped together, spent hours on the beach, talking and wishing and planning their futures.

And now it's like they never existed. Like it was all just a dream . . .

Of the three of them, Joanie's house had been the only one left standing after the hurricane. There were some shingles gone, and some windows blown out, but the floodwaters had risen only over the front porch and into one small section of their living room. Nobody had expected the storm to be so fierce, so destructive, so deadly. People had done the usual sandbagging, the usual boarding up of windows and doors, the usual hoarding of groceries and water. They'd felt confident to stay at home and ride out this hurricane as they had so many others in the past.

Only this hurricane was different.

And by the time people realized just *how* different, it was already too late.

The beaches, of course, were the first to go. Houses and businesses, docks and boats, hotels full of tourists—everything tossed like confetti, everything split like kindling. Huddled with her mother under a mattress, Miranda felt their whole house fall to pieces around her.

Later, she wondered how they'd managed to survive at all.

Many hadn't.

Friends . . . neighbors . . . loved ones . . . pets—in the aftermath of the storm, as the death toll rose, the shock and grief became unbearable. Without homes or utilities, without the most basic of necessities, thousands of people turned helplessly to overcramped shelters, and their once-beautiful community became a wasteland.

Miranda still couldn't remember everything that happened after the storm. Only that Joanie's father had rescued them, coming in his boat and hauling them out of the rubble. For a week Miranda and her mother and Marge's family stayed together at Joanie's house, discussing their options and what to do. While the grown-ups decided their fate, Miranda and her two best friends clung to one another and cried.

God, how she missed them.

Joanie was still in Florida. Miranda had called her that very first day in St. Yvette, and both of them had cried all over again. Marge's family was staying with friends in Wisconsin, Joanie told her, and gave Miranda the address and phone number.

"Mom says I can't run up Aunt Teeta's long-distance bill." Miranda had forced back a fresh wave of tears. "And you know I don't have my cell phone or computer anymore. I don't know how much I'll be able to call."

Joanie's voice was heavy and sad. "So many people have moved away already. So many of our friends. We're not going to graduate together, but, Miranda, you've *got* to keep in touch. We *all* do. Promise me. Promise me we'll always stay close."

"I promise." Yet even as she said it, Miranda knew in her heart that things would never be the same.

That she and Marge and Joanie would never be the same. *I wonder what you two are doing right now? Thinking of me? Missing me as much as I miss you?*

It hurt too much, remembering. Every time she did, her heart felt broken all over again. *Nobody understands how unhappy I am . . . how alone. Nobody cares.* She hated feeling sorry for herself, but she didn't even know who she was anymore.

Worse, though, was the shame. This shabby apartment over a garage, this nothing little town. Handouts and charity and having to ask for every single thing. And now this . . .

My grandfather. The lunatic.

No . . . as much as she loved and missed her best friends, she doubted she'd be calling them again anytime soon. *Not till I have something to be happy about, not till my life gets better. Which means* never. Pushing those thoughts firmly from her mind, Miranda got up from the couch. She'd taken only a couple steps when suddenly she stopped, frowning, sniffing the air.

Smoke?

That faraway hint of smoke again . . . the same thing she'd smelled that day as she and Mom drove into town. Just like before, no more than a thought—here and then gone again. Puzzled, she crossed the room and peered out the open window above her bed.

No smoke there . . .

The garage stood quite a distance behind Hayes House—

the main house where her grandfather and Aunt Teeta lived. Miranda could see only part of it across the sprawling expanse of lawn and the moss-covered oak trees that shadowed the grass. Of course, she had no idea what the inside of that house might look like—she'd been forbidden even to step through the door. But outside there were gnarled old trees all around, and wrought-iron benches for sitting, and a shady veranda with tall, brick columns. There were azaleas in front, and an herb garden in back, and at night the perfume from all those lovely plants soaked the hot, humid air, floating all the way up to her bed, almost sickeningly sweet. Behind the house, the yard stretched for nearly half an acre, before finally sloping down to a tall stone wall and the park that lay beyond.

Miranda had heard all about Rebel Park. It was the sacred resting place of southern soldiers—not only from the Civil War, but from every war since—and St. Yvette's consummate pride and joy. A tasteful blend of memorial and family recreation, open seven days a week but securely gated at night, a place where people could make use of the walking path, as well as pay their respects.

From here, Miranda's view consisted of lush grass; a large, tranquil pond; the oversize statue of a Confederate drummer boy; and towering magnolia trees. She was glad the actual graveyard was on the opposite end of the park. She couldn't imagine looking out her window and seeing it there, so close, every single day.

From somewhere in the distance, faint voices rose and shouted, many voices together, yet too muffled to understand.

She thought she heard a car backfire—once . . . twice . . . five times. She decided it might be kids setting off firecrackers instead.

She felt uneasy all of a sudden. Nervous to be here alone, though she wasn't sure why. She'd never been afraid to stay alone before, but she couldn't stop thinking about that mysterious odor of smoke. Heavy yet faint; disturbingly real, yet with no more substance than a dream.

"I'm being ridiculous." It made her angry to feel so unsettled. Angry and vulnerable and fiercely defensive. "I must have imagined it."

A cold breath touched the back of her neck.

"No," a voice whispered. *"No . . . you're wrong."*

4

"WHO'S THERE?" Panicked, Miranda whirled around. "Mom, is that you?"

From where she stood, she could see the entire room, even the tiny bathroom through its open doorway. She could see her lone reflection in the full-length antique mirror near the corner. She could see that the whole apartment was empty.

And yet . . . something was here.

Slowly . . . steadily . . . the temperature seemed to be dropping. The air hung heavy and still. She wanted to scream, to run, but her own voice was paralyzed, and her feet stayed rooted to the floor.

"No . . . you're wrong . . ."

It spoke again, that voice. Coming from a place she couldn't find, from a person she couldn't see. A whisper she heard perfectly, though the room was deathly silent.

A distinctly male voice. The voice of a stranger. A voice so hollow, so hopeless, it sent chills down to the very pit of her soul.

Miranda choked out a cry. She didn't realize she'd been holding her breath; she had no idea how long she'd been standing here, transfixed by the empty apartment around her.

But now she could feel the sticky heat, hear the whir of the fan and the buzz of a housefly at the window screen.

Had she slipped into a daydream? How much time had passed? She remembered now: she was supposed to go with her study group; they were stopping by to pick her up. Had she missed them? Had they come and gone without her even hearing? Maybe they'd assumed she wasn't home. Or maybe . . .

A prank?

Her cheeks burned at the thought of it. Maybe they'd played a trick on her—hey, let's scare the new girl with her Ghost Walk idea! Maybe they were down there even now, with their tape recorder and spooky voices, waiting for her to come out so they could all have their big laugh. Or maybe they'd run off already—this'll freak her out, make her *really* think she's crazy!

Miranda flung open the door. She couldn't see a car outside, but that didn't mean the group wasn't hiding somewhere. And though she wasn't exactly sure whether she was trying to get *away* from the source of the voice, or get *to* the source of the voice, she stumbled out onto the landing and down the steps at breakneck speed.

Too late, she saw the figure at the bottom of the stairs—the figure starting up as she was running down. Caught by the momentum, she didn't even have time to shout a warning before the two of them collided full force.

"Whoa! You trying to kill *me* or just *yourself*?"

Miranda reeled from the blow. As a pair of arms steadied her, she staggered back and gazed up at the young man blocking her way.

He was easily six feet tall—long and lean in his muddy workboots, worn T-shirt, and jeans low on his hips. The curved hollows of his cheeks were accentuated by strong, high cheekbones, and she could see taut ridges of sinewy muscle along the length of both arms. His skin looked naturally tan. He had thick waves of jet-black hair tousled almost to his shoulders, and his sensuous lips were pressed hard into a frown.

He reminded her of some wild gypsy.

Once her initial shock had passed, Miranda was furiously annoyed. "What's wrong with you? It's not like you didn't see me coming. Why didn't you get out of my way?"

"And let you fall?" His eyes reflected mock horror. They were the blackest eyes she'd ever seen. "But I'm so much more comfortable to land on than the driveway, yeah?"

The driveway, like so many back roads around town, was a narrow, rutted path of crushed oyster shells. Miranda's anger turned down a notch.

"You could've warned me," she muttered. Her heart had stopped pounding, though she still felt seriously shaken. "How long have you been out here?"

He wasn't frowning at her now. His face was calm and expressionless, which was almost more unnerving. "I'm not stalking you, if that's what you mean."

"Was someone just out here with you?"

"No."

"Are you sure? You weren't talking to anyone a minute ago?"

"There's nobody here but me. And I'm pretty sure I'd know if I was talking to myself."

"Look . . . I *know* I heard a voice."

This time he raised an eyebrow, his gaze sweeping over the empty yard. "And just how long you been *hearing* this voice?"

Was he teasing her? Being sarcastic? Whatever it was, Miranda didn't appreciate it. "Who are you, anyway? What are you doing here?"

"Miss Teeta sent me to fix the air conditioner."

Miss Teeta. Miranda still wasn't used to all this old-fashioned southern courtesy, so ripe with tradition and respect—the yes ma'ams and no sirs and gentle obsession with good manners. The conclusion she'd finally reached was that adults and old people were treated with the utmost politeness, but if you were friends with them, you could preface their first name with Miss or Mr. *Miss Teeta, the real estate lady. Miss Wanda, at the beauty shop. Mr. Louie, who brings the mail each day.* Even Mom had already lapsed into the etiquette of her upbringing—Miranda had heard her referring to the neighbors down the street as Miss Emmeline and Mr. Henry.

"So . . . you gonna let me in?" the young man asked. His voice was deep and slightly husky. Definitely a southern accent, but with something else—*a trace of French, maybe?*—mixed in. Sort of musical and mysterious. *Sexy, even . . .*

"How do I know you're telling the truth?" Miranda stood her ground. "You could be a burglar."

Cocking his head, he jerked his chin toward the apartment. "Me, I'd have to be pretty desperate to rob this place. Not much profit these days in lace doilies and gumbo pots."

So he *had* been in the apartment before. Still trying to

maintain her dignity, Miranda conceded with a curt nod and led the way upstairs.

"Mmmm . . . bet you're really hot," she heard him mumble behind her.

"Excuse me?"

"With the air-conditioning broken"—his tone was all innocence—"it's gotta be over a hundred degrees in here."

As the screen door closed behind them, he strode over to the window unit and immediately began an inspection. Miranda stood watching a moment, then took a seat on the couch. There was no whispery voice in here now.

Could I have imagined it?

"I've told Miss Teeta a thousand times, it's no good to keep fixing this ole piece of junk. Everything's gotta die sometime." The young man seemed to be talking more to himself than to her. As Miranda watched, he wrestled the air conditioner off the sill and set it carefully on the floor.

The prospect of spending even one more minute in this heat was unthinkable. "You mean you can't fix it?"

"I can fix anything, *cher*."

"That's not my name," she corrected him. *And aren't you just pretty impressed with yourself, Mr. Repair Guy.*

For a split second he looked almost amused, but then his features went unreadable once more. While he knelt down to resume his work, she gave him another curious appraisal. She hadn't noticed those scars on his arms before—faint impressions, some straight, some jagged, some strangely crisscrossed. She wondered briefly if he'd been in an accident when he was younger.

Her eyes moved over the rest of his body. He was busy unscrewing the back off the air conditioner, his movements quick and fluid. She saw him glance at her, and she quickly looked away.

"Sorry about what happened," he said. There was an awkward pause before he added, "To you and your mama—the hurricane and all. Must be tough, what y'all are going through."

Miranda stared at him as he bent forward, his hair falling down around his face, shielding it from view. "How do you know about that?"

"Everybody knows about that. And if they didn't already know before you came, I'm sure they knew five minutes after you got here." He shrugged, but didn't look up. "Small town. You'll get used to it."

No, you're wrong. I'll never get used to it. I'll never get used to people knowing my business or invading my privacy. Only Marge and Joanie shared those things with me. Only them.

"I hate it here." The words were out, bitter and angry, before Miranda could stop them. Embarrassed, she turned her attention to the floor. *Great. Now I'll probably be quoted on the six o'clock news . . .*

Repair Guy, however, didn't seem at all offended. "You'll change your mind."

"What do you mean, I'll change my mind?" Another flash of anger went through her. "You don't even know me."

"The town, it has a way of pulling you in." He squatted back on his heels. He wiped his face across one sleeve of his T-shirt, leaving a smear of dirt on his forehead and down his left cheek. "And maybe I know you a whole lot better than you think."

Flustered, Miranda groped uselessly for a comeback.

"You really did hear someone before, didn't you?" He fixed her with a calm, deliberate stare. "And what about the screams? Have you heard those, too?"

5

Miranda couldn't move. It was as if every muscle had frozen in place and her mind had gone completely blank.

She had a sense of his scrutiny, a sense of her own confusion, an endless silence—but it wasn't till the screen door burst open that she was finally able to stumble up from the couch.

"Why, here y'all are!" With a delighted laugh, Aunt Teeta hurried in, her plump arms spread wide, her blue eyes sparkling. "I didn't see your truck outside, Etienne! I was afraid maybe you wouldn't have time for me today."

Etienne? Miranda shot him a startled glance just as Aunt Teeta caught him up in a hug. Hadn't those kids in class been talking about someone named Etienne?

"Hey, Miss Teeta," he said. "Uncle Frank had to borrow it—he'll be passing by in a minute to get me." He still hadn't smiled, Miranda noted, but he didn't seem to mind Aunt Teeta's enthusiastic show of affection.

"All right now, tell me." Releasing him, Aunt Teeta cast a hopeful look at the air conditioner. "Can you fix it—one more time?"

"You know I can."

Another hug. Another laugh. It was always that way with Aunt Teeta. Arms open wide to hug everybody in sight, and that big, warm, contagious laugh that made everyone within earshot laugh right along with her.

Except Miranda didn't feel much like laughing.

"So how do you like my handyman?" Aunt Teeta greeted her, pulling Miranda close. "Isn't he a genius?"

Miranda managed a nod.

"I wasn't sure your mama told you he was coming," Aunt Teeta went on. "But I see you two have already met."

Repair Guy answered smoothly. "We sort of . . . ran into each other."

"Well, I'm so glad. Etienne, this is my niece, Miranda. I wasn't exaggerating now, was I? About how beautiful she is?"

"No, ma'am, you weren't exaggerating at all."

With a silent groan, Miranda glanced longingly at the door while her aunt bustled back across the room.

"And Miranda, this is Etienne Boucher. I'm surprised y'all don't know each other from school."

"I've been working the last few days," Etienne said.

"It's one of those special programs, Miranda." Aunt Teeta's voice lowered, as though sharing some great secret. "He goes to school part-time, and the rest of the time he works. And he *still* manages to charm all the ladies in town."

For the first time, Etienne seemed almost embarrassed.

"And my, but he cleans up good—I've seen him." Winking at Miranda, Aunt Teeta was perfectly deadpan. "It just goes to show you—you can't judge a greasy ole book by its cover."

Hooting with laughter, she gave Etienne one last hug, then headed outside. "I've got some houses to show this afternoon," she called over her shoulder. "But the door's open, and there's iced tea and pecan pie. You know where to find them."

"Thanks." Etienne hoisted the air conditioner into his arms. "Another time, maybe."

"Whenever you can, hon. You know you're always welcome. Oh, and about the heat in here—"

"I'll make sure Uncle Frank brings a unit by and gets it running. Y'all can use it till this one's fixed."

"Darlin', you are my hero of the day!"

"Wait up—I'll walk out with you."

Miranda could only stand there and watch them go. She couldn't believe it. *"And what about the screams?"* he'd said. And now he was acting as if nothing had happened. He'd totally blindsided her, and now he was leaving. *"Have you heard those, too?"*

She started after him, but suddenly noticed the clock. Those kids from her class would be here any second to pick her up, and she wasn't halfway ready.

Damn. Why did I ever agree to study with them? She'd never be able to concentrate. She'd never be able to come up with any ideas. Not now. Not after what had happened to her today, not after what Etienne had just said.

Who is *this guy?*

She barely managed to change clothes before a horn blared from the driveway, sending her reluctantly downstairs.

"Hey!" Parker exclaimed. "A woman who's actually on time. You paying attention, Ash?"

Parker sat behind the wheel of a gleaming red convertible—a

BMW, Miranda recognized at once—with Ashley perched next to him, and Roo smoking a cigarette in the backseat. Etienne was leaning against the car, head lowered, arms crossed on Parker's door. As Miranda got closer, he reached casually for Roo's cigarette, took a drag, then handed it back again. Gage was nowhere to be seen.

"Mosquito bait." Scooting over, Roo stared at Miranda's bare legs. "You should've worn jeans."

"Her shorts are fine," Ashley argued. "I brought bug spray."

Roo had added more makeup, Miranda noticed—more black around the eyes, a black outline around the lips—and the black hair with its purple streaks was now gathered into a strange, twisted configuration on top of her head. Miranda tried not to stare, but she couldn't help it. As Roo slid over to make room, Miranda was taken with the girl's exotic eyes—their pale color of soft, smoky green. Heavy-lidded eyes, daunting in their boldness, yet, at the same time, distant . . . almost dreamy. It was unsettling to look into those eyes. Miranda wondered if it was unsettling for everyone.

"—we'll see y'all there!"

Startled, Miranda realized that Ashley was talking to Etienne, who'd pulled back from the car. In the next second, Parker had revved the engine and shot onto the road, making conversation next to impossible.

"Parker, for heaven's sake, *slow down*!"

The BMW decelerated smoothly into the speed limit. Parker grinned as Ashley glared at him.

"Quit showing off," she scolded, then turned her attention to

Miranda. "I don't know how much of St. Yvette you've seen so far, but I really think you'll like the Falls. It's a ways out of town though, so people sort of forget about it."

"I don't." Roo frowned. "I go there a lot."

"And that way we sort of forget about you, too." Parker spoke up. "So it works out great."

Determined, Ashley kept on. "There's hardly ever anybody out there. That's why we like it so much."

"Well, that and the poisonous swamp. And the man-eating diamondback water snakes. Don't forget those." In the rearview mirror, Parker's eyes widened dramatically. "And then one day . . . the new girl in town went off to the Falls with her friends." His voice deepened, horror-movie style. "And she was never seen again."

"Parker, will you stop? That's not funny."

Though Parker was laughing, Miranda didn't think it was funny either—especially since she'd just suspected them of trying to terrorize her. Not that she suspected them anymore—not after Etienne's disturbing comment—but then again, what did she really know about these kids? What did she really know about Etienne?

Her thoughts grew darker and anxious. *Mom said we'd be safe here in St. Yvette; Mom said our lives would be normal. But that was before I knew about Grandpa, before I heard that voice and those screams in the night—*

"—the Falls," Ashley was explaining once more. "Closer to the water than it used to be. I wish they'd fix it so it wouldn't flood."

This time Miranda did her best to focus. "So . . . it's like, a waterfall?"

"No." Roo exhaled a stream of smoke. "It's like, a cemetery."

"A *real* cemetery?"

"I told you this was a bad idea." Taking a last puff, Roo tossed the cigarette. "I told you it would freak her out too much."

"I didn't say I was freaked out. I just asked if it was a real cemetery."

"Actually, it's a park *and* a cemetery—" Ashley began, but Roo cut her off.

"There was a big battle here during the Civil War. And afterward, there were lots of dead Yankee soldiers who couldn't be identified. So when nobody claimed their bodies, the town built a cemetery for them." She paused, chewed thoughtfully on a short, black fingernail. "Originally, it was called Site of the Fallen Union. But over the years, it got shortened to just the Falls."

"And therein lies the irony!" Parker grinned. "Because, as we all know, it wasn't the *Union* that ended up falling."

Straining forward, Roo tilted the rearview mirror so that Parker's face disappeared from view. He calmly readjusted it.

"There's so much Civil War stuff here in St. Yvette," Ashley said. "Especially on the Brickway. Did you know that practically everything on the Brickway is over two hundred years old?"

Miranda swept windblown hair from her eyes. "I think Aunt Teeta mentioned something about that."

Aunt Teeta had mentioned quite a lot of things about St. Yvette, but Miranda had paid little attention. She'd never been particularly interested in history—not of where she'd lived before, or anyplace else. But one thing she'd learned in her short time here was that these townspeople were fiercely proud and protective of their heritage. And they never seemed to grow tired of talking about it.

"The Brickway goes in a circle," Ashley explained. "About a mile long from start to finish, with—how many buildings?" Glancing at Roo but getting no help, she guessed. "Fifteen? Twenty?"

Miranda made a supreme effort to be polite. "All I know is that it's a street made out of bricks, and it's about a block away from Aunt Teeta's house."

"Oh, that's right!" Ashley remembered. "Hayes House is your family's house! Well, it isn't actually *on* the Brickway, but it's still considered part of the Historic District. We have a really nice museum here—it's run by the Historical Society. And it has guidebooks and brochures and all kinds of information. And Roo and I were thinking—"

"*You* were thinking," Roo corrected, though Ashley ignored her.

"—we were thinking the Brickway might be the perfect place to put your Ghost Walk."

"It's not *my*—" Miranda began once again, but Ashley didn't even slow down.

"So if each of us took a few buildings and did some research on them, I'm sure we could find lots of great scary stories, right?"

"The Falls is supposed to be haunted," Roo said, though she couldn't have sounded more indifferent about it.

"So much for folklore," Parker added. "Have any of us ever seen one single ghost in all the times we've been there?"

"Not all those bodies at the Falls got buried in tombs," Roo explained. "A lot of Union soldiers were dumped in shallow graves, or mass graves—and there's no telling how many ended up in the bayou. There were probably hundreds never even found at all. I mean, they couldn't have picked up every body part lying around."

"So be careful, Miranda," Parker warned. "You might hear a whole lot of little phantom feet marching around there."

"Ewww!" Ashley jerked back in alarm.

"Ah, don't worry," Parker soothed her. "That's why we always bring Roo along. To scare creepy things away."

Roo shot him a glance. "Then how come *you're* still here?"

Without warning the car swerved into the oncoming lane. As the girls screamed, Parker veered back on course and looked immensely pleased with himself.

"Will you quit doing that!" Ashley was furious. "I *hate* when you do that! Don't you realize how dangerous it is?"

"Oh, no, Parker. Please. Do it again." Roo stared grimly at the back of his head. "I just love that sensation of flying through the air and splattering into a tree."

Parker didn't seem the least bit contrite. "*As* I was saying—"

"You've said enough. Now quit being a jerk, and keep your eyes on the road." Still visibly shaken, Ashley twisted around to face the backseat. "The Falls has really gone downhill. It's not nearly as nice as it used to be. Not at all like the Confederate cemetery in town."

Roo grimaced. "Hard to believe Rebel Park was once a battlefield. All that suffering and death."

"I thought you liked suffering and death," Parker threw back. "I mean . . . you always *look* like suffering and death."

"Parker, *watch where you're going*!" Ashley's voice went shrill. "For God's sake!"

As the speedometer dropped down again, Miranda shut her eyes and clutched the edge of her seat. "So Rebel Park, the one behind Hayes House, was the actual battlefield?"

"I'm not sure." Ashley considered a moment. "I mean, it was a huge battle. So the park was probably only part of the battlefield."

Once more, Parker looked in the rearview mirror. "Back then, all this area was farmland and woods and swamps. That's where most of the fighting happened. The town was pretty much spared—mainly because the Union army used it for their headquarters."

"Parker's mom works at the Historical Society." Roo glanced at Miranda. "He really isn't that smart."

Though Miranda had opened her eyes again, she felt edgy and distracted. Something was tugging at the corners of her mind, something vaguely familiar that she couldn't quite identify.

"—slaughter," a voice said.

Miranda jumped. She looked at Roo, who was gazing levelly back at her.

"The battle of St. Yvette was a complete slaughter," Roo said again. "The Confederates never had a chance. You can read about it—all the accounts are equally gruesome."

Parker winced. "Can you tell by now that she's really *into* gruesome?"

"There was so much smoke, it was like nighttime. They couldn't even see the sun."

"Guns and cannons," Parker clarified, while Ashley threw each of them a pleading glance.

Feeling more anxious by the minute, Miranda tried her best not to show it. Roo's eyes were still fixed on hers in a bold, unwavering stare. Almost as though the girl sensed her sudden vulnerability and was closing in for the kill.

"They said the air was actually wet." Roo's tone was somber. "Wet and red. From all the blood spraying everywhere."

Reaching back, Ashley pounded Roo on the knees. "You are *making* that up! Just to be disgusting! Now *stop* it right—"

"Actually, she's not," Parker broke in. "Making it up, I mean. She *is* disgusting."

From the look on his face, it was obvious how much this pained him, taking Roo's side. "The battle of St. Yvette was one of the bloodiest ever recorded around this area. But then, the Civil War was also the bloodiest war up to that time."

And the nag was still there, that persistent little nag in Miranda's head, refusing to be ignored. It pushed her to the edge of her seat and leaned her in close to Parker.

"Why was it the bloodiest?" she asked him.

Nodding, Parker spoke louder. "Partly because of the bullets. Up till then, bullets were round—they didn't hit their targets that well, and they tended to bounce off bone. But during the Civil

War, there were these new conical bullets that were heavier and more pointed. A lot more accurate. A whole lot more blood. Bad infections, too. When a bullet like that tore through a guy's skin, it took dirt and parts of his clothes and who knows what else with it. It was pretty much a death sentence."

"Bet you're glad you asked." Roo slanted a look at Miranda.

But Miranda had sunk back into her own uneasy thoughts. She knew what it was now, that restlessness in her mind—the memory of that strange, familiar smell. And while Parker had been talking, she could *swear* that smell had come to her again—a faint odor of smoke mingled with . . . *what? Sulfur? Flesh? Blood?*

"Oh my God," Miranda murmured.

"Oh, Miranda, I know." Ashley was quick to sympathize. "I can't stand to hear about blood either. I can't stand to look at blood. I can't even stand to think about it! So y'all talk about something else, okay?"

As Ashley went on to scold Roo and Parker, Miranda scarcely listened. What she'd heard and smelled earlier had seemed so totally real. And now this—this Civil War battle—was it related somehow? She'd never even heard of the battle of St. Yvette. Never studied a single detail about it, never read a single historical account. Didn't have the slightest knowledge about artillery smoke or bullets.

So how could this be possible, when it all sounded crazy, even to herself? *Because I can't be* sure, *can I? How can I be absolutely* sure *that I've smelled the battle smoke—that I've heard the cries of the wounded and dying?*

Once again she felt overwhelmed with uncertainty. *I must have seen something about that battle—on TV maybe, or in a magazine. Because the other can't be true, it's too* impossible *to be true.*

And what on earth had ever possessed her to think it?

6

Restlessly, Miranda tried to concentrate on the scenery flying past. It occurred to her that she hadn't noticed any buildings for a while—other than an abandoned gas station and a couple of rotted barns. Trees closed in from both sides of the road, and the road itself had begun to narrow, winding on beneath scattered canopies of moss. When Parker made a sudden left turn into the woods, Miranda felt as if they were all being swallowed alive.

What have I gotten myself into?

The paved road began to disappear. Soon it was nothing more than a trail of mud and crushed oyster shells rutted deep with tire tracks, and barely wide enough for the car. Trees grew even thicker here, shutting out the light. Moss brushed over the top of her head, and she slid lower in her seat.

Even the air had changed. Heavy and wet and overly ripe with smells, and a promise of water close by. These smells were different from the wind-and-surf beach she was used to. These smells were secret and primal and dark.

"Here we are," Parker announced, and the car lurched to a sudden stop. As he killed the engine, a wave of silence engulfed them.

Miranda sat there, eyes and ears straining to adjust. Straight ahead of her, among moss-shrouded trees, was the Union cemetery they'd told her about, and beyond that, the murky waters of Bayou St. Yvette.

"Come on!" Ashley called, and Miranda realized everyone else was out of the car. "This way!"

But Miranda didn't move. She couldn't stop staring at the cemetery.

In a halfhearted attempt at maintenance, someone had recently clipped back weeds and underbrush, leaving a few stone urns holding plastic flowers. But the old tombs—no more than a dozen and built aboveground—lay scattered at odd angles with no hint of order. Some resembled low-lying slabs, suggesting only one or two occupants; others stood nearly as tall as Parker, indicating several inner burial compartments, stacked one upon another. None were marked with names. No grass grew between them. Peeling whitewash hung like scabs, leaving gaps in the powdery brick and rotted plaster. Some tombs had actually sunk into the ground; others were partially washed away, victims of too many floodwaters, she guessed.

Hundreds dead and only these few pitiful graves.

Remembering what Roo had said earlier, Miranda wondered just how many abandoned soldiers had lain in mass graves all these many years, or in the overgrown tangle of the woods, or at the bottom of the bayou.

Despite the sweltering heat, she rubbed a chill from her arms. That heaviness in the air was growing worse—oppressive almost—the way a room could feel when it held too many people.

With a sheer effort of will, she climbed out of the car and

caught up with the others. They were sitting at an old picnic table in a small, concrete shelter.

"Oh, there you are!" Ashley motioned Miranda down beside her. "Wasn't I right? Isn't it nice here?"

Miranda thought fast. "Well . . . there's atmosphere, that's for sure."

"I could never come here all by myself. But when Roo's mad or sad or worried about something, this is where she always runs away to."

"Yeah." Parker sighed. "Too bad she always runs back home again."

"And thank you so much, Ash." Roo forced a saccharine smile. "For sharing my secret place with everybody in the whole entire universe."

"Oh, Roo, I didn't—Look, there's Etienne. I hope he remembered to pick up Gage."

Miranda craned her neck for a better view. What she saw was an old muddy pickup truck lurching slowly along the road, then coming to a stop about thirty feet behind Parker's BMW. There was a half trailer hitched to the back—both it and the truckbed were full. Among the cargo, Miranda could pick out lawn mowers, ladders, chain saws, and a generator.

Jumping casually to his feet, Parker flashed an endearing smile. "Just stay put now, ladies—I'll see if they need any help. I have to get the cooler out of my car, anyway."

Miranda caught the quick glance Roo shot him—something between curiosity and outright suspicion. "Don't bother," Roo said, just as casually. "I'll do it."

Before Parker had a chance to respond, Roo turned and started walking. Parker's expression tightened for a second, then went carefully neutral as he headed for Etienne's truck.

"Wait, Roo, we'll go with you." Ashley gestured to Miranda. "There's some blankets in the trunk, and I forgot the darn bug spray."

Miranda was only too glad to join them—any distraction to keep her mind off the day's unsettling events.

Reaching the convertible, Ashley popped the trunk and started digging inside. Roo immediately hauled out a small ice chest and opened the lid.

For a moment Roo stood there, staring down into the cooler. Then, pulling out a beer, she turned to Ashley and held up the can.

"Nice, Ash. Star quarterback busted for drinking. *Again.*"

"He's not getting busted. And he's *not* drinking—not like before. Especially not since our last fight."

"So what's this?" Roo's glance moved between Ashley and Etienne's truck, where the three guys were deep in conversation. "A root beer in disguise?"

"It's not like he's the only guy at school who has a beer once in a while. It's no big deal."

"It will be when his coach finds out."

"Well, Coach doesn't ever have to *find* out." The implication was clear. "Unless *somebody* tells him."

"Nobody has to tell Coach anything, Ashley. It's amazing all the things you can find out about a guy when he pees in a cup."

Roo gave a mock wave. "Surprise! Good-bye, Parker! Good-bye, scholarship! Good-bye, multimillion-dollar career!"

"He's not even playing right now—not till his shoulder's completely healed. And anyway, one little beer won't make any difference."

"He's scary enough when he's driving and *hasn't* been drinking." Roo's tone was mildly chastising. "Or haven't you noticed?"

Ignoring the comment, Ashley reached back into the trunk, grabbing some blankets and the bug repellent.

"You're not helping him, you know," Roo persisted. "You're enabling him. You're just afraid he'll dump you if you don't go along with what he wants."

Ashley tossed her things at Roo. "Here. You bring these. I'll take the cooler."

It was obvious to Miranda that the argument was over—though she seriously doubted if either side had won. Unsure what to do, she watched Ashley hoist the cooler and march away.

"Love really is blind." Roo let out a gloomy sigh. "Love is also dangerous, insane, and highly overrated."

There was a long pause before Miranda finally asked, "Are you speaking from personal experience?"

"No, from *Ashley's* personal experience. Sisters are *also* highly overrated."

"You two are sisters?" Miranda hadn't meant to sound so shocked, but Roo took it in stride.

"Why are people always so surprised by that? Yeah, we're

sisters. Stepsisters, actually. But our parents got together when we were both three years old—so we've never *felt* like stepsisters. We're not anything alike though."

No kidding. Miranda almost smiled.

At the sound of approaching voices, she turned to see Parker, Gage, and Etienne walking past. Etienne mumbled something she couldn't quite catch. Parker kept his eyes straight ahead, while Gage shot them a quick glance.

Roo tossed the blankets into the backseat, then reached for Miranda's arm. "Stand here and hold your breath."

Miranda felt the first cold squirt of bug spray. Before she could move, Roo had doused her from top to bottom, and she was choking on fumes.

"There. That should do it." After pitching the can into the trunk again, Roo slammed down the lid and leaned back against the car. She fished a cigarette and matches from her jeans pocket. Then she lit up and inhaled a slow, satisfied breath. "So what do you think of Etienne?"

The abrupt question caught Miranda completely off guard. She said the first thing that popped into her mind. "He came to fix our air conditioner."

"Yeah, everybody calls Etienne when something breaks or doesn't work right. He can fix anything. He's got the touch."

"So he said," Miranda recalled.

"Besides, he really needs the money."

Miranda felt suddenly awkward. It wasn't her business to discuss Etienne's private life—yet she couldn't help being a little curious.

"He and his mama run swamp tours back in the bayou." Roo flicked ashes into the trampled weeds. "Tourists really like that kind of thing, don't ask me why. He works construction jobs, too. Mows lawns, cuts trees, takes fishermen out in his boat. Stuff like that."

"Quite a résumé."

"And not bad to look at either." Roo arched an eyebrow. "Or haven't you noticed?"

"I don't even know him."

"You don't have to know him to notice."

Miranda hedged. "Well . . . sure. I guess he's kind of cute."

"Cute? Kind of? I'd say *that's* the understatement of the century."

"Does he have a girlfriend or something?" As Roo flicked her an inquisitive glance, she added quickly, "He keeps calling me Cher."

Clearly amused, Roo shook her head. "It's not a name, it's a . . ." She thought a minute. "It's like a nickname . . . like what you call somebody when you like them. Like 'hey, love' or 'hey, honey' or 'hey, darlin'. It's sort of a Cajun thing."

Miranda felt like a total fool. No wonder Etienne had gotten that look on his face when she'd corrected him about her name.

"His dad's side is Cajun," Roo explained. "That's where Etienne gets that great accent."

Miranda's curiosity was now bordering on fascination. She knew very little about Cajuns—only the few facts Aunt Teeta had given her. Something about the original Acadians being expelled from Nova Scotia in the eighteenth century, and how they'd finally ended up settling all over south Louisiana. And how they'd come to be so well known for their hardy French pioneer stock, tight family bonds, strong faith, and the best food this side of heaven.

"Before?" Roo went on. "When he walked by? He was talking to you in French. Well . . . Cajun French, actually."

"He was?" Miranda wanted to let it go, but the temptation was just too great. "What'd he say?"

"He said, 'Let's get to know each other.'"

A hot flush crept up Miranda's cheeks. It was the last thing she'd expected to hear, and she was totally flustered. Maybe Roo was making it up, just poking fun at her—after all, she didn't quite know *what* to make of Roo.

"Oh," was the only response Miranda could think of.

"He and Gage are cousins, you know."

This was even more shocking than Roo and Ashley being stepsisters. "I had no idea."

"First cousins. Their mothers are sisters—twins. Etienne's mama got cancer a few years ago. She was so sick for a while, we were all scared. She's better now though. They're a really close family—Gage always says it's like he and Etienne each have two moms. And Gage's daddy helps them out a lot—he owns a fleet of trawlers—he hires Etienne on with his crews during shrimp season."

"What about Etienne's father?"

"Dead."

"I'm so sorry."

"Don't be." Roo shrugged. "Didn't you notice those scars on Etienne's arms? His daddy beat him—and his mama—on a regular basis."

Miranda looked away. The unexpected reality of it sickened her. This was something that happened on crime shows, not to people she knew.

"We better get back," Miranda said, not wanting to hear any more. Gathering up the blankets, she tried to switch gears. "So, are you . . . and Gage . . . together?"

"What? Gage and me?" Wryly amused, Roo took another puff of nicotine. "Here's the thing about Gage and me. We've lived next door to each other since kindergarten. There's not much about each other we don't know."

"So . . . best friends forever? That sort of thing?"

"We did have sex once." Roo was matter-of-fact. "But then we decided—why ruin a perfect friendship?" Holding her cigarette at arm's length, she casually studied the black and purple lipstick smudges around its filter. "He was *amazing*."

"I . . . see." Miranda couldn't tell if she was being teased, shocked, or confided in. "Thanks very much for sharing."

"Of course, he'd be completely mortified if he knew I'd told you. He has this real problem about sharing personal stuff."

Roo pushed herself away from the car, dropped her cigarette butt, and ground it underfoot. Then she walked off without a word, leaving Miranda to trail behind. By the time the two of them reached the cemetery, the others were already engaged in a lively discussion.

"There's always the Historical Society. And the Ladies of the Southland." Lounging back on top of the picnic table, Gage drew up one knee and draped his arm across it. "Parker's mom could help with that."

Parker recoiled in mock horror. Taking the blankets from Miranda, he spread them on the ground, plopped down, and pulled Ashley down beside him, not bothering to hide the beer he was drinking. "No! No way! Leave my mom out of this."

"Just see if she'll talk to us, Parker," Ashley insisted. "Think of it as investigative reporting."

"Hey. Lois Lane. Mom and I don't like seeing each other any more than we have to. What part of *no way* don't you understand?"

Etienne was leaning against a tree, arms folded over his chest. Now that Miranda knew his family background, it was all she could do not to stare at those faded, telltale marks over his skin.

"What's up, Boucher?" Roo greeted him. "Is that your screwdriver, or are you just glad to see me?"

While everyone groaned, Etienne spread his arms wide. "You just have that effect on me, *cher*."

Roo grabbed a soda from the cooler, then settled herself comfortably on a low-lying tomb. She motioned Miranda to sit with her.

"We have to decide how to start our research," Ashley said. "Like, should we look for information on the whole town, or just one specific area. Roo and I decided we should all focus on the Brickway."

"*You* decided we should all focus on the Brickway," Roo mumbled, popping the tab on her can.

Gage nodded. "Ashley's right. If this is a walking tour, some kids in our class might not want to walk very far."

"If, in fact, anybody wants to walk on this tour at all," Parker couldn't help adding. "Come on . . . we're not *really* going to do this ghost stuff, are we?"

Ashley rolled her eyes. "Well then, maybe we should have transportation. Maybe we could use our cars?"

"*Our* cars? Etienne and I are the only ones with wheels."

"What a perfectly brilliant idea, Ash." Roo shot her sister a bland look. "Ghost BMW. No . . . wait. Ghost Truck. I'm all tingly with dread."

"Or Ghost SUV?" Despite Ashley's wounded expression, Parker clasped his hands beseechingly at Gage. "Oh, pretty please, can we use your mom's minivan?"

Ashley's lips tightened. "Parker, this is serious!"

"Look, I know it's half our grade." Easing back down, he took a swig of beer and tried to reason with her. "But let's face it—the whole thing's pretty stupid. And impossible."

"It's not stupid. And why is it impossible? All we have to do is research old places that might be haunted."

"And just how do you propose we do that? Oh wait, I know—let's just knock on people's doors. Excuse me, we're doing a survey—are there any creepy ghosts living in your house? Ash, come on. We can't force things to be haunted just so they can be close enough to walk to."

A disappointed silence fell. For several minutes everyone seemed lost in thought, till Etienne unfolded himself from the tree.

"Don't y'all know anything about your own town?" He walked over to the cooler and pulled out a beer. To Miranda, who watched him, he moved with all the grace and stealth of a predatory cat.

"Well, I'm not going to flunk this project," Ashley said crossly, "just because Parker's an idiot."

Roo promptly frowned. "Where's your compassion? Parker can't help being an idiot."

"Okay now, listen." Holding up both hands, Etienne motioned for quiet. "I think Ashley's idea is the way to go. Say we start at the Battlefield Inn. Follow the Brickway going east, past the park. We got us all those old buildings to pick from—there's gotta be plenty dark stories there, yeah? So if we do the whole mile circle of the Brickway with our little tour stops, I'm guessing it should take about an hour."

Ashley gazed at him admiringly. "Which is exactly how long Miss Dupree said our presentations should be!"

Approving looks passed back and forth. After a brief pause, Etienne continued.

"That Ghost Walk in New Orleans." He turned to Miranda. "A lotta atmosphere, yeah?"

Miranda did her best to remember. "Sort of a winding route—I mean, it was easy to lose all sense of direction, and a couple times the guide swore we were lost."

"For effect."

"Definitely for effect. There were alleys and backstreets and little courtyards. Lots of closed-in places, lots of shadows and dead ends. Low doorways we had to duck under, things like that. And sometimes ghosts came out of the dark and scared us."

"Right there on the tour?" Ashley's eyes widened. "The ghosts actually let you see them in person?"

"No," Parker said. "Only in spirit."

"Actors, Ashley." While the others laughed, Miranda tried to hold back a smile. "Just people *pretending* to be ghosts."

Ashley looked immensely relieved. "Oh, I get it! Like a big outdoor haunted house!"

"Come on, y'all. This has gotta be about more than just scaring people," Etienne reminded them.

The laughter died down. All attention shifted back to his face.

"It's about the town," he went on. "Finding out about the history of St. Yvette and—"

"Okay, we get it," Parker broke in impatiently. "The history of the town. All its evil secrets and unsolved mysteries; and the skeletons in its closets; and the curses; and the big, bad, bloody murders; and the crazy weirdos—"

There was a brief, uncomfortable silence as all eyes focused on Miranda. Even Parker had the grace to look embarrassed.

"No offense," he mumbled.

"Okay! Great!" Ashley did her best to divert attention. "Miss Dupree wants a rough outline Monday. So let's start working on ideas and meet again tomorrow." Jumping up from the blanket, she chattered just a little too brightly. "Outside the inn, ten o'clock. Oh, Etienne—you can come, right?"

"Sure." Slowly he ran a hand back through his hair. "As long as I'm at work by one."

"Perfect! We can walk the route and time it. And pick out which buildings are . . . historic."

"They're all historic," Roo said.

"Well . . . scarily historic."

"If each of us looks up just one or two buildings, it shouldn't be that hard." Gage slid lightly to his feet. "I don't mind doing some research tonight."

Parker stretched and stood, wrapping his arms around Ashley and nuzzling her neck. "Yeah, that's exactly what we had in mind, too. Right, Ash? Some good, basic, investigative research."

"Forget it." Pushing him off, Ashley tried to keep a straight face. "Only if you're a ghost."

Roo raised her hand. "No problem there. I'll be glad to kill him."

It didn't take long to pack up. They gathered their things, and made one last survey of the area. Miranda was still wondering how she could approach Etienne, get him alone, ask him to explain those strange comments he'd made back at the apartment. Puzzling over this, she noticed Parker gulping the last of his beer. In true quarterback style, he drew back his arm and let the can fly toward one of the tombs.

It hit its mark, bounced off, and ricocheted across several more graves. Foam splattered onto the nameless markers and ran down into the weeds.

"Touchdown!" he roared. "And the crowd goes *wild*!"

But it wasn't a crowd that came bursting through the trees just then. Wide-eyed and stumbling and gasping for breath.

The old man stopped just a few feet away. At first glance, he could have been a corpse risen from some lost grave, his stringy white hair matted with leaves and twigs, his torn clothes a muddy shroud, his gaunt face and bony arms smeared with dirt and blood. He swayed to one side, shaking violently from head to toe. And then, as the others stood paralyzed, he gestured frantically toward the woods.

"Can't you hear him?" the old man mumbled. "He won't stop. He won't rest. And God forgive me . . . I'm so tired . . ."

Miranda felt a slight movement behind her.

She heard Roo whisper in her ear.

"Well, Miranda . . . meet your grandfather."

Miranda couldn't believe it.

Jonas Hayes? This scary old man babbling incoherently in front of her? With the terrified face and snarled, scraggly beard? And looking nothing at all like the grandfather in her photograph?

Because she *knew* what her grandfather looked like; she'd *kept* that photograph.

Even though Mom had taken it away from her that first time and put it back in the box on that high shelf in the closet. And even though Mom had forbidden her ever to snoop through that closet again.

Miranda had done it anyway.

She'd waited for Mom to leave the house, and the very next chance she got, she'd taken the photograph and hidden it in a brand-*new* secret place, among her most cherished treasures.

She'd looked at it so many times.

And on that fateful day of the hurricane—for some strange reason she still didn't understand—she'd suddenly had an overwhelming urge to pull the photo out from the loose floorboard under her bed and stuff it deep down inside one pocket of her jeans.

She loved that picture. When she and Mom moved into the garage apartment, she'd slipped it, all crumpled and dog-eared, beneath her mattress for safekeeping. She didn't even have to look at it anymore to recall her grandfather's face—she'd memorized that face perfectly through the years.

That kind-looking, quiet-looking scarecrow of a man. Craggy and rail-thin, with a thick mop of graying brown hair. With the neatly trimmed beard and the long arms and those sad, sunken eyes—eyes as pale blue and faded as his summer linen suit.

And now *this*?

This total raving lunatic, scarcely able to stand on his own two feet?

No, this was *not* her grandfather.

"That's not him," she murmured to Roo.

"Yes, it is."

"You're crazy."

"No," Roo whispered back. "*He* is."

"Why can't I see it?" The old man's voice was almost pleading. "I'm his only chance . . ."

As he glanced back through the trees, Miranda could swear that his skin turned pale beneath its layers of grime. She realized that Etienne was walking toward him. And now that the initial shock had passed, everyone else began to stir cautiously behind her, their voices low and muffled.

" . . . the hell's he doing here?"

" . . . belongs in a straitjacket—"

"Ssh, don't let Miranda hear you . . ."

But Miranda had already heard. Her heart was beating so fast, she thought it might explode.

"It's okay, Jonas. You know me. Calm yourself down."

Etienne's voice was low, but firm. He held up both hands in a nonthreatening appeal.

Confused, the old man darted his eyes from side to side, before settling his gaze once more on Etienne.

"I'm tired," Jonas murmured again.

"I know you are. That's why we're gonna take you on home—"

"Then who'll watch out for him? For *all* of them? After I'm gone?"

"Don't you be worrying about that. You and me, we'll figure something out."

Etienne had reached the old man's side. For a second it seemed as if Jonas might bolt, but then a deep breath shuddered through his entire body.

"I never told you about him." His head lowered; both arms hung limply at his sides. "I should have . . . but I never did . . ."

"There's a lotta time for that," Etienne assured him. "Whatever it is, you can tell me about it later, yeah?"

With a strange sense of detachment, Miranda watched the bizarre scene playing out. It took several moments to realize that her classmates had crowded in around her. Wary glances were being traded back and forth. Ashley looked scared to death; Parker's expression hovered somewhere between disbelief and outright laughter. And though Gage and Roo had their heads bent together, Miranda could still make out whispered snatches of conversation.

"Who's he talking about?"

"I don't know."

"Well, who do you *think*?" Roo persisted.

"I think he's scared and confused." Abruptly, Gage cut her off. "I think *he* doesn't know what he's talking about. Just let it go, Roo."

Miranda blocked out as much as she could. *I don't believe it. I* won't *believe it. He can't be my grandpa.* And yet she heard herself asking, "Is that really my grandfather? What's wrong with him?"

"I told you," Roo said. "He's crazy."

Parker jabbed Roo hard in the ribs. "Roo, shut up."

"Well, it's true. How come nobody wants to say what's true?"

"Not now," Gage murmured, but more firmly this time. "Parker's right—just be quiet."

Roo's reply was a grunt and a shrug. Miranda felt someone squeeze her hand, and realized it was Ashley.

Then, without warning, the old man staggered and hit the ground. Before anyone could grasp what was happening, Etienne knelt beside him and eased him carefully onto his back.

"Call 911!" Etienne shouted.

Parker automatically began patting himself down, searching through all his pockets. "Shit. Where's my cell?"

"I have mine—" Gage began, but Ashley's voice stopped him.

"It won't do any good. We're out of range here, remember? There's no signal!"

Emotions battled in Miranda's heart. She wanted to run *to* her grandfather—she wanted to run *away* from him. She couldn't do either one. She couldn't even move.

"Get him in the car!" Etienne ordered. And then, when

nobody volunteered, his tone sharpened. "Why are y'all just standing there? *Allez!* Hurry up!"

Everyone scrambled except Miranda. As Parker, Roo, and Gage raced forward to help, Ashley began tugging her away.

"Come on." Urging Miranda into a run, Ashley headed for the BMW. "Do you know your aunt's phone number? Your mom's?"

Numbly, Miranda shook her head. "Aunt Teeta's working." *And Mom won't come.*

She climbed in the back of the convertible where she'd sat before. To her surprise, Etienne and Gage lowered the old man into the seat and rested his head awkwardly across her lap. Ashley had buckled herself into the front. With some hasty and expert maneuvering, Etienne managed to squeeze in beside Miranda, while Parker jumped behind the wheel and fired up the engine. Etienne tossed his keys to Gage, who immediately ran to the truck with Roo.

"My seats," Parker moaned. "Who's going to clean all that?"

Ashley was not amused. "Your family has a maid and a gardener. And enough money to replace your car every time it gets a speck of dust on it. Now *drive*!"

The car lunged forward. Before Miranda knew it, they were already halfway to the main road.

All she could do now was stare down at this stranger's face—this slack, rawboned face with its age lines crusted in dirt, and the blood already dried in those deep, wrinkled creases of . . .

Sorrow? Pain?

No, it's something worse than pain, isn't it, Grandpa? Something much worse than pain . . .

For a split second, her mind filled with shadows.

"What happened to him back there?" she finally asked. "Who was he talking about? What was he running from?"

Ashley offered Miranda a sympathetic smile, then shook her head in bewilderment.

Straining forward, Etienne tapped Parker on the shoulder. "Take the bayou road. It'll be faster."

"Where we going?" Parker called back to him. "The clinic or the hospital?"

"Too far to the hospital—it'll have to be the clinic for now. They can always move him later if they need to."

"No!" As cold fingers clamped onto Miranda's wrist, she tried desperately to pull away. She heard Ashley's cry and the squeal of tires as Parker struggled to free himself from Ashley's flailing arms.

"No . . . no clinic." Still clinging to Miranda, Jonas Hayes fixed her with a gaze so pleading it nearly broke her heart. Then his fingers began to relax. And the words he spoke next were choked with emotion.

"Why . . . you're Miranda," he whispered. "You're my granddaughter."

An icy current surged through her. As she returned his gaze in shocked silence, it was as if they were the only two people in the car.

"I'm begging you." His eyes closed now, wearily. "No

emergency room. Too many questions . . . too many stares. Please . . . just take me home."

Miranda glanced helplessly at the others. Etienne looked grim; Ashley was as close to her door as she could get; Parker watched uncertainly in the rearview mirror.

Not even sure why she was doing it, Miranda leaned toward Etienne. "Maybe we *should* take him home. Maybe he'd be more comfortable there, with Aunt Teeta."

"We don't know what's wrong with him or how bad he's hurt," Etienne answered. "He needs a doctor. You can call your aunt from the clinic."

Miranda hesitated. Her grandfather had lapsed back into unconsciousness, his grip loosened, his hand still covering hers. *This hand of a stranger,* she thought again. *And yet . . . he recognized me. He knows who I am.*

"Take him home." Miranda's voice was loud and firm. "I'll stay with him."

The mood in the car changed instantly. Miranda could almost swear she heard a collective sigh of relief from the front seat.

But not from Etienne.

He was staring at her, his expression unclear. She wasn't sure if she should feel noble or guilty about the decision she'd just made.

"Aunt Teeta will be back soon." For some reason, she felt the need to defend herself. "I'd rather not do anything till then. I mean, maybe this has happened before. She'll know how to handle it better than we can."

Etienne started to say something. His lips parted, then settled into a thin line. Miranda deliberately peered out the back windshield at Roo and Gage in Etienne's truck.

No one spoke the rest of the trip. It was only when Parker sped into the driveway of Hayes House that Miranda's grandfather stirred again.

"You'll help him, won't you?" He wasn't talking to Miranda this time; he seemed to be talking to no one. "Find what he's looking for . . . what he's lost . . ."

Miranda longed to ask more questions, but brakes were squealing and Etienne was already out of the car. As the truck slammed to a stop behind them, Gage hit the ground running.

"Let's get him in the house!" Etienne shouted. "Gage, you go around to the other side and—"

"No . . . no . . . you're not listening." Even as Parker turned off the engine, the old man was struggling to sit up. "You have to help him! Why won't you believe me? Why won't anybody believe me . . . ?"

The only thing Miranda could do was stay put while the three boys pulled Jonas Hayes off her lap. Ashley retreated to one side of the driveway and nervously chewed her bottom lip.

"I can walk," the old man said weakly. He waved the boys away, then sagged against the passenger door, his dazed eyes scanning the house, the lawn, and the faces of his rescuers. Miranda wasn't sure he even knew where he was. When Gage and Etienne propped him up between them, he didn't resist. Slowly they turned him toward the veranda.

"It's okay, Jonas," Etienne assured him. "You just need to rest yourself, that's all." He took a few steps, then glanced back at Miranda. "You gonna help us here, or what?"

Startled, she saw the accusation in his gaze.

"You're the one who wanted to stay with him," Etienne reminded her. "It's not gonna do a whole lotta good if he's in there and you're out here."

The truth of it hit her then—all those things she should have considered first, before making her snap decision. She'd been forbidden to meet her grandfather. She had no idea where to put him or what to do with him once they got him inside. And her mother would be absolutely furious.

But before she could answer, Jonas Hayes broke away. He jerked free so suddenly that Gage and Etienne nearly went sprawling to the ground.

"You're the one, Miranda!"

The voice of her grandfather reached out to her. She could hear the desperation in it, and the sorrow. His eyes, so wild before, now fixed on her with the utmost gentleness, like a silent prayer.

"You'll have to do it, Miranda." The old man's tears spilled over. "You're the only one who can."

As everyone watched in amazement, Jonas Hayes stumbled off across the yard. He half climbed, half fell up the steps of the veranda. Then the front door closed, and he was gone.

8

"WELL! OKAY, THEN!" Parker smacked his palms together, sounding much too relieved. "Looks like we're through here, huh? So I guess we'll be going now!"

He jumped quickly into the front seat, motioning the others to hurry. Ashley didn't waste any time. Roo followed, but seemed doubtful. Gage and Etienne stood talking for a moment before finally climbing into Etienne's truck. As the BMW jumped the curb and fishtailed onto the street, Miranda saw Ashley waving good-bye.

"Don't forget!" Ashley called. "Tomorrow, ten o'clock! In front of the Battlefield Inn!"

With a sinking heart, Miranda watched them go. How could they abandon her like this? Leave her here with this crazy old man? She turned and gazed miserably at the house. She'd had the sincerest intentions earlier when she'd offered to stay with her grandfather. When he'd recognized her and said her name, all her emotions had taken over. She'd honestly believed he was going to be okay.

So what am I supposed to do now?

She had no idea when Aunt Teeta would be home. She couldn't just wait around and do nothing in the meantime. What if her grandfather got confused again, and sick, and terrified like he'd been at the Falls? She had to go inside; she had to check on him. *Why didn't I listen to Etienne?* Etienne had been right—her grandfather belonged in a clinic with doctors.

But he's not in a clinic. And it's my fault he's here, and there's only me now to take care of him.

Miranda drew a deep breath. Squaring her shoulders, she walked to the front door of Hayes House and gave a tentative knock. It didn't really surprise her when no one answered. Summoning all her courage, she let herself in.

She wasn't sure what she'd expected. In her daydreams, she'd always pictured Hayes House as a kind of small plantation, something straight out of *Gone with the Wind.* She knew from Aunt Teeta's letters that the house was very old, that it had survived the Civil War but had been updated and added onto throughout all the generations. That it was close to the Historic District, located on a shady side street about a block off the Brickway. And that it backed up against one quiet area of Rebel Park.

Now, as she moved slowly across the threshold, Miranda let her eyes wander over the hardwood floors, the wide staircase, the high ceilings. Through half-open pocket doors she could see what must be the living and dining rooms. The wallpaper looked old, the furniture was dusty, and there were brown stains on the ceiling where water had leaked in. It might have been a grand house once, but now it felt sad and tired. And it was hard to think of Mom growing up here—Mom, who loved open spaces and plenty of light.

Miranda gazed a moment longer. *Still . . . Mom would think this place has potential.* Before, when Mom ran her own interior design studio, Miranda had seen her work miracles out of the shabbiest impossibilities. She couldn't help wondering what Mom could do here.

The muffled sound of a voice brought her back to attention. It seemed to have come from above her, though she couldn't be sure. Approaching the staircase, Miranda peered up at the landing, then stopped and listened. Yes . . . it *was* a voice.

Grandpa?

Calling for me?

She knew she hadn't imagined it. For an endless moment she stood there, trying to decide what to do. He hadn't wanted anyone to help him earlier—it would probably be better if she just left. And those weird things he'd been mumbling? *What if he really* is *crazy, like Roo said?*

A cold wave of fear rippled through her.

Just go, Miranda. Leave now.

Yet she put her hand on the banister. And she started up the stairs.

The second floor was much darker than the first. As twilight slanted in through a stained-glass window, it bathed the landing with soft, multicolored pools of light. A long, empty hall stretched out before her, and she could see heavy doors on both sides, most of them shut. She didn't want to be alone here—she didn't want to be here at all—but she'd reached the first doorway now, and had found what she was looking for.

His eyes were closed. He was lying on a narrow, wrought-iron bed that took up one wall of a narrow, cluttered room. A room that might just as well have been a museum.

No, more than a museum. A shrine.

For it was exactly that—an overflowing, overstuffed memorial to the Civil War. Faded photographs of soldiers and battlefields. Hand-rendered portraits of officers dressed in gray. A mounted gun with bayonet, a small collection of knives. An old-fashioned doctor's bag complete with surgical instruments. Rebel caps and a shaving mug, papers and pens, a bent pair of spectacles without lenses, a tobacco pipe. And row upon row of dusty jars, rusty tins, and musty boxes containing God knew what. There was even a sword with a dull, stained blade and a moth-eaten sash around its handle.

Curiosity got the best of her. Quietly, careful not to wake him, she began lifting lids off the jars and boxes and tins. Eclectic assortments, she saw at once—yet everything was neatly organized. Bullets and various-style buttons. Scraps of rotted cloth. A locket . . . some rings. Gold chains of different lengths; a short strap of braided leather. Cutlery so tarnished, she doubted it would ever come clean. Crumbling pages of a Bible. Locks of hair tied up with brittle ribbons . . .

These are real things; they belonged to real people. Real people who had lives and who used these things before they died . . .

She picked up a small, round tin from the nightstand. As fine hairs prickled at the back of her neck, she glanced at the bed and saw her grandfather watching her.

Miranda dropped the tin. It clattered down onto the floor and rolled noisily out of sight beneath a dresser, but she was powerless to retrieve it. She couldn't look away from her grandfather's face. That surprisingly powerful gaze that held her, that unsettling gaze of infinite calm and profound knowing. Another shiver went through her, though it was different this time. For a split second, it was almost as if that gaze had opened to her—allowing the briefest glimpse of immeasurable wisdom and immeasurable pain . . .

"Miranda," he whispered.

His eyes began to change. Pale, blue eyes growing kind, glowing warm, with a tenderness and clarity that pierced her heart.

This was the grandfather of her photograph.

The grandpa she'd hoped for, the grandpa she'd prayed for and imagined for so long.

And as his hand lifted and beckoned, she walked to his side and offered him a smile, half fearful, half shy.

"I've been waiting for you," he said softly. "All this time. So many years. I was beginning to think this day would never come."

She didn't know how to answer. His voice was still so weak, his face so chalky white. She felt his long, frail fingers close around her hand.

"It always skips a generation," he mumbled. "That's why your mama won't ever understand."

"Grandpa, I don't . . ." Miranda hesitated . . . shook her head. He was obviously still delusional; she didn't have a clue what he was talking about.

"They'll come to you because they know you can see them.

They'll speak to you because they know you'll hear." The old man gave a restless sigh. "It's a burden sometimes, all that listening and helping. But you can't turn them away."

I shouldn't have done this. I'm just making him worse.

Casually, she tried to free herself, but he only squeezed her hand tighter. "Promise me, Miranda. Promise me you'll never turn them away."

He was growing more agitated now, more insistent. Miranda feared what he might do if he worked himself into another frenzy. Not wanting to risk it, she gave him a solemn nod.

"Yes. I promise."

What have I done now?

But the change in him was remarkable. Relief shining from his eyes . . . peace drifting over his face.

"Good girl," he whispered. "I knew I could trust you."

Glancing away, she wrestled with her guilt. She'd promised, and he'd believed her. She'd promised him something, and she didn't even know what it was.

"Let him help." Her grandfather's voice was fading. As Miranda looked down at him once more, his body went limp with exhaustion, his ramblings lowered to murmurs. She wondered if he'd already slipped into his strange, private dreams.

"Ssh . . ." Freeing her hand, she placed it gently on his forehead. "Ssh . . . just rest now . . ."

"It's lonely, Miranda. He'll help you. Let him do that."

She stepped back from the bed, watching the rise and fall of her grandfather's chest—his deep, easy breathing of sleep. All around them, the shadows had grown darker. They'd lengthened and thickened and crept in from the musty hall, and now they slid along the walls and over the headboard, covering the old man's face like a death mask.

"Oh, Grandpa," Miranda whispered, "I wish I knew what you were talking about."

"I think," said a voice behind her, "he's talking about me."

9

All the strength drained out of her. As Miranda whirled around, a scream rose up and caught silently in her throat.

At first he seemed merely a shadow, one shapeless form among many. But when he shifted and started toward her, she recognized Etienne's tall silhouette etched sharply against the gloom.

"You're with him. That's good." Etienne's voice, like his arrival, was quiet and matter-of-fact. "I was hoping you would be, but I couldn't be sure."

Miranda didn't answer at first. Their earlier conversation—his knowing about the screams—flashed back to her, and she pressed against the dresser, trying to put distance between them.

"Sorry." Etienne moved closer. "I didn't mean to scare you. I thought you knew—"

"Knew what?" Though the intrusion hadn't disturbed her grandfather, Miranda felt wary and unnerved.

"Knew I was here," Etienne finished.

"All I know is that you seem to show up—*uninvited*—at very weird times."

"Okay, you're upset, I understand that. But I left to take Gage home. And you and Jonas needed a little time alone together."

"Why would *I* care whether you left or not? And who are *you* to say what I need?"

Etienne's gaze drifted to that elderly face upon the pillow. "It's what *he* needs."

"Oh, really? And I suppose he told you that?"

"He didn't have to tell me, *cher*. You're practically the only thing he cares about."

It was a revelation she certainly never expected. Swallowing a lump in her throat, she watched Etienne cross to the window, angle himself against the wall, and stare out at the gathering dusk.

"Gage didn't want to leave either," Etienne added offhandedly. "But I talked him into it."

Miranda scarcely heard the remark. "What did you mean just now? What you said about my grandpa and me?"

"Why? Is it so hard for you to believe?"

"To tell you the truth . . . yes."

"Your *grand-père*, he's saved every letter you've written to your aunt Teeta. Every picture you've ever sent. He talks about you like he's known you for your whole life. Like the two of you've been together forever." Etienne's tone went thoughtful. "Well . . . maybe you really have."

"Why would you say that? We've never met each other, never communicated. For ten years I never even knew he existed."

For a moment Etienne didn't respond. Then slowly he turned from the window, his black eyes narrowed hard upon her face.

"But Jonas, he always thought—always wondered—if that connection was there between you and him. And he knew if it was . . . then none of the other stuff mattered."

Miranda wished he would stop; she didn't want to hear any more. Yet at the same time, a fearful curiosity had sparked inside her, *wanting* to hear, *needing* to hear . . .

"He told me I'd know for sure when you heard their voices," Etienne went on. "And he said to ask you about the screams. He said only *you* would hear their screams at night."

Her curiosity vanished now, replaced by a growing panic. *This can't be happening to me.* It squeezed her heart and choked her words, though she fought to stay calm. Her hands clenched at her sides. She willed her voice not to tremble. "I don't even know what you're talking about."

"Look, Miranda—"

"I don't know about any voices."

"But you heard one in your apartment today, yeah? We *both* know that—"

"No. It was a mistake. I only thought I did . . ."

"I guess it'd be easier to believe that. *Safer* to believe that." Despite her angry glare, Etienne's voice softened. "Your *grand-père,* he cares about you. He knows what it's like. He wants your life to be happy."

"I'll be happy when you leave. Why'd you come here anyway? Why don't you just go?"

She was starting to shake uncontrollably. Deep, painful chills that ached all the way through. She couldn't get warm. She couldn't concentrate on what Etienne was saying. She hugged herself and tried to stop shivering, and that's when she realized Etienne's arms were around her.

"Your *grand-père,* he wants me to help you, *cher,*" Etienne insisted. "So you won't be alone in all this."

The chills began instantly to melt. As Etienne pressed her firmly to his chest, she could feel his faint stir of breath through her hair, the length and shape of his body against hers. Her pulse quickened; her thoughts spun. She had to escape—from this room and this house, from Etienne and the way he was holding her, from these crazy things he was saying . . .

Miranda pushed him away.

"I told you, I don't know what you're talking about. My grandpa doesn't know anything about me, and neither do you. There's nothing to help me with. I don't *need* any help. And I'm not lonely."

"I didn't say you'd be lonely." Etienne seemed to be studying her, as if she were some unusual specimen under a microscope. "I said you'd be *alone.* But in this case, you might end up being both."

"I'm leaving. *You* can stay here with Jonas Hayes."

Shoving past Etienne, she headed for the door, but his calm voice followed her.

"You *have* heard the screams, haven't you? And he *told* you you'd hear things. He *told* you you'd see things. Things other people can't hear or see."

Miranda froze with one hand on the door frame. Etienne continued, unfazed.

"I've seen what this does—this gift of his. I see every day what it does to your *grand-père.*"

"He's sick!" Even as the words left her mouth, she wished she could take them back. Feeling guilty and frightened and angry, she whirled to face Etienne. "He's just a sick, crazy old man. We should have taken him to a doctor like you said."

"Miranda—"

"You saw him at the cemetery. Is that your idea of a rational person? I mean, what was he doing running around in the woods like that anyway? He ought to be kept somewhere."

"So, what . . . you're saying he should be locked up?" Etienne's face went rigid. "For years he was caretaker at the Falls. And he still likes to go there—do some exploring, clean up the cemetery, fish a little."

"But that doesn't explain the way he was acting. Everyone says he's a lunatic. So why are you defending him? Why do you even care about him?"

Etienne held her in a long, cool stare. And yet there was something in his eyes that Miranda hadn't seen till this moment . . . something distant and almost sad.

"Because," Etienne said quietly, "he's my friend."

A heavy silence sank between them. For just an instant, Miranda felt as if she were seeing a different person standing before her—a stranger with Etienne's face. The briefest glimpse of loss and shame and vulnerability, the cold defiance of fierce pride.

And then it was gone. As quickly as it had come, it vanished again, leaving her to wonder at the mystery.

She heard the crunch of tires below in the driveway, the slamming of car doors. The familiar sound of voices—Aunt Teeta's and Mom's.

"You better get yourself outta here," Etienne told her. "Before your mama finds out."

"How do you know about—"

"Turn left at the bottom of the stairs and go two rooms down. There's a side door through the pantry; I'm just about the only one who ever uses it, and it's never locked. You can cut through the backyard—nobody'll see you with all those trees."

"But what about Grandpa?"

"Don't worry. I'll make sure Miss Teeta knows about him."

Miranda didn't waste any time. While Etienne went out the front door, she made a quick getaway, reaching the apartment well ahead of her mother. When Mom finally came in, Miranda was already sitting on the bed amid scattered piles of homework.

"Congratulate me!" Mom greeted her. "I got the job!"

Miranda couldn't have cared less about the job. In light of all that had happened today, a job hardly even seemed significant.

"Great." Miranda forced a smile. "Congratulations."

"I start tomorrow." For the first time in weeks, Mom sounded almost happy. "It's a renovation project—one of the oldest plantations on the bayou. Belle Chandelle? You remember Aunt Teeta telling us about it? The company was very impressed that I'd had my own design studio. They said my experience is just what they need!"

"That's good, Mom."

"Then afterward I picked up Teeta, and we stopped for a quick bite. We *did* come by here first, honey, to see if you wanted to eat with us."

When Miranda didn't respond, Mom did a quick appraisal of the books and papers on the bed.

"So how was your study group?"

"Fine."

"Think you'll make some new friends?"

"I guess."

"Well, it sure feels nice in here now, doesn't it?" Awkwardly, Mom groped for more small talk. "A lot better than it did before. So I'm assuming the air conditoner got fixed."

"It's a loaner."

A long pause followed. Then, "Miranda . . . about our discussion—"

"Not now, Mom, okay? I really need to get this done."

Mom's relief couldn't have been more obvious, though a slight frown creased her brow. "That's fine, honey. Maybe tomorrow, huh?"

"Maybe."

"Did you have dinner? Aunt Teeta and I are going to sit in the backyard and have ice cream if you—"

"No thanks."

She was glad when Mom left. There was too much to think about, too much to worry about, too much to figure out. The events of today swam crazily through her mind—the kids she'd met, the Ghost Walk they were planning, the eerie voice she'd heard, the Falls, her grandfather, Etienne . . .

Etienne.

Etienne, who seemed to know far more about her than she knew about herself . . .

"He told *you you'd hear things."* Etienne's words haunted her. *"He* told *you you'd see things. Things other people can't hear or see."*

"You're insane, Etienne Boucher. You and Grandpa and everyone else in this stupid town are all completely insane."

But what if it were true?

Because I did *hear a voice, and I* have *heard those screams . . .*

With one angry swipe, Miranda knocked all her books and papers to the floor.

What if everything Etienne said is true?

What does that make me?

10

THE SCREAMS CAME BACK THAT NIGHT.

Tossing and turning, Miranda tried to shut them out, to obliterate them once and for all. Only now they were *louder*—louder than they'd ever been—and the *voice* was there, too, drifting beneath them . . . muffled yet every bit as clear—

"No . . . you're wrong . . ."

That hollow male voice—*he's young . . . twenty at the most.*

"I swear to you—for the love of God!"

That raw, hopeless voice—*and his throat's dry, he can taste blood, his lips are cracked . . . he needs water.*

"I'm the one you want . . . only me."

Like drowning waves, the voice and the screams flowed over her. Once again Miranda fought them, but they wrapped her in a cold embrace and drew her down into darkness.

She was lost in that darkness.

Lost and stumbling in that horrible darkness . . . yet not alone.

She couldn't see them, but they were there. Couldn't find them, couldn't touch them, but they were real. Real hands clawing and groping . . . real eyes vacant and staring, moving so close around her, just beyond her reach. Pain and shock and grief and rage—

she could feel them all, the unbearable essence of them as they whispered the very words her grandfather had spoken . . .

"You're the one, Miranda . . . you're the only one who can—"

Bolting upright, she gasped for air. The apartment was sweltering hot, her flimsy nightgown completely soaked with sweat. As an unfamilar glow filtered through the darkness, it tinted the shadows red and thickened them into fog.

A deep, unnatural silence filled the room. Though she strained her eyes, she couldn't see anything—not the walls or the light from the bathroom, not the door, not even her mother's bed. As if, slowly and stealthily, that eerie red haze was shutting her off from the rest of the world . . . *no, no, not haze. Smoke!*

"Mom?" She wanted to throw back the covers, jump out of bed, and run to her mother, but suddenly she was so *scared,* too scared even to *move.* "Mom, are you there? Please answer me!"

Something's burning. We have to get out of here!

"Mom?" Miranda choked.

The smoke was swirling with nightmares, macabre silhouettes bursting into bright orange flames.

Fire!

Panicked, Miranda lunged at the darkness. Her fists pounded, and her legs kicked. The sheets felt tight, trapping her, and she struck out with flailing arms. As the smoke softly, gradually began to fade, her eyes opened to light.

For a second she didn't know where she was. Then the walls came into focus, and the air flowed around her, gentle and quiet and cool.

"Mom?"

Groggy and disoriented, Miranda sat up. The covers were tangled at the foot of the bed now; her head was throbbing, her stomach churned. She felt like she'd been run over by a truck.

"Mom, what time is it?"

Reaching for the clock, she let out a groan. *Nine forty-five?* Mom was probably at work already. *Why didn't I ask her to wake me?* She groaned again as a knock sounded at the door, and she stumbled over to answer it.

"Roo said you'd forget," Etienne greeted her.

"I didn't forget." Conscious of her thin nightgown, Miranda stepped behind the door.

"And Roo said even if you didn't forget, you still wouldn't be there on time."

His hair was damp, as though he'd just washed it. His black jeans fit casually over his narrow hips, and his black T-shirt had BOUCHER SWAMP TOURS stamped across the front in faded red letters.

"You should be feeling proud of yourself," he added offhandedly. "So far she hasn't told me one word about boiling you in oil. Not many people can pass the Roo test."

"Is that supposed to thrill me?"

"It thrills *me*. You sure don't want Roo putting a *gris-gris* on you. *Very* bad luck, *cher*."

"I have to get dressed," Miranda grumbled.

"I'll wait."

"I don't need you to wait for me."

"You might get lost."

"It's only a fifteen-minute walk to the inn, right? How lost could I get?"

She felt his eyes rake over her. She doubted if those eyes ever missed much.

"Bad night?" he asked her.

Miranda hesitated. Was he trying to be funny? Self-righteous? But the expression on his face wasn't joking or smug, and she didn't feel like answering any questions right now.

"I'll be out in a minute."

"Your *grand-père*? Miss Teeta says he's better," Etienne said. "Just in case you were wondering."

"Great. Maybe today he'll do something else for the whole town to talk about."

"The town, it won't talk if it doesn't know." Etienne's voice hardened. "I don't think you give your friends enough credit."

"What friends?" But she shut the door before he had a chance to respond.

She'd just assumed her classmates would tell everyone what had happened at the Falls—what a raving nutcase Jonas Hayes had been. It never occurred to her that they might keep it to themselves, and now she felt embarrassed and confused. Etienne had called the others her friends, yet she hardly knew them. Miranda realized she didn't quite know *what* to think—about *anything.*

Guiltily, she threw on her clothes, then smoothed her hair back behind her ears. She wished Etienne hadn't stopped by for her; she wished she'd thought up some brilliant excuse to stay home. She didn't feel like researching today, didn't feel like being with anyone or having to make conversation. She felt horrible, and she knew she looked horrible, too. *Well, how else would I look with no sleep?*

For the memory of her nightmare still clung to her. The smoke, the fire, the screaming. Despite its dreamlike aftermath, it hadn't *seemed* like a dream while it was happening—all those details, so frighteningly vivid.

She frowned at herself in the bathroom mirror.

Swearing under her breath, she brushed her teeth, then headed out the door.

Etienne was waiting for her at the end of the driveway. As Miranda approached, she could see Gage there, too, and the minute he smiled, she could feel her spirits lift. She walked between them, trying to match their long strides, then finally gave up and trailed behind. It was Gage who stopped and waited for her. Etienne slowed down but kept going.

Nearing the Battlefield Inn, they spotted Ashley and Parker sitting together on the front steps. Ashley immediately jumped up and started waving.

"There y'all are! We just got here, too! Isn't this fun!"

"Yeah," Parker grumbled, "I love spending Saturday morning out in the hot sun doing a crappy homework assignment."

"It's a beautiful day. Don't be such a whiner."

"If you say so. Can we please just get this over with? Look, I've got all this junk my mom gave me. So I don't see any reason to hang around here and waste time."

Reaching over, Ashley took the manila envelope he was holding. "I've already looked through it, and it's wonderful.

Brochures and little booklets and handouts—things like that. Plus, copies of actual newspaper articles, the history of the town. I mean, we've all heard *some* of the legends around here, but there's a lot of stuff I didn't know about."

"Fascinating. I'm overwhelmed with fascination."

"Mrs. Wilmington got us all this from the Historical Society. She's in charge of their museum, you know. Wasn't that sweet of her?"

"I'm overwhelmed with sweetness." Parker made a gagging sound in his throat. "In fact, let's nominate sweet Mrs. Wilmington for Mother of the Year."

"Parker, be nice."

"I'm always nice. You, of all people, should know how nice I am." Jumping to the sidewalk, he suddenly took Gage by the shoulders. He looked Gage up and down; he looked behind Gage's back. As the others started snickering, Parker stepped away again, his expression shocked. "That's *it*! I *knew* something was wrong. You're missing your worse half!"

Gage pointed to the old-fashioned bakery across the street. "She walked on ahead. She was hungry."

"Wow." Parker's eyes went wide. "I'm just not used to seeing the two of you separated. You look different. It's kind of scary."

Even Ashley couldn't help but join in. "What's *really* scary is when you see those people who spend so much time with each other? And they start to look alike?"

Etienne nodded at her, as if Gage weren't even present. "What do you think people like that *do* all the time they're together, anyway?"

"Ugh! Stop!" Parker gave an overly dramatic shudder.

As if on cue, Roo strolled out of the bakery, carrying a huge cinnamon roll in one hand and a giant cappuccino in the other. She wore a black taffeta miniskirt, black tights, black ballet slippers, and a black tank top over a purple T-shirt. Watching her a moment, Parker turned to the others and sighed.

"Look at her. Fashion Goddess of the Dark Realm."

"She's creative," Ashley emphasized. "And her realm isn't always a bad place to be."

"Neither is hell. If you're the Antichrist."

This earned Parker a slug on the arm. Grinning, he pulled Ashley close and kissed her.

"Don't even ask," Roo announced as she joined them. "These are mine, and I'm not sharing."

Gage promptly tore off a fourth of the cinnamon roll and popped it in his mouth. Etienne took a third of what was left. Roo stood there looking down at her practically empty napkin.

"You didn't need that, anyway," Ashley insisted. "All those calories."

Parker gave Roo a serious once-over. "Since when has Roo cared about calories? No, wait. Since when has Roo cared about clothes? No, wait. Since when has Roo cared about how she looks?"

He stared at Gage. Gage stared at Etienne. Etienne stared at Parker.

"Since when has Roo cared about anything?" they all asked in unison.

Feeling a little envious, Miranda observed the good-natured

teasing. The kids back home hadn't shared this kind of camaraderie. Not that they hadn't been close—their own special group of girls and guys—but what Miranda saw here was different.

Stronger, somehow.

Like a real family.

Miranda refocused on the three boys. Roo didn't seem the least bit bothered by their comments. As Gage reached for the last bite of cinnamon roll, Roo stuffed it quickly into her mouth. Etienne just as quickly snatched the cappuccino from her other hand.

Giving Etienne a shove, Roo gestured knowingly in Miranda's direction. "I told you she'd forget."

"I didn't forget," Miranda defended herself for the second time.

"I told you she'd be late."

"Okay," Miranda grumbled. "I'll give you that one."

Roo looked smugly pleased. She took back her cappuccino.

"I think we should get started." Ashley, as usual, seized command of the situation. "Did y'all come up with any good ideas? I brought stuff for us to take notes with."

Parker grudgingly accepted the pad and pen she handed him. "Wow. Just what I always wanted."

"You'll thank me when you get an A on the project."

"I can think of other things I'd rather thank you for."

A memo pad came down on his head. Wincing, he rubbed his scalp and shot Ashley an injured look.

The six of them started walking, heading down the east side

of the Brickway, pausing often along the route. Other than the information Parker had gotten from his mom, Gage was the only one who'd bothered to do any actual research last night. Now he pulled a crumpled list from his pocket and read out interesting facts from time to time.

"Like the courthouse," Gage began, while Parker immediately dismissed the idea.

"Yeah, yeah, we all know about the courthouse. Every town in America has a haunted courthouse."

"We didn't." Miranda looked curiously at Gage. "What about the courthouse?"

"Supposedly, Judge Girard sentenced a lot of innocent people to death. Legend has it that he attended every single hanging, and that he'd actually laugh each time another body swung from the noose."

Roo's tone was matter-of-fact. "He liked to see them twitching."

"The thing is," Ashley picked up the story, "I guess a lot of prisoners really hated that judge."

Parker snorted. "You think?"

"When they spoke their final words, they cursed him." Gage's voice lowered. "One morning the judge was found dead in his own courtroom. Hanging from the rafters. Most people *didn't* believe it was suicide."

"Some people swear they've seen the judge's ghost," Roo finished.

Parker was obviously pleased with the outcome. "Yeah! The only good judge is a dead judge."

"Parker Wilmington the Sixth!" A slug from Ashley. "You stop that right now!"

"Parker's dad is a judge," Roo explained. She and Miranda had fallen behind the others, and out of earshot. "Parker really hates his dad."

Though Miranda had no desire to get involved, she couldn't help stating the obvious. "He doesn't sound like he's real fond of his mom either."

"He's not. His folks are into all the big social and political stuff around here. Parker hardly ever sees them; they're never home."

"But . . . I'm sure they love him, right?"

"Would *you* love Parker if he were *your* son?"

Miranda didn't know whether to laugh, be sad, or both. She decided on a more positive approach.

"He really likes Ashley."

Roo's shrug was noncommital.

"What I mean is," Miranda tried again, "he seems to really care about her."

"Sometimes I'm not sure what he cares about." Another shrug as Roo stared at the back of Parker's head. "He'll get thrown off the team permanently if they catch him drinking again. And his dad expects him to get a full football scholarship. Which Parker doesn't want to do."

So Parker's deliberately trying to get kicked off the team. Keeping the obvious conclusion to herself, Miranda asked, "What *does* Parker want to do?"

"Self-destruct would be my guess."

Suddenly aware that part of their crew was missing, the others stopped and waited. Roo and Miranda caught up to them, and the walk continued.

Despite her distracted state of mind, Miranda couldn't help being fascinated by the Brickway. Things about the old South that she'd watched on TV and in movies, things she'd read about in books—all that long-faded past was coming to life around her. Whether antebellum house or step-front shop, each held the promise of mystery and romance.

"Maybe we should start with commercial buildings," Gage suggested. "I think we'll have a better chance of getting inside than we would with most of the houses."

Ashley consulted the contents of her envelope. "What about the park?"

"Yeah! They're having the Rebel Rouser there today!" Parker's eyes shone with the possibility of escape.

At Miranda's questioning look, Ashley elaborated. "It's like a fair—all the money's used to maintain the park. The Ladies of the Southland sponsor it every year."

"They're this women's club," Gage said. Then, as an afterthought, "They do garden tours."

"And tea parties." Parker daintily crooked his little finger, as if holding a china teacup. "They wear hats. With fake flowers on them. And plastic fruit."

Chuckling, Gage shook his head. "Let's forget about the park. That could be a whole other tour by itself."

The others readily agreed. As they moved down the sidewalk, Ashley linked her arm through Miranda's and kept up a steady flow of information.

"Here's the museum—the one Parker's mom is in charge of. It belongs to the Historical Society. And that over there? It's all closed in now, but it was the original public market. You know, like a farmer's market? And that's Grace Church. And that's the library."

"Actually, I found out it used to be a funeral parlor." Gage smiled, glancing at Ashley.

Ashley shuddered. "I bet there's *tons* of creepy stories about *that*!"

"And a lotta other buildings maybe you wouldn't expect." Without breaking stride, Etienne pointed out a charming yellow house on the opposite side of the street. "Mama said a Dr. Fuller used to have his office in that place. Who knows who might've been sick or died there."

"Ewww!" Ashley stopped in her tracks. Gage promptly plowed into her from behind.

"We should do some research on voodoo, too," Roo reminded them. "Lots of people around here practiced secret voodoo rituals."

"How do you know that?"

"Why *wouldn't* she know that?" Parker returned. "She of the Deep Underworld who keeps decomposing mice and many other dead things in her locker."

Roo's stare was calm disdain. "*One* mouse."

"We still don't know how it got in Roo's locker," Ashley explained, looking distressed at the memory. "But she threw her books in and squashed it."

"It was hiding. How was *I* supposed to know it was there."

"Maybe if you cleaned out your locker once in a while?"

"Hey!" Snapping his fingers, Parker gave an exaggerated gasp of excitement. "I think we should put Roo's locker on our tour! The mummy of the murdered mouse!"

Gage held back a smile. "Why don't we just put *Roo* on our tour?"

"No, no, *mon Dieu,* way too scary." With one smooth motion, Etienne crooked his arm around Roo's neck and pulled her sideways against him. Roo tried to elbow him, but he expertly dodged the blow. "Okay, I think we got it, yeah? What information we have now, that's where we're gonna start. And once we get into all that research, we'll probably be finding even more ideas."

He seemed to be waiting for Miranda's confirmation. Realizing the others were staring at her, she quickly nodded. "Anything dark, mysterious, unsolved, or unexplained. As long as you don't make it up. The Ghost Walk's all about having fun and giving people a good scare. But it's also about factual events, the real history of the town."

"Well done," Gage murmured.

Doing her best to pay attention, Miranda wiped a hand across her brow. The morning had started out hot and humid, but she hadn't expected the temperature to rise so quickly. No one else looked uncomfortable, she noted. *Maybe I'm just tired from last night.*

"This fancy house?" Ashley still had Miranda firmly in tow. "Can you believe it started out as a one-room feed store? The family that built it had a little boy who died. I don't remember the exact details, but there's a newspaper article about it in this stuff from Parker's mom."

Miranda gave Ashley a puzzled frown. It suddenly occurred to her that she'd scarcely heard anything the girl was saying.

"What about that building over there?" Miranda asked.

"That one? Oh, that's the bank."

"Not the bank." Halting abruptly, Miranda spun Ashley halfway around. "That one."

Ashley caught her balance at the last possible second. Bewildered, she followed the point of Miranda's finger. "You mean Magnolia Gallery?"

"It's not a gallery," Miranda murmured.

Coming up beside them, Gage shot her a quizzical glance. "Yes, it is . . . an art gallery. Not just paintings though. We have a lot of local—"

"No." Her voice had gone stubborn. She realized the others had gathered close, watching her in quiet dismay. "Before that."

Gage glanced from Parker to Roo to Etienne. "Hasn't it always been a gallery?" Receiving only shrugs, he skimmed the list of research he'd done.

"No, that's not it!" Out of patience now, Miranda's tone sharpened.

God, it was so *hot* out here! Why were they all staring at her again? And why did she suddenly have such an overwhelming urge to go over and look at that building?

"Miranda?" Ashley asked worriedly, but Miranda didn't answer.

Pushing Ashley and Gage aside, she hurried across the street to the old building set back behind magnolia trees. Stately white facade; high, round columns; tall French shutters; upper-floor balconies—all the details rushed over her, familiar somehow, as if she'd seen them all before. She took the wide front steps two at a time and shoved open the massive doors. She paused expectantly on the threshold.

Music?

Her body grew even warmer, curiously detached. A strange but not unpleasant sensation of being removed to some different place—some close but hidden place where she could watch herself frozen there in the doorway. She could feel her mind opening, her heart searching, her senses reaching out . . .

Yes, definitely music. The tragic refrains of a finely tuned orchestra.

And a voice—such a voice!

An angel's voice!

Soaring to heaven and back again in sweetly pure soprano . . .

Again Miranda felt the pull. The pull to give in and go farther, the urge to completely let go.

The swishing of skirts and handheld fans, the clinking of crystal glasses, flow of fine wine, heady sweetness of roses . . .

The final fall of a curtain . . .

And one voice.

"Nathan . . . why?"

The angel's voice, sad and alone . . .

Sobbing . . .

Now silent.

Miranda whirled around. She was here, right here on the threshold of the gallery, and she could see the others gathered in behind her on the steps. Parker and Ashley, Roo and Gage and Etienne—all of them just standing there, watching her with half-stunned expressions. After what seemed an eternity, Etienne started toward her, but Gage got to her first.

"It was an opera house," she mumbled. Letting the door's swing shut, she peered up into Gage's startled eyes. "And something terrible happened here."

11

The rush, the heat, the eerie detachment were gone.

No roses now, no ghostly sounds.

Instead, Miranda felt as though a raging fever had broken, leaving her weak and shaky, but remarkably clearheaded. She remembered every detail—every sight and scent and sound. She recalled her senses heightening to almost painful intensity before fading back again to normal.

And she was positive that time had come to a standstill, even while passing her by.

Oh my God . . . did I really say that out loud?

Etienne had stopped midstride. She could see the way he was looking at her—beyond curious, beyond surprise, almost as if he'd suddenly recognized who—or what—she truly was. The others, exchanging wary glances, hadn't moved.

It was Parker who finally broke the silence. Slapping both hands on his knees, he doubled over in forced laughter.

"Man! That was *great*! You really had me going there for a second!"

But Ashley's voice held a slight tremor as she snapped at him. "Parker, have you completely lost your mind? What is wrong with you?"

"Well, don't you get it? The way she set us up like that? It was brilliant!" Straightening, he grinned from ear to ear. "Hey, Miranda, did you take acting lessons at your old school? I think *you* should be the guide on this Ghost Walk thing—I mean, you were convincing as hell!"

"Um . . . excuse me?" Roo's stare was as condescending as her tone. "Reality check here. I don't think she was acting."

"Well, sure she was. She—" Parker broke off. Realizing he was the only one laughing, he glanced at Miranda's blank face, at Gage standing uncertainly beside her, at Etienne's fixed expression. Then he laughed again, though not as loud as before. "Y'all aren't buying this, are you? She's just screwing with us."

"*Were* you?" Ashley murmured, her wide-eyed gaze on Miranda. "Is that supposed to be part of the tour?"

Roo pulled a cigarette from one pocket, matches from another. She lit up, crossed her arms over her chest, and blew out a long curl of smoke.

Avoiding Etienne's stare, Miranda forced an amused smile. "Come on, you guys, how would I know anything about an opera house?" *Could I have read it somewhere?* "How would I know anything about *any* of these buildings?" *Could I have heard it from Aunt Teeta?*

Ashley immediately looked relieved. "So you *were* acting! Oh, Miranda, that was so good—you really have it down! I totally believed you!"

"She wasn't acting," Roo said again.

But Miranda couldn't listen to any more. Etienne was standing next to her now, and Gage was on her other side, and she was beginning to feel trapped. She had to get away from here.

"Sorry." Faking a look at Etienne's watch, she bolted down the steps and past the others. "I didn't realize how late it was—I promised Aunt Teeta I'd help her with something. See you later!"

She hurried along the route they'd taken, knowing full well how lame her excuse had been. She thought she heard someone call her name, but she didn't stop, and she didn't look over her shoulder. Had she managed to convince them that she'd been making everything up? For what else *could* she have done at the mercy of an event so totally unexpected and unforeseen? She could hardly believe it herself—how could she ever expect *them* to?

Yet she *did* believe it. Because this time was different.

This time she hadn't been afraid or alone or confused like she'd been before, when the voice had spoken, when the screams had come. This time she hadn't been lost in some nightmare. There had been a real opera house, a real tragedy within its walls, and though she wasn't sure how or why she could have known this, she was certain about it now. She just *knew*.

I have to go home. She had to escape before *it*—whatever *it* was—happened to her again. As she picked up speed, it dawned on her that there was one person who would understand.

I have to talk to Grandpa.

Miranda walked even faster. She prayed no one had followed, but there were footsteps behind her, gaining steadily.

"Miranda! Wait up!"

She pretended not to hear. When Etienne grabbed her arm, she gasped as he swung her around to face him.

"Come on, *cher,* where you going?"

"It's a mistake!" Miranda insisted. "What I said at the gallery. I don't know anything about it—I made it up!"

"You know you didn't."

She tried to shake him off, but he only held her tighter. "Etienne, please—I need to talk to my grandfather. I need him to explain. I need to understand what this *is*—what's *happening* to me!"

"He already told you. You can communicate in ways the rest of us can't. With people the rest of us can't."

"Dead people." Miranda could barely choke out the words. "That's what you're saying, isn't it? That suddenly I've got this—this horrible power . . ."

"*Gift, cher.*"

As his eyes fixed on hers with calm intensity, she found it impossible to look away. She wondered if those eyes had ever shown the slightest trace of fear. She wondered why her own fears seemed to be calming inside her, leaving only a quiet resentment in their place.

"So I'm supposed to believe that. And accept that. Like it's perfectly normal."

"Yes. Your *grand-père,* he always helped them. When they had secrets they needed to share. When they were in pain. He was the only one they could turn to."

Miranda's heart was an icy knot. "Please don't tell me this."

"You need to hear the truth. And I promised him."

"This is crazy. You know that, right? Things like this don't happen to normal people." Biting her lip, she fought back sudden tears. "Why did that hurricane ever have to hit? Why did I ever have to come here in the first place?"

"Because," Etienne said gently, "maybe this is the place you're supposed to be."

His solemn words struck deep. With a puzzled frown, she gazed into his night-black stare.

"I heard what Jonas said to you yesterday," Etienne reminded her. "He asked you not to turn them away."

Thinking back to that strange conversation, Miranda gave a reluctant nod. "I *have* heard things. Voices. Sounds. And those screams Grandpa told you about. And something happened last night, too—I couldn't be sure what was real and what wasn't." She paused, her brow furrowing. "And now today. No warning, no time to think. What if it happens again?"

"It *will* happen again."

"I don't like being surprised. I don't want people staring and laughing at me."

Etienne sounded thoughtful. "There's only one person I know of who was laughing back there just now. And some people, they laugh just to hide how scared they are."

She knew he was referring to Parker, but it didn't ease the sting. "Parker can't be half as scared as I am."

"Listen to me, *cher*." Sliding his fingers beneath her chin, Etienne tilted her face toward his. "You got a lot on your shoulders right now—a lotta thoughts, a lotta questions, a whole lotta things to get used to. It doesn't seem real to you—and it probably won't for a while. But you better accept it. 'Cause, if you're anything like your *grand-père*, it won't be going away."

His honesty did little to reassure her. She noticed the rest of the group approaching now, and the urge to escape grew stronger.

"Aunt Teeta's waiting for me," she mumbled.

Twisting free, she took off once more, determined to put as much distance between herself and the others as she could. Thank God she didn't have far to go. She rounded the last corner and could finally see Hayes House ahead of her. She saw the neatly lettered sign on the curb stating PRIVATE HOME—NO TRESPASSING. And she saw a mass of people crowded along the driveway and across the lawn.

That's weird . . .

As Miranda started to run, neighbors continued to gather, all talking somberly to one another while they watched the house. For the first time she spotted several police cars and an ambulance. With rising dread, she forced her way through curious onlookers and up the front steps.

It was Mom who met her at the door. Mom with an expression much too serious, and a hint of tears glistening in her eyes.

"Mom?"

"It's your grandpa," Mom said quietly. "He's gone, honey. Teeta found him about half an hour ago . . . dead in his room."

12

THE AWFUL REALITY WAS SLOW TO SINK IN.

It seemed forever that Miranda stood there, regarding her mother in stunned disbelief.

She felt Mom take her arm and steer her gently inside the house, then close the door behind them. She heard Aunt Teeta crying. She could hear the hushed voices of police and paramedics, the creaking of footsteps on the second floor, the muffled maneuvers on the stairs as a stretcher was carried down.

Mom coaxed her into the nearest room—what Miranda had guessed to be the living room on her first visit here.

Yesterday. It was just yesterday.

How could that be? She'd finally found her grandfather. After all these years, all her dreams and imaginings, she'd met him at last. She'd talked with him, held his hand, touched his face. She'd been happy and disappointed; she'd been hopeful and had her hopes dashed. She'd been angry and yearning and horrified and confused, and she'd been given a shocking, secret revelation that she couldn't comprehend and certainly didn't want.

There would be no understanding now.

No answers, no explanations, nothing.

"It always skips a generation . . . that's why your mama will never understand . . ."

"Maybe this is the place you're supposed to be . . ."

Words pounded in her head. Grandpa's words, Etienne's words, useless words, meaningless words. She'd been afraid of her grandfather—she'd been embarrassed and ashamed. But now she was all mixed up. Now she didn't know *how* she felt.

I know I loved him. Tears filled her eyes at the realization. *And I really* wanted *to love him.* Had he known? Had he been able to see beneath her resentment and defenses? Had he been able to see that love in her heart?

Miranda looked down at the glass of water Mom was putting in her hand. The two of them were side by side on the couch, though she didn't remember sitting. She wondered about her mother; she searched Mom's face for telltale signs of emotion. But what she saw were features like stone, a dazed expression, and movements strangely mechanical.

Miranda waited till her grandfather had been taken away. Should she comfort Mom? Strong, stoic Mom who never asked or even liked to be comforted? Mom hadn't shed a tear when they'd left Florida, their friends, the empty rubble of their old life. Mom had been in total control, and she'd *taken* total control. *Does she feel guilt? Sadness? Pain? Regret?*

Miranda didn't know. And there were no clues to tell her.

"I need to check on Teeta," Mom said softly. "I guess you and I will be moving into the house now. I'm sure she's going to need us."

Miranda could only nod. Mom sounded so calm and practical, already making plans. *Just like when Dad died.* Setting her glass on the coffee table, Miranda stood on shaky legs.

"I think I'll go outside for a while."

"Not where people can stare, honey. They're like a pack of vultures out there, wanting to know every detail."

How could she be like that? Miranda wondered. Even now, in the midst of another tragedy, Mom was obsessed with what people thought. Fighting down a wave of anger, she slipped out the side door that Etienne had shown her. The trees hid her from view, and without hesitating, she hurried along the back wall and away from the house.

She hadn't intended on going to the park.

She just suddenly found herself at the entrance.

Swept inside by the crowd, Miranda was immediately assailed by a carnival-like atmosphere. *Oh, right. The Rebel Rouser today.* The air was filled with laughter; rich smells of barbecue, boiled shrimp, fried fish, and grilled burgers; the pounding, earsplitting rhythm of a zydeco band. From a petting zoo, goats and sheep bleated nervously as squealing kids chased them with handfuls of food. Bells clanged for lucky prizewinners at dozens of game booths. Flags flew, men in Civil War uniforms flirted with hoop-skirted ladies, and from somewhere in the distance came the boom of a cannon and the muffled discharge of guns . . .

Miranda stopped in her tracks. Yes . . . she was certain now that what she'd heard from her window yesterday hadn't been a car backfiring or kids playing with firecrackers . . .

"They *were* gunshots," she mumbled. *But not these gunshots.*

A chill clawed through her veins. How many other things had

she seen and heard since coming to St. Yvette? Things she hadn't paid attention to, things she should have noticed?

But how could I have realized? I didn't know! I didn't know till now—and now I don't want *to know!*

Forcing down panic, she moved on. She'd hoped to lose herself here—to blend in, be inconspicuous, retreat from the rest of the world. *How many clues have I missed? How many signs have I ignored?* She couldn't stop thinking about it. Why wouldn't it leave her alone?

She wandered farther into the park, along winding, tree-shaded pathways, looking for a place to sit down. The muggy heat had grown way past stifling. The sun blazed down without a cloud in the sky. In the wider, more open spaces, both Rebel and Yankee regiments impressed spectators with various marching and marksmanship skills, while in a small amphitheater, folksingers performed nostalgic Civil War ballads. Miranda paused briefly at each, then continued on to the cemetery.

Unlike the Falls, the Confederate Cemetery had been lovingly cared for. Located on a gentle rise, its grass was lush and green, its graves peaceful and undisturbed. Each tomb looked freshly whitewashed, banked with masses of flowers and foliage, decorated with vintage photographs, religious figurines, yellow ribbons, rosaries, and votive candles that flickered among the crosses. Markers and memorials stood proudly. Every name and message was distinct.

Spotting an empty bench, Miranda went over and sat down. It was a beautiful spot, facing the graveyard across a flower-bordered path, but the beauty did little to console her. As families strolled past, she thought of her grandfather—all the things left unsaid and undone, all the unexpressed feelings and unanswered questions.

A fine sheen of sweat glazed her brow. She was feeling warmer by the minute—warm from the inside out—getting so hot, she could hardly stand it. She wondered vaguely if someone had set up a grill nearby; she could see fine tendrils of pale, gray smoke curling through the air.

I just never expected Grandpa to die. I just never expected any of this.

Leaning forward, she propped both elbows on her knees . . . covered her face with her hands. She wanted to cry, but she felt so empty. When she finally lifted her head again, she was surprised to see even more smoke in the air, floating slowly in her direction, bringing with it a faint, familiar smell . . .

That smell! That smoke!

Only now the odor was stronger—more recognizable—and thoughts and images were tumbling wildly through her brain. Sweat and sulfur, dirt and blood and open sores, stagnant water, charred flesh, ashes, and hot, hot metal . . .

Miranda stiffened and looked around. There weren't any grills in sight, no cookouts, no food vendors. Not a single blade of grass stirring, not a single leaf rustling on a tree, though the smoke kept drifting toward her.

Alarmed, she jumped to her feet, waved her arms, tried to fan back the smoke. It was getting thicker, and with a slow, sick awareness, she watched it darken to red. *Like last night . . . oh, God, just like last night . . .*

"Please!" A dark haze was all around her now, she couldn't see the path anymore, not even six feet away. "Can someone help me?"

And, yes, thank God, someone *was* coming to help! She could see the vague silhouette materializing in front of her . . . the shadowy hand reaching out . . .

She realized then why he hadn't been completely visible at first. Why he'd blended so perfectly into the smoke. The tattered, gray uniform he was wearing . . . the dark smears of blood on his face and his clothes. *Was he from one of those reenactment regiments she'd been watching?* Yet his body seemed to hover there, suspended.

"For Miss Ellena," he whispered.

Miranda was totally paralyzed. All she could do was watch helplessly as he came forward to meet her.

"Take it . . . the rose . . ."

That sorrowful voice. That raw, empty, pleading voice, heartbreaking in its anguish.

That voice Miranda knew, for she had heard it before.

"Who are you?" From some distant place inside her head, Miranda knew she hadn't spoken aloud. Yet she heard the echo of her question, and she understood somehow that the young man heard it, too. "Who *are* you?"

The answer came like a death rattle.

"Nathan."

"What do you want?"

His face began to appear through the gloom. *Pale hair, bleached skin, eyes like bottomless, black holes. Sunken cheeks streaked with blood, parched lips caked with blood, but none of that as horrible as the blood soaking his uniform, as the wide, crimson stain blossoming over his shirt, directly over his heart . . .*

"Take it," he murmured. *And those lifeless eyes staring, staring, all the suffering there, the hopelessness, the aching regrets . . .* "Help me . . ."

As a faint, ragged breath stirred the air, Miranda felt something slide across her upturned hand. Not a rose, as he'd said, but something like twine . . . a short length of twine, knotted or twisted or woven . . .

Braided? She couldn't see it in her open palm. *Braided twine?*

"For Miss Ellena," he whispered. "The rose . . . the rose . . . the . . ."

And he was fading now, just as his voice was fading, just as the smoke was fading . . . fading to nothing but shadow . . .

She felt the sun.

She heard the people.

As the park came back into jarring focus, Miranda blinked against the light and looked down.

Her hand was empty.

And she was crying.

13

That night for the very first time, Miranda slept in Hayes House. Or rather, *tried* to sleep, in between tossing, turning, checking her windows, and keeping an eye on her door. Even the mirror made her nervous—not to mention the closet, the space under the bed, and every shadow in every single corner.

That poor soldier . . . that poor, tragic soldier.

Nathan, he'd called himself.

She couldn't stop seeing his face, hearing his voice. *"Take it . . . the rose . . . the rose . . ."* And his blood, his sorrow, his unbearable pain . . .

No matter how much Miranda longed to deny it, ignore it, and forget it—in her heart she couldn't.

She didn't remember coming home from the park. She'd suddenly found herself locked in a downstairs bathroom, crying into a towel and unable to stop. When she finally slipped out to the kitchen, no one seemed to have missed her, and she was relieved that Mom was too distracted with Aunt Teeta and pending funeral arrangements to focus on her.

But later, lying there in her mother's childhood room, Miranda almost wished she had someone to talk to. Not just about the soldier, but about so many other things. News of death traveled quickly in St. Yvette, and there'd been a constant procession of neighbors throughout the day, bringing casseroles, cakes, and condolences. She'd spent most of her time being introduced to people she didn't know and didn't care about knowing. She'd felt confused about her grandfather—how she should feel and how she should show it. She'd wondered what to say to her mother, who seemed rock solid, and what to say to Aunt Teeta, who was devastated.

Her only source of comfort had arrived later that evening, when she'd started down the hallway to go outside and found Gage at the front door.

"Are you okay?" was the first thing he'd asked. And then, before she'd been able to answer, his arms were around her in a gentle hug. Miranda had fought back unexpected tears and felt herself surrendering—just as unexpectedly—to his concern.

"We weren't really sure what to do," Gage explained as she led him into the deserted study at the back of the house. He'd waited till she sat down before taking the chair across from her. "We all wanted to come, but we didn't know how you'd feel about it. We didn't want to make you uncomfortable."

Miranda simply stared at him. "Nobody needed to come."

"We *wanted* to come."

She hadn't known what to say. Despite her best efforts, she'd felt embarrassed and strangely touched. "I've only known you guys for two days."

"Sometimes that's long enough."

When he smiled, she couldn't help smiling back at him. After a moment, he leaned toward her, his voice more solemn.

"Do they know what happened to your grandfather?"

"They're pretty sure it was a stroke. And that it was quick, so he didn't suffer."

Gage hesitated. "Did what happened at the Falls yesterday have anything to do with it?"

"I don't know. Maybe we should have taken him to the clinic."

"I think Etienne was right, Miranda—I think we did the best we could."

"Etienne hasn't been by this afternoon." She'd been startled when the words popped out—she hoped they hadn't sounded—what? Judgmental? Disappointed? The truth was, she'd honestly expected him to show up at the house, at least for Aunt Teeta's sake.

Gage's eyes were full of sympathy. "They were pretty tight, Etienne and your grandfather. I know Etienne's heard the news, but I haven't talked to him yet. He . . ." Again Gage paused, as though choosing just the right words. "I know he'll be really upset. And he never lets anybody see him that way."

"Macho thing?" Miranda couldn't help asking.

A dimple flashed in Gage's cheek. "Something like that, I guess."

They'd lapsed into a companionable silence. To Miranda, it felt so good just to sit there with him, not feeling the need to pretend or explain or keep up any sort of appearances. He'd seemed in no hurry to leave, and she'd been glad for him to stay. And when his attention focused on the comings and goings out in the hallway, she'd taken that chance really to study his face.

Yes, there were definitely resemblances between Gage and

Etienne—the same high cheekbones, lanky frames, and dark good looks. She guessed both their mothers were beautiful. But what was even more apparent up close was the stark contrast in the boys' eyes. One, soulful and sensitive . . . the other, suspicious and blatantly defiant.

"You're staring," Gage mumbled.

As Miranda realized she'd been caught, the two of them laughed self-consciously. Gage lowered his eyes and slid back in his chair.

"Do you know when the funeral is?" he'd asked her.

"I heard them talking about Tuesday."

"Let us know for sure."

"But—"

"So we can be there."

"But—"

"Because." His hands went up to ward off her question. "Because we want to, okay?"

"Okay."

"Oh, and um . . ." Frowning slightly, he traced one finger across his upper lip. "I'm not sure it's the right time to bring this up . . ."

"No, go ahead."

"That building you wondered about this morning? Magnolia Gallery?"

The change she'd felt had been immediate—that tightening in her stomach, that tensing of her nerves—though Gage didn't seem to notice. In fact, he'd seemed almost *too* casual as he continued talking.

"I've been trying to find some information on it. I haven't really come up with much yet, but what I've got so far is pretty interesting."

Miranda swallowed nervously, half expecting him to bring up her odd behavior of that morning. But Gage only cleared his throat and looked down at the floor.

"I thought . . . maybe later . . . when you feel better? Maybe we could talk about it."

"Yes. Later's good. I'd really like that."

"Great. Well . . . I better go." As the two of them stood, he'd fished in his shirt pocket and handed her a folded slip of paper. "Here's my cell phone number. And Etienne's. In case you . . . you know . . . need anything."

"Thanks."

Giving her another hug, he whispered, "I'm sorry, Miranda. Just remember I'm—we're—thinking about you."

His body was warm and strong, and there was nothing the least bit shy about the way he held her. Miranda had a sudden, silly urge just to stand there in his arms and never leave. But instead, she pulled free and walked him to the door, her mind in turmoil. *Should I tell him? About what happened in the park today? And how I knew about the opera house?* Because somehow she was sure Gage would listen . . . somehow she was sure he'd understand.

"Gage?"

Stopping on the walkway, he'd turned to look back at her. "Yeah?"

"Nothing. Just . . . thanks."

"I didn't do anything."

"Yes, you did. More than you know."

That dimple again, and a modest shrug. "See you."

Exhausted, Miranda had dragged herself through the rest of the evening. After the last visitor had gone, she and Mom and Aunt Teeta had sat together in the kitchen, picking at the vast assortment of food, but eating little. Aunt Teeta showed Miranda her new room—a cozy little hideaway tucked up on the third floor—then immediately went to bed. While Mom insisted on tidying up, Miranda made a quick run to their apartment to fetch nightgowns and toothbrushes.

And now she couldn't sleep.

It had been a long and grueling day, a bizarre and upsetting day. Even with her soft mattress and feather pillows and the privacy she'd been longing for, Miranda could only pitch restlessly back and forth and stare wide-eyed into the darkness.

This room had been Mom's, Aunt Teeta had told her—this room was where Mom had spent all her growing-up years. It sat right at the top of the narrow third-floor staircase, small and sparsely furnished and nestled snugly back under the eaves. Instead of air-conditioning, French doors stood open to a small sunporch where screened windows on three walls allowed for breezes, but could also be shut against bad weather. There'd been many a slumber party out there, Aunt Teeta recalled—girlfriends staying up till all hours, talking and giggling throughout those long, carefree summer nights. At one end of the porch a door led out to a flight of wooden steps. The banister was overgrown with ivy and honeysuckle vines, and the steps went all the way down to a thickly shrubberied back corner of the house.

Miranda wondered if her mother ever thought about this sunporch, about this room, about childhood. If her mother ever had any happy memories at all . . .

Memories . . .

But Miranda had her own memories to deal with tonight. Memories trudging heavy through her brain and flashing back at her like snapshots, making her heart race and her head pound. The walls seemed to be squeezing in. The stagnant air whispered with faraway screams. Unable to fight it any longer, she jumped up and made for the door, not even bothering with the bedside lamp.

Smart, Miranda. Real smart.

She'd forgotten how dark the staircase was. Groping along the wall, she couldn't find a light switch anywhere, but she *could* follow the sudden rumble of Aunt Teeta's snoring. With a relieved sigh, she reached the dimly lit second-floor landing, then continued on down toward the kitchen.

That's when she heard the crying.

Miranda froze at the foot of the stairs. *Oh, please God, not again.* Yet almost at once she realized *this* crying was different. Not the same ghostly sounds as before, but almost as heartbreaking. And very, very close by.

Still fearful, she peered through the kitchen doorway. The room was mostly in shadow, though a pale, silver moon shone in at the window above the sink. Then, as her eyes adjusted to the gloom, she finally recognized the figure at the table. Mom sitting there with her head lowered on folded arms, and her whole body shaking with sobs.

Miranda had never seen her mother cry like this before. In fact, she couldn't remember having seen her cry at all since Dad died. Mom—the strong one, the invincible one—always unflappable in the face of every situation, no matter how bad.

Startled, her mother gasped and looked up in alarm. "Oh, Miranda, it's you. What's wrong, honey, can't you sleep?"

Just like that, in total control again. While Miranda could only stand there and watch helplessly.

"Mom?" she whispered.

For an endless moment their eyes locked. Mom's hands fluttered uselessly toward her coffee cup, as if searching for some viable excuse.

"Mom . . . what's wrong?"

Her mother's shoulders sagged. Miranda moved slowly across the floor and took the empty chair across from her.

"What are you doing up?" Mom asked again.

"I was . . . thinking about stuff."

"Me, too." Mom made a feeble attempt at a laugh. "Well, your grandpa, mostly. But a lot of other stuff, too, I guess."

From her mother's red, puffy eyes, Miranda could tell she'd been crying for a long time. Now she asked cautiously, "What were you thinking about Grandpa?"

"About . . . oh, time, I suppose. How fast it goes. How much it can end up robbing you, if you let it."

Mom idly stirred her cold coffee, gazing down at her spoon.

"We were so different, Miranda—your grandpa and I. Teeta

was younger, and she was always closer to Daddy. I was the one closer to Mother, and after she died, I felt . . . I don't know . . . excluded, I guess. Teeta was always so good, and I was always the rebellious one."

"You!" Miranda couldn't hide her shock.

"Yes, me. And don't get any ideas." Mom frowned in mock sternness. "Daddy was . . . different. Teeta always seemed to understand that. Accept that."

"How do you mean?"

"He was . . . I don't know. Just *different.* Sort of quiet, never shared much. Strict with us and overly protective—at least that's how I saw things when I was growing up. He had his hobbies, his books . . . He kept to himself a lot. I never knew what he was thinking. But Mother—well, she was so animated, so happy all the time. You always knew where you stood with Mother, and people really loved her. But Daddy had these . . ." She shrugged. "Moods. That's what Mother called them. His moods."

Miranda said nothing. Simply waited for Mom to continue.

"I don't know how else to describe it, just that he'd get . . . *weird* about things. Like when Teeta and I would have our hearts set on going somewhere. And at the last minute Daddy would tell us we *couldn't* go, that something *bad* had happened there, and he'd forbid us to even step foot *near* the place."

"So . . . what'd you do?"

Mom gave a rueful smile. "We didn't go. No matter what Daddy said, no matter how irrational he sounded, and no matter how much Teeta and I argued—Mother would put her foot down, and we'd stay home."

"*Had* anything bad happened in those places?"

"Who knows? Daddy never explained how he knew about these so-called 'bad' things. Or where—or who—he got his inside information from." Mom's sarcasm was tempered with sadness. "Whatever the reasons, he completely believed them. And Mother completely believed *him*."

Chills raked at Miranda's spine. She didn't want to hear any more about Grandpa or his warnings, yet something held her tightly in her seat. Something that compelled her to keep listening.

"There was *one* time though." Mom's brow furrowed in thought. "I remember Teeta and I were going to a carnival in the next town. But sure enough, at the very last second, Daddy said we couldn't go. We were devastated. I wouldn't speak to him for days. Then about two weeks later, we found out five girls had been raped at that carnival."

The chills were growing steadily worse. Miranda could feel herself starting to tremble.

"Apparently every night this carnival worker would pick out a certain girl in the crowd to follow. He'd go up to her, looking very upset, and say he was worried about his wife—that she'd gone into one of the public restrooms but hadn't come out again. He'd say he'd been waiting for a long time, and he'd ask the girl to go in and check on her. Well, of course, all the girls wanted to help. He'd take each of them back to the very farthest shelter, back where nobody else was around. Then he'd pull a knife. And when it was over, he'd threaten them—tell them he knew where they lived, and if they ever said a word, he'd find them and kill them and kill their families, too."

"My God, those poor girls. They must have been so terrified."

"Thank goodness one of them finally found the courage to talk. She and her parents went to the police. But the carnival had left town by then . . . and the guy had left the carnival."

"Did they ever find him?"

"Yes. But . . ." Mom looked slightly incredulous at the memory. "After the news got out, Daddy walked over to the police station one morning and said he knew where the rapist was. Told them the guy was in River Camp—a town about five hundred miles from here. He gave them a physical description, down to the missing ring finger on the guy's left hand. The trailer park where he was staying, the color of the trailer, and the backcountry road where the park was located."

"Well, that was good, right?"

"Except that Daddy'd never been to River Camp. Never in his life."

"So..." *No. I can't ask. I* won't *ask.* "How did Grandpa know?"

"That's what the police wondered—along with everyone else in town. Daddy said he'd stopped at the gas station and overheard a man talking on the pay phone outside. And that when the man saw Daddy watching, he jumped in his car and took off before Daddy could get the license number."

Kind of lame. But kind of believable, too. Miranda's hands clenched together on the tabletop. She couldn't even look at her mother now. She could barely choke down the fear in her own throat.

Intent on the story, Mom didn't seem to notice. "But after Daddy went to the police, I heard him and Mother talking in their room that night. I didn't mean to listen—I was right outside their door, on my way downstairs. I think . . . Daddy was crying. I'd never known him to show that much emotion before, and it scared me. Mother was trying to comfort him, I guess, talking real quiet. I heard Daddy say something about another victim, and a hayfield, and that's how he'd known where the rapist was. That one of the *victims* told him."

Stop, Mom, please stop, don't say these things, don't make them true, don't make them real—

"I couldn't believe what I was hearing. I thought Daddy was very sick—*mentally* sick—that Mother had just been protecting him and not telling us the truth. And then . . ." Pausing, Mom drew a deep, shaky breath. "And then, a few days later, there it was in the newspaper. The police found a girl's body dumped in an old hayfield on an abandoned farm. Only a mile from where the carnival had been. They said she'd probably been there about three weeks."

Without realizing it, Miranda reached across and touched her mother's hand. "So you believed him *then*, right?"

It was a heartfelt plea. But one, Miranda knew at once, that her mother couldn't recognize.

"Of course I didn't believe him." Mom's tone bordered on

regret. "Because things like that are impossible. When Daddy was in one of his moods, we never knew *what* he might say—*what* he might make up."

"But . . . the rapist. Did they catch him in River Camp?"

Mom's lips pressed into a grim line. "They caught him, convicted him, and sent him to prison for life."

"And . . ." Miranda paused, her heart fluttering out of control. "And the girl in the hayfield. *Did* he kill her?"

A long silence fell between them. And even before her mother spoke, Miranda knew what the answer would be.

"Yes," Mom said at last. "He confessed to everything."

For an instant, Miranda felt the kitchen receding around her—she felt a thousand different emotions battering her from all sides. She was shivering violently now; she didn't know what to say. *Argue? Defend? Confess? Explain?* Clamping her arms tight around her chest, she fought to keep her voice level.

"Did your mother believe your dad?"

Mom wasn't looking at her now. Instead, she twirled her coffee cup slowly between her palms. "Oh, Mother always stood by him, no matter what. But things just got worse after that."

"How?"

"Well, maybe I should say, *Daddy* got worse after that. Or his *moods* got worse after that. Or maybe they'd been that bad all along, but till that night when I heard him and Mother talking, I just didn't realize *how* bad."

"Did you ever tell Aunt Teeta what you heard?"

"Of course. We started watching Daddy more, and he started

having more moods. We'd hear him talking to himself—sometimes for an hour, sometimes even longer—except it was like . . . like he was talking to another person. Of course, there wouldn't be anybody else *there.* And especially after Mother died—then we'd hear him having long conversations with *her.*"

"So what'd you do?"

"Well, it was obvious he was having a breakdown. But you didn't talk about things like that in St. Yvette; families kept personal things to themselves. Even though all our neighbors knew about it. Something like that's pretty hard to hide."

"Small town?"

Miranda was getting used to the cliché. Mom gave a faint smile.

"Small town," she agreed. "And Daddy became the small-town eccentric. People pretended not to notice the glazed look in his eyes, or the way he'd walk down the street, discussing things with invisible friends. Everyone considered him fairly creepy, but harmless. And naturally, Teeta refused to put him away. And naturally, I couldn't stand knowing what other people thought of him—*and* of us. The stares, the gossip, the jokes. I was embarrassed. And ashamed."

Briefly her eyes met Miranda's. As a wistful look passed over her face, she cleared her throat and pushed away her half-empty cup.

"I wish I could have been like Teeta. Maybe if I'd tried to understand Daddy more . . . help him more . . . "

It must have been so hard for you, Mom . . . so hard being

Grandpa's daughter. A million questions rose up in Miranda's mind, but she recognized the fragile edge to her mother's voice. Biting hard on her bottom lip, she resisted the urge to keep nagging.

"But at the time," Mom continued tonelessly, "all I wanted to do was get away from him. Away from *here.* As far away as I possibly could. And then I met your dad . . ." She hesitated, drew a ragged breath. "And I *did* get away."

Her mother's eyes had gone distant now. Tears trickled down her face. "Honey, I loved your dad so much. And then you came along, and things were even more perfect. I never dreamed that anything bad could happen to us—to your dad. That someone so young could have a heart attack . . . could be here one minute, so full of life, then be taken from us the next."

"Oh, Mom . . ."

"No, honey, I'm okay. When your father died, your grandpa and Aunt Teeta begged me to come back here. They wanted to take care of us. To help us and watch you grow up. But I just couldn't. I just couldn't come back to all the gossip and staring and everything else I'd put behind me. All I could see were the same things happening all over again. I didn't want you to grow up the way I had."

"Why didn't you ever tell me this before?"

"I guess . . ." Mom ran a weary hand over her wet cheeks. "It was just easier not to. Not to involve you in things you couldn't possibly have understood. Children shouldn't have to carry their parents' burdens."

"But maybe I could have helped you."

A wan smile touched her mother's lips. "You help me just by being you. And by being happy. That's all I could think about after the hurricane—keeping you safe and happy. But we *had* to come here, Miranda; we didn't have a choice. And I was scared. And I'm *still* scared, but I'm ashamed of myself, too."

"Mom, *why*?"

"Because you didn't get to meet your grandpa, and all he ever really wanted was for us to be a family."

Miranda felt tears on her own face now. "And do you really believe that? That we can be a family again? A *happy* family?"

"Yes. I do." Mom's voice was firm. "And I want you to believe it, too, Miranda. I tell your dad every day how proud I am of you, and how brave you are, and what a great life you're going to have."

"Really?"

"Well, of course. Why do you sound so surprised?"

"I never . . . I guess I never realized you thought about him. I mean, you never talk about him. Not to me, anyway."

Now it was Mom's turn to be surprised. "Oh, honey, how can you say that? Your dad was my whole world—and I know he was yours, too. And I thought if I brought up memories, it would just make both of us too sad. I wish I could wave a magic wand and make everything like it used to be, when he was here and everything was good. But I can't. And someone *had* to be strong. Had to be strong then *and* now, to hold you and me together."

Miranda felt another wave of emotions surge through her. For the moment, every suspicion, every bad thought, was forgotten.

"I'm here," she insisted. "You have me."

"Thank you, honey." Bending forward across the table, Mom tenderly kissed her brow. "I know that. And I promise I'll try to be better."

"Me, too, Mom. Me, too."

14

After her midnight talk with Mom, Miranda slept peacefully the rest of the night, even waking up much later than usual. She spent most of Sunday at home, meeting and greeting more neighbors, making room in the refrigerator for more food, jotting down more names for thank-you notes. From time to time she caught her mother smiling at her, giving an appreciative nod. Since Aunt Teeta was too upset to be of much help, Miranda was glad to give Mom some much-needed support.

To her surprise, Ashley, Roo, and Parker dropped by together, bringing a perfectly arranged tray of gourmet hors d'oeuvres from Mrs. Wilmington's favorite deli, a fresh pot of jambalaya from the girls' mother—Miss Voncile—and a homemade pie from Roo.

"We don't know *what* kind of pie exactly," Parker said, his face perfectly composed. "But I've heard it's the thought that counts."

A slight frown settled between Roo's brows. She'd changed the streaks in her hair from dark purple to bright orange.

"It's something I haven't tried before," she said solemnly. "It's made with cottage cheese."

Ashley instantly looked alarmed. "You didn't use the cottage cheese in the fridge, did you?"

"What other cottage cheese would I use?"

"For God's sake, Roo, that's been in there for weeks. It's nasty by now."

"Well, I'm sure the cooking part must have killed the bacteria, if that's what you're worried about."

Despite Parker's vivid portrayal of death by poisoning, Miranda made a special point of exclaiming over the pie. Then she dumped it in the trash can as soon as they left.

By late afternoon, she was beginning to feel trapped. The steady stream of visitors had finally dwindled, so she went out onto the veranda and sat in the porch swing, swaying back and forth, lulling herself into a doze. When she heard her name being spoken, she jumped guiltily, only to find Gage seated beside her.

"Didn't mean to wake you," he said.

"You didn't."

"Uh-huh."

"I was just . . . thinking."

"Do you always snore when you think?"

"I was *not* snoring."

"I could hear you all the way down the street."

Despite his insistence, she saw the teasing in his eyes. She looked around for the rest of the group, but he appeared to be alone.

"Feel like getting away?" he asked her.

"That obvious, huh?"

"The Tavern has the best burgers in town, if you don't mind walking."

"Just let me grab my purse."

After a quick check-in with Mom, Miranda was ready to go. The Tavern was at the opposite end of the Brickway and mostly uphill, but in spite of the heat, she welcomed the fresh air and exercise. Gage seemed in no particular hurry to get there. Side by side, they settled into a leisurely stroll, discussing various points of interest along the way.

"You know, I never thought much about St. Yvette before this project," Gage confessed.

"I never thought about my own town either. I guess when you live in a place, you just take it for granted."

"Now that I've started doing some research, there really is this whole dark-history thing going on. Bad stuff behind closed doors. Buildings that look so normal from the outside . . . but terrible tragedies inside."

"You *have* been doing research." She waited for him to bring up the gallery, but he didn't.

"It's interesting. Sad sometimes . . . scary sometimes . . . but definitely interesting."

I can certainly agree with that. Once again she toyed with the idea of confiding in Gage. Once again, she kept quiet.

"You just never know about people, do you?" Gage went on seriously. "You think you know somebody so well. Then it turns out you don't know them like you thought you did. Maybe we never really know anybody at all. Even the people we're closest to."

"Or maybe, *especially* the people we're closest to."

His lips hinted at a smile. "Maybe that's because we're so used to seeing certain people a certain way. The way we *want* to see them. It sort of gives us tunnel vision."

Now it was Miranda's turn to grow thoughtful. "Have *you* ever been disappointed? By people you thought you knew?"

"Wow. There's a loaded question."

"Or . . . have you ever trusted your instincts, and then found out you were completely wrong?"

"I let Roo talk me into playing doctor once when we were little." Gage sighed. "Unfortunately, she *really* meant *play doctor*. She decided my mosquito bite needed surgery and cut my knee open with a pair of blunt scissors."

Miranda's expression flinched between pain and laughter.

"I still have the scar." Gage cast her a sidelong glance. "But that's not what you were asking, is it? I'm guessing this has something to do with your grandfather."

Reluctantly, she nodded. "I just wish . . . can you tell me anything about him?"

"I didn't really know him."

"But you must know something about him."

Was Gage deliberately hedging? She couldn't tell.

"Why don't you ask your mom?" he suggested. "Or your aunt?"

"I just couldn't, especially not now. Not with what they're both going through."

"Then talk to Etienne. He spent time with your grandfather."

And confided in him, too, Miranda thought uneasily. "How did they get to be friends?"

Gage's only answer was a shrug. Miranda decided to keep trying.

"How is Etienne, anyway? About my grandpa, I mean. Has he gotten in touch with you yet?"

"No. He'll come out when he's ready."

"Are you close to him?"

"You mean, where we live?"

"No, Roo told me that you and he are cousins. I just wondered if you're close to him."

"Nobody's close to him," Gage said matter-of-factly. "But if anybody *were* close to him, then I guess it'd be me."

"So where *does* he live?"

"He and his mom have a little place down on the bayou. About a mile or so from the Falls."

Should she admit that Roo had told her about Etienne's past? "What about his dad?"

"He died."

Gage was facing forward, yet Miranda still caught the subtle change in his expression. The slow, rigid set of his jawline. The carefully fixed stare. Almost as though he were watching something too distant for her to see.

"Sorry," she murmured. "That's too bad." Then, after a split-second pause, she took a chance. "How did it happen?"

Another shrug from Gage. His straight-ahead stare didn't waver. "He had an accident."

She wondered why Gage didn't elaborate. Was it one of those personal things he didn't like discussing? Had Etienne asked him not to mention it? Whatever the reason, Miranda took the hint and let the subject drop. She could see The Tavern coming into view on a small cul-de-sac. When they got there, Gage held the door for her, and they went inside.

They found an empty booth in a back corner away from the noise. Miranda couldn't help noticing how many girls perked up as Gage walked through—waitresses and customers alike, calling his name, delighted to get his attention. Miranda recognized serious flirting when she saw it. Gage, on the other hand, seemed not to realize the obvious.

After ordering hamburgers, the two of them settled back in their seats and talked generalities—the high school volunteer program, favorite and not-so-favorite teachers, the football team, movies they loved, books they hated, and, ultimately, hurricanes.

"It never happens to somebody you know," Gage said. He angled himself into the corner, one elbow resting on the table, a Coke in his other hand. "It always just happens on the six o'clock news."

"You're right. And that's why you still can't believe it, even when it *does* happen to you. You just want to change the channel and watch something else."

An awkward silence followed, as if Gage were working up the courage to ask something personal. When he finally did, Miranda was caught off guard.

"I . . . just keep thinking. I mean, about you and . . ." Gage avoided eye contact. "I guess you must really miss everybody. And the way everything used to be in your life."

Thank God he wasn't looking at her. It was all she could do to force back tears. "It's all gone. Nothing will ever be the same."

"I'm sorry." Gage's voice lowered.

And then, without warning, the need to talk about it became overwhelming. "We lost everything when the hurricane hit. Our house, our furniture, our car, our clothes. Everyday stuff you don't even think about. I probably won't see my friends again for a really long time. Maybe never. And there's just this huge hole in my heart."

Gage kept silent, but his eyes had gone sad.

"I know Mom's really worried about money, too. I mean, she just found a job yesterday, but I know Aunt Teeta's helping us a lot." Miranda paused, embarrassed. She didn't know why she'd told him that; she didn't know why she was telling him *any* of this. As the waitress set down their food, she was thankful for the interruption; another second and she'd have been bawling her head off. *No more moments of weakness, Miranda. Way too risky, feeling that much at one time.*

"I shouldn't have said anything—" she mumbled, but Gage immediately stopped her.

"It stays between us, okay? Maybe this just happened to be the right time, when you really needed to tell somebody. And . . . you know . . . I'm glad it was me."

An unexpected warmth spread through her. She twisted her napkin in her hands. "Maybe we should talk about something else."

He smiled that smile. Picking up the bottle of ketchup, he poured it liberally over his Ultra-Supreme-Everything-But-the-Kitchen-Sink Burger.

"That building you were interested in . . ." He agreeably

switched the subject. "Magnolia Gallery. I told you I found some information about it."

"And . . ." Miranda was all ears.

"And . . . you were right. It *was* an opera house."

"It . . . are you sure?"

"It was originally built in the early eighteen hundreds. But a long time after the war, it changed from being the opera house to being the gallery."

A shiver of excitement went through her. She could hardly sit still as Gage continued explaining.

"St. Yvette might have been small, but it was known for its culture back then. There were lots of rich planters around here, and I guess that original opera house was all about prestige. And I guess some pretty famous people performed there."

Music . . . applause . . . swishing of fans . . . roses . . . a curtain falling . . . a voice singing . . .

Miranda drew in a slow breath. "Really? Like who?"

"Nobody I ever heard of." Gage chuckled. "But I guess some of them came all the way from Europe."

While the waitress refilled their glasses, Miranda chewed thoughtfully on a French fry. "Where'd you find this out?"

"The Internet didn't have much at all. So I stopped by the library yesterday and started looking through their private collection on St. Yvette. We can't take any of it out, but we can always go back there and do more research. The Historical Society might have some information, too. I thought maybe we could go there tomorrow after school."

Miranda wasn't sure she could hold out till tomorrow. She

was amazed at Gage's findings, at how closely they matched the impressions she'd received. And now that this eerie reality began to dawn on her, she wanted to find out all she could.

"Gage, did it say that anything bad happened at the opera house?"

"You mean, besides opera? That's pretty bad."

She couldn't help smiling. "Are you sure something *else* bad didn't happen?"

"I'm not sure at all. But *you* seem pretty sure."

Miranda tried for casual surprise. "I do?"

"And you seemed to know an awful lot yesterday about a place you'd never seen or heard about before."

It wasn't said accusingly, not even suspiciously. More like a gentle reminder. And once again Miranda felt torn. Gage obviously knew something was going on. And though Etienne was the one her grandpa had advised her to trust, she'd trusted Gage enough to share other personal things with him. *So why can't I tell him about the voices, the screams, the soldier in the park—*

Startled, she felt a slight pressure on the tip of her chin. She hadn't noticed Gage leaning toward her, napkin in hand.

"You have mustard," Gage murmured, "right . . . there."

She held very still while he cleaned it off. She wanted to concentrate on the opposite wall, but it was impossible to look anywhere but at him. Those big, brown eyes with their long dark lashes . . . innocent and wise at the same time . . . incredibly sweet . . . amazingly sexy . . .

"*He was* amazing . . ." Roo had said.

As the memory of Roo's confession caught her off guard,

Miranda tried once more to look away from Gage. To focus on anything but his eyes. The fantasy potential there was both endless and irresistible.

"One of the books I found showed some old playbills." To Miranda's relief, Gage drew back to his own side of the table, intent again on research. "There were a few pretty bad photos of the building, too. It didn't say when they were taken though."

Miranda fidgeted with her napkin. "What about entertainers?"

"Their names and their acts were listed on the playbills. Singers. Actors. Dancers. Clowns." His frown was genuinely disturbed. "Why are clowns so creepy?"

"You're afraid of clowns?"

"I didn't say that. I just said they're creepy."

Miranda watched him, amused. The best defense was an even better offense.

"You're staring," Gage mumbled.

"I can't help it."

"Why? Do I have a messy face, too?"

"No." Miranda couldn't resist. "You have dimples."

He squirmed self-consciously. "I guess."

"I bet you get teased a lot."

"Is there some relevant point to this?"

Miranda did her best to keep a straight face. "Just that they're so cute."

"Stop it."

"Are you blushing?"

"Shut up."

Oh, Gage, you have no idea . . . if Marge and Joanie were here right now, they'd jump all over you.

Still flustered, Gage signaled the waitress. But it was someone else who walked over instead.

"Private conversation?" Etienne greeted them.

"No," Gage answered, a little too quickly.

"*Intimate* conversation?"

"I was just telling him about his . . ." Miranda began, but Gage looked so trapped, she didn't have the heart to bring Etienne into it. "Just telling him about—"

"We were talking about the gallery," Gage broke in. "That building she was wondering about."

Etienne glanced purposefully from Gage to Miranda and back again. "I don't know, from where I was standing over there, you were looking a little embarrassed."

"The opera house. I was telling her what I found out."

"Okay, if you say so."

"It's true!"

"And I said okay. I believe you. You gonna eat the rest of those fries?"

Gage slid his plate across the table as Etienne slid in beside Miranda. Etienne shot her a secret wink.

"It's not the thing with the dimples again, is it?" he asked innocently. "I don't know what it is with girls, the way y'all love his—"

"Why are you here?" Gage asked. Getting to his feet, he pointed toward the restrooms. "I'll be right back. *You* can leave the tip."

"I was going to anyway."

"No, I'm paying for my own." Miranda picked up the tab, but Etienne's hand came firmly down on hers.

"Gage and me, we are *nothing* if not true southern gentlemen. And a lady *never* pays on her first date."

Now Miranda was flustered. "It's *not* a date. We really *were* talking about that building."

"I know that." Shrugging, he yanked a napkin from the metal holder. "I also know Beth, your waitress. She's the one who heard you teasing Gage."

"You are so bad."

With a vague frown, Miranda settled back to watch him eat. Unlike Gage, it didn't seem to bother him, being the object of her scrutiny. She could only marvel at his focus.

"Magnolia Gallery," she said at last, "Etienne . . . it *was* an opera house."

"You sound surprised."

"I . . . I don't know what to think."

"How about the truth?"

For a long moment, she gazed down at her plate. It was the intensity of Etienne's stare that made her look up again.

"I'm sorry I didn't pass by your house." His voice, though lower now, had tightened. "I should have. I wanted to."

"Don't apologize. You were my grandpa's friend. This must be really hard for you."

Etienne didn't answer. Resting his elbows on the table, he wiped his mouth with the napkin, then crumpled the napkin in one fist. Miranda wondered what he was feeling. She understood that sense of loss, of being left behind. But with Etienne, it was almost impossible to know what emotions he was hiding.

"Maybe . . . maybe there's something of Grandpa's you'd like to have?" she suggested. "To remember him by? I could make sure you get it."

He seemed to mull this over. "Thanks. I'll think about it."

"I'd really like to."

The hard lines softened around his mouth. "I know," he said quietly.

Well . . . I guess this is as good a time as any. She hadn't been able to tell Gage, but Etienne . . . "Something happened to me in the park yesterday. And I know I didn't imagine it."

This time she'd definitely piqued his interest. He seemed about to question her when Gage suddenly leaned over the back of their booth.

"I just remembered," Gage said to Miranda.

Etienne shifted easily to one hip, fished into his pocket, tossed some money on the table. "What's that?"

"The *name* of the opera house."

Gage stood aside as the other two got out. He added his own money to Etienne's.

But Etienne was only half listening. "Come on, I'll give y'all a ride."

"So what is it?" Miranda asked. "What's the name?"

Gage squeezed in close to her as they pushed their way to the door. "The Rose."

"The *what*?"

"The Rose Opera House." Gage's expression turned curious. "Have you heard of it?"

Quickly Miranda shook her head. They were at the truck now, and she climbed in tensely between the two boys. Etienne started the engine, and her mind raced back, back to yesterday, to the old building and the sweet smell of roses . . . to the park and the ghostly plea: *"Take it . . . the rose . . ."*

Connections, somehow? Coincidences?

"Miranda? Here's your house."

"What?" Both Gage and Etienne were looking at her. She managed a sheepish smile. "Oh. Sorry. You guys want to come in?"

She was conscious now of Etienne's thigh against hers. And of Gage's arm along her shoulders, resting lightly on the back of the seat. The guys seemed to exchange a mutual glance.

"Better not." Etienne shrugged. "Night job."

"Homework." Helping her out, Gage walked Miranda to the door. "Don't forget about the Historical Society. Right after school tomorrow."

"I won't. And thanks for tonight, Gage. I had a really good time."

Smiling, he turned and headed back to the truck as Miranda let herself in.

Surprisingly, no one seemed to be around. Aunt Teeta's door was closed, and though the TV still blared from the den, Miranda found her mother sound asleep on the couch. Deciding not to wake her, she shut off the television, covered Mom with an afghan, then hurried upstairs.

The Rose Opera House!

Is that what the Gray Soldier—Nathan—was trying to tell me? Not a flower, but a place*? That must be it—why else would I have known about the gallery once being an opera house?*

Flopping down on her bed, she gazed numbly at the ceiling. More puzzle pieces fitting together . . . but still so unbelievable . . . still so impossible!

No . . . not impossible. The truth. Grandpa knew the truth. And you know it, too, Miranda.

Turning off the bedside lamp, she closed her eyes and drifted. The darkness was sultry and still, a deep hole to hide in. She wished she could turn off her mind as easily as she could turn off the light, but her thoughts refused to cooperate. *If only I could find answers . . . figure things out . . .*

The Rose Opera House.

"For Miss Ellena . . . take it . . . the rose . . ."

"Help me."

Miranda shuddered as Nathan's words echoed over and over in her head. Like a song, like a spell. Over and over and over again . . . exhausting her into sleep . . .

Miranda was floating . . . surrounded by darkness, suspended in time. And there was a faint, faraway voice . . . like an echo underwater . . . rippling softly . . . shimmering sadly . . .

Miranda strained to hear.

"Take it . . . for Miss Ellena . . ."

She was apart from everything—she was part of everything; he could see her—she was invisible; she suffered with him—she was at peace—*helpless and trapped in the smoke and the fog and the downpour of rain and the earth running dark, dark crimson with blood . . .*

"Help me," Nathan said to her. The soldier in gray, the young man with the helpless, haunted face. *"You're the only one."*

And his pale, outstretched hand . . . a short length of twine, woven, knotted . . . only *this* time her fingers brushed over it, *this* time her fingers closed around it.

Miranda touched his hand. His skin was ice cold; her fingers passed right through.

"*Take it . . .*"

Jerking upright, she saw the figure beside her bed.

The figure veiled in shadows, just beyond reach of the moonlight through her windows.

She tried to cry out, but couldn't; her heart leapt into her throat and stuck there as she gasped for breath.

"No!" Miranda choked.

She closed her eyes, willing him away. When she opened them again, he was gone.

Yet Miranda wasn't comforted. Tears ran down her cheeks; her covers were damp with sweat. She reached for the lamp on her nightstand, then suddenly froze.

She was holding something. Something clutched tightly in her hand.

Puzzled, she spread her fingers and looked closer. In the room's pale glow, she could see the small, familiar object nestled there against her palm.

"Oh my God . . ." she whispered.

It was a piece of braided twine.

15

Praying no one would hear her, Miranda sped downstairs to use the kitchen phone. As she punched in Etienne's number, she was still shaking.

"Please, Etienne," she whispered. One ring. Two. "Please pick up."

She had to tell someone. There was nobody here she could talk to, and she had to tell someone what had just happened, what she'd just found.

Three rings. Four.

Her grandpa had told her to trust Etienne, and she wanted to—more than anything right now, she *wanted* to trust him. *And I* need *to trust him. Because he's the only one now who'll believe me.*

Five rings. "Come on, Etienne, where are you?"

"Yeah?" That deep, husky voice, slightly breathless. "Yeah, hello?"

"Etienne—"

"Miranda? What's wrong?"

"I'm sorry. I hope you weren't asleep."

"Me, no, I never sleep." His tone sharpened. "Something's wrong, I can tell. What is it?"

Hesitating, she cupped her hand around the phone and

glanced nervously over her shoulder. She took a deep, steadying breath, barely managing a whisper. "I need to talk to you. I need your help."

"Wait for me in your room."

"What! Now?"

Realizing he'd hung up, Miranda stood there, still clutching the receiver. She hadn't actually asked him to come by—she'd have been thankful for just a comforting conversation over the phone.

But now that he *was* coming, she felt better . . . *and* safer. She only hoped he'd get here fast.

Reluctantly she crept to her bedroom, pausing on the threshold to make sure she was alone. She switched on every lamp, put on her robe, and curled back against the headboard with her pillows around her. She figured Etienne would sneak in the side door downstairs, so when she heard footsteps out on the sunporch, her heart nearly stopped.

"Miranda, it's me," Etienne said softly. "You okay?"

Ducking his head, he slipped through the low doorway. As he stopped beside her bed and gazed down at her, Miranda went limp with relief.

"How'd you know where my room is?" she asked.

"Your *grand-père,* he had me fixing things in here the week before you came. He was always hoping you'd live in this house."

The reminder stabbed painfully through her. Trying not to cry, she gestured past Etienne toward the sunporch. "How'd you get in?"

"What, you think I don't know how to pick a lock?"

She couldn't tell if he was teasing or not, but his eyes were dead serious, sweeping the room with one keen glance. "What's going on, *cher*?"

But now that he was with her, she couldn't say it. All she could do was point to her nightstand and the piece of knotted twine she'd tossed there when she'd run for the phone.

Etienne's brow furrowed. "This?" And then, when Miranda finally nodded, he scooped it up to examine it more closely. "What the hell is it?"

"I don't know."

"So . . . what am I missing? Where'd you get it?"

"Nathan gave it to me," she whispered, but not loud enough for Etienne to hear. She watched him hold it near the lamp, turn it carefully over in his palm. It was about six inches long, narrower than a pencil, and shone dull in the lamplight, the color of rust.

"It's solid . . . really tight. But it's not twine . . . I don't think it's any kinda string. See here, how it's braided?" Etienne shot her a sidelong glance. "More like hair, yeah? Like a piece of braided hair?"

Miranda couldn't look at it anymore; it made her skin crawl. "You're not serious, are you?"

"It's been braided once . . . and then back over itself." Etienne's long fingers stroked the woven edges. "And look—there's something on each end . . . hard to see, they're so tarnished. Like some kinda clamps or clasps—what, to keep the hair from unraveling?"

"Etienne, *please* tell me you didn't just say—"

"Hair. I think this is human hair."

Clutching a pillow to her chest, Miranda fought off a fresh wave of horror. "Then what does it mean? And why did Nathan give it to *me*?"

"Nathan? Whoa, now. Just a minute. Who's Nathan?"

"The Gray Soldier." She was shaking again; she could hear her words tumbling out all wrong. "That's his name—the soldier in the park. Except he wasn't real. I mean, he was *real*—but a real *ghost*. And then tonight when he was here . . . tonight in my room when—"

Abruptly she broke off. The confusion in Etienne's eyes had faded to understanding; his face blurred through her tears.

"Start at the beginning." Slowly he sat beside her on the bed. "And don't leave anything out."

Somehow she was able to do it—to recall her experiences in detail; to answer his occasional questions; to explain as best she could. She knew Etienne believed her, yet she longed to know what he was thinking. She wished she could see inside that calm, black stare, into the carefully guarded places of his mind.

As Miranda finished, Etienne refocused his attention on the braid. "So where does this fit in with everything?"

"And all the stuff about roses?" Miranda added. "I smelled them at the gallery that morning . . . Nathan talked about a rose . . . and then tonight Gage tells me the name of that opera house was the Rose. Those can't be just coincidences."

"You got any idea who Miss Ellena is?"

"None."

"And I'm guessing this Nathan, he's in the Rebel army, him wearing that gray uniform and all."

Again, she nodded. "He was so sad, Etienne. I don't know how to describe it exactly, but . . ." Miranda made a futile gesture. "*More* than sad, even. *Worse* than sad. Just empty . . . completely lost."

The room fell silent. Only night sounds now, mingled faintly beyond the open windows. She was all too aware of Etienne's gaze, though she'd closed her eyes. And sensing he might reach for her, she picked up another pillow to hug, and leaned her head back against the wall.

"So I guess this is how my life's going to be from now on," she murmured. "Just like Mom said it was for Grandpa. All kinds of bad surprises coming out of nowhere."

"Not all bad," Etienne answered quietly.

Opening her eyes, Miranda fixed him with a bitter stare. "Being scared all the time? Having to see the very worst tragedies? And hear the very worst sufferings? How can I—how could *any* person—be expected to live that way?"

"'Cause you've got to." Etienne was firm, though not unkind. "'Cause like it or not—*want* it or not—it's who you are. Look, your *grand-père,* he loved you so *much.* Do you think for one second he'd have wanted you hurt or unhappy?"

"Then why didn't he just tell me how I could escape the family curse?"

"If he'd thought it was a curse—and if there'd been a way out—I'm sure he'd have told you. For your sake."

Despite her resentment, Miranda needed to believe that. She remembered the last time she'd seen her grandfather, and her smile began to fade. "So what happens now? What can I do about it?"

"Not turn them away."

Just what Grandpa said.

"Listen to them. And help them." As Etienne's voice softened, some deep, hidden emotion flickered briefly in his eyes. "Your *grand-père,* he made a whole lotta differences in their world. And when *they* found peace . . . then *he* found peace. Let them guide you."

"You mean, like Nathan? Is *he* trying to guide me?"

"Think about it. When you see him—when he talks to you—besides feeling sad for him, what do you know? Down here in your gut, what do you really *know*?"

"I know . . ." *Yes, Miranda, look inside . . . you* do *know.* "I know . . . he wants me to deliver a message. I know the message is really important. And I know it's for someone named Miss Ellena."

"So that's where you need to start, yeah? With what you know."

"But how will that help him if I can't figure out the rest?"

"You *can,*" Etienne assured her. "And I'm gonna help you. Whatever kind of research we need to do, we'll take each clue as it comes. And right now"—he held up the braid, dangling it between his fingers—"this is the best clue we've got."

Miranda's face went grim. "Well, the only clue we can actually see and touch, anyway. Even if we *don't* know what it is."

"But something might come to you, yeah? Maybe if you just look at for a little while . . . or hold it in your hand?"

"No. I can't." As more tears threatened, she fought to control the quiver in her voice. "I don't want to see him in my room again. I'm sorry . . . I just can't."

"Ssh . . . it's okay. I'll take it with me, how's that? You need to rest anyhow, and I need to go."

Almost fearfully, Miranda looked up again. She watched Etienne get to his feet and slip the braid into the front pocket of his work shirt. She watched him bend over to peer solemnly into her eyes.

"The next few days are gonna be hard, *cher*. The wake and the funeral and all. You gotta be strong, you gotta be good for your family . . ." His voice trailed off. His hand brushed lightly over her hair. "Jonas, he was always so proud of you," Etienne whispered. "Now I know why."

The words stayed with her long into the night. Long after Etienne had left her, long after her eyelids finally closed.

And *"Who'll watch out for them?"* she heard her grandfather whispering. *"For all of them? After I'm gone?"*

16

Somehow Miranda dragged herself through Monday.

She didn't remember falling asleep the night before, or if any ghostly voices had sought her out in dreams.

Exhausted and depressed, she was already in a foul mood by the time she got to school—and the morning went steadily downhill from there. She'd translated the wrong chapter in her Spanish workbook; she'd completely forgotten about a math assignment. She flunked a pop quiz in English lit. Parker was in her first class, Ashley and Gage in her third, and she could swear they were acting differently toward her today. Evasive, she noted, and somewhat distant. She even caught Parker staring from time to time, but when she made eye contact, he quickly looked away.

She told herself that it was all in her mind, that she was being paranoid—yet she couldn't shake the feeing that something was wrong. When noon rolled around, she decided to hide out in the library. She didn't expect Ashley to show up at her locker before she could escape.

"Have lunch with us." Ashley smiled, as friendly as ever. Almost *too* friendly, Miranda couldn't help thinking. "We've got this great spot outside where we always eat."

Miranda had seen them and their great spot on her first day of school. The close-knit group eating at their special table, in their own private corner of the schoolyard. Now Ashley's invitation made her feel irritable and trapped. She had too much on her mind; she needed to find a quiet place, be alone, sort things out. She didn't *want* to be part of their group. They'd forced her into it, and now everything was a mess. They were getting too close to her, and now her life was worse than ever.

"I'm not hungry," she insisted, slamming her locker door.

Instantly sympathetic, Ashley laid a comforting hand on her arm. "Are you worried about that quiz? Don't be. There was a death in your family—Mr. Klein's really understanding about things like that. All the teachers are. Trust me, he won't even count that grade."

"I just can't eat right now, okay?"

"You don't have to eat. We need to talk about the project—get your opinion on some things before we turn in that outline."

Miranda cringed. She'd forgotten that their project outline was due today, but Ashley was quick to reassure her.

"We didn't want to bother you with it, Miranda. You had enough on your mind this weekend. Anyway, Gage and I put something together. Like we always do, when we're working with Roo and Parker." She paused for a long-suffering sigh. "But I think the outline's good. Very good and very thorough."

"Then you don't need my opinion," Miranda replied stubbornly. "I'm sure whatever you did is perfect."

"We really need you, Miranda. Please come. The group's not complete without you."

Don't you get it? I don't want *to complete the group, I* never *wanted to complete the group. I want to be left alone.*

Without giving Miranda another chance to refuse, Ashley practically dragged her down the hall. There were a lot of kids eating outside, some at wooden picnic tables, others at round umbrella tables, many on benches, steps, and blankets, or just grabbing quick snacks at the vending machines. Miranda saw the four familiar faces in their usual hangout—Etienne among them—but again she sensed that something had changed. As if they were all studying her. And trying not to. And hoping she wouldn't notice.

"Hey, there you are." Gage immediately slid over to make room. "We tried to catch you after class, but you disappeared."

Miranda settled beside him. Parker was gulping down a Coke, watching her over the rim of his cup. Ashley sat down next to Parker, her smile fixed firmly in place. Standing, Etienne leaned casually against the table. Roo was the only one who met Miranda's eyes.

"You met a ghost," Roo said. "How cool is that?"

Parker choked, spitting ice in all directions.

There followed a moment of stricken silence. Then, turning to Roo, Gage shook his head in disbelief. "Very nice. Hell of a lead-in."

"Subtle as always," Parker muttered, brushing ice chips and cola off the front of his shirt.

Even Ashley looked distressed. As Roo's words began to sink in, Miranda could only sit there in stunned silence, pinned by five pairs of eyes. Then she turned slowly to Etienne.

"You . . . told them?" Her voice hardened with the pain of betrayal. "You told them what happened?"

"Right, like we're not already involved." Roo gave a dismissive shrug. "Like we all didn't see you freaking out at the gallery yesterday."

Parker and Gage closed ranks. "Roo, shut up."

"What? What's the big deal?"

Throughout the exchange, Miranda kept watching Etienne, searching for some sign of remorse. But his stare—and his words—weren't the least bit apologetic.

"Look, with all of us, there's a whole lot better chance of figuring things out. I thought Gage might know what the braid was. Or Parker might've seen one sometime at the museum. You and me, we can't think of *everything*, yeah?"

"So you *told* them," Miranda repeated, still shocked.

"It was the right thing to do—the *smart* thing to do. And they needed to know."

"You had no right." Pain had turned to anger now. Miranda's throat squeezed tighter and tighter. "You wanted me to trust you."

"And I meant it."

"You were supposed to keep this secret. This is a secret thing."

"Get used to it," Parker snorted. "No secrets in *this* motley crew."

Taking her elbow, Gage turned her gently back toward the others. "It's okay, Miranda. We—"

"We'd just like to help." Ashley broke in.

It was all Miranda could do not to break down. Numbly she

stood up and started walking away, but what Etienne said next, stopped her.

"Your *grand-père*, it's what he wanted, Miranda."

"No," she replied, fixing him with a bold, accusing stare. "He wanted *you* to help me, no one else."

"I *am* helping you."

"How? By sneaking around behind my back? By making fun of me?"

"Uh-oh," Parker mumbled. "Soap-opera time."

"Listen to me." Before Miranda could take another step, Etienne blocked her path and caught her firmly by the shoulders. "I already told you, I *saw* what it did to Jonas. And I'm *not* gonna let that happen to you."

There was cold, hard truth in his eyes. And a determination so strong, it nearly overpowered her.

"Miranda?" Ashley's concern broke the tension. "Please?"

Etienne released her. As Miranda reluctantly faced the group around the table, she could see every intent expression waiting for her response.

"We really can help you," Ashley said softly. "Please let us."

Miranda turned back to Etienne. His gaze was sure and steady.

"You need friends, *cher*. And we're your friends."

Seconds dragged by while she tried to think. She was hurt and confused; she was flattered and touched and even strangely relieved. The reality of her life was crowding in on her, much too close, much too quick.

"It wouldn't be so scary with us around." Roo said philosophically.

Tipping his cup, Parker shook more ice into his mouth and slanted Roo a look. "Not true. It's always scary with you around."

"Give us some credit." Gage winked at Miranda. "We might surprise you if you give us a chance."

"You don't have to be in this alone," Ashley insisted.

Yet despite the positive support, Miranda couldn't shake her bewilderment or her doubts. "Why are you doing this?" she asked them. *You're already friends, and people like you don't let strangers into your exclusive little group. Besides that, how could you possibly understand what you're getting into, when I don't even understand it myself?* "You don't even know me."

"Etienne threatened us." Yawning loudly, Parker gave a long stretch, then wheezed as Ashley punched him in the ribs. "I'm *kidding*! Hey, I'm *kidding*, okay? *Damn*, Ashley!"

"You might as well say yes, Miranda," Ashley persisted as if Parker weren't there. "Because we're going to help you find out about poor Nathan one way or another."

"How?" Miranda challenged. "*How* are you going to do that?"

"Well . . . we . . . don't know yet. We're still . . . still . . ."

"Trying to decide if I'm as crazy as my grandpa was?" To Miranda, the uneasy silence spoke volumes. It lasted only a second, but that was long enough for her heart to drop. "Look, you guys." Her tone came out harsher than she'd intended. *What was I thinking? I should have just kept on walking.* "This is private, okay? And I don't need any help, and it really doesn't matter if you believe me, so—"

"I believe you," Gage said quietly.

"You know *I* do," Roo echoed.

"And me." Ashley's head bobbed up and down.

Scowling, Parker glanced at each of them. Then he folded his arms across his chest, leaned back, and scowled harder. "Well, I don't believe her. I don't believe any of y'all, and I think you're *all* crazy. But . . . what the hell."

"Well, *cher.*" Etienne faced Miranda. "The sooner we start, the better, yeah?"

The bell rang then. Grateful for the distraction, Miranda trailed the others back across campus. She was just starting into the building when Etienne suddenly took her arm and steered her into an alcove where they couldn't be seen.

Flustered, she peered up at him. He wasn't holding her now, but the alcove was small, and their bodies were practically touching. As his eyes fixed on hers, she realized he'd moved nearer, and there was nowhere she could go.

Her pulse began to race. He was standing so close—*too* close—and she wanted him closer, even as she wanted to push him away. She was afraid he might actually hear her heartbeat or her quick intake of breath.

"Miranda," Etienne murmured, "I promised to help you. To protect you."

His stare never wavered. His lips were only inches from her own.

"I keep my promises."

Before Miranda could react, Etienne was out of the alcove and backing slowly away, one corner of his mouth hinting at a smile.

17

When Miranda met Gage after school, she found the whole group waiting there with him.

"Gage said y'all were going to the museum," Ashley announced. "So it only makes sense for *all* of us to go."

"Yeah, you two didn't want to be alone, did you?" Roo shot Gage a sly glance, hiding a smile as he looked away.

Ashley tugged excitedly on Miranda's arm. "Then we can research our Ghost Walk *and* Nathan's ghost at the same time!"

They headed toward the Brickway, while Ashley systematically checked off topics in her notebook.

"Okay, here's how we figured things out. Are y'all listening?"

Parker instantly looked suspicious. "Who figured what things out?"

"Parker, were you paying *any* attention in class when I handed in our outline? Research for the project, of course. And who *else* would do it? Gage and I *always* do all the work."

"Not true." Roo frowned. "I contributed."

"You criticized. And complained. A lot." Not bothering to hide her annoyance, Ashley continued down her list. "I'll take the courthouse."

"No, I want the courthouse," Parker insisted. "I'm all into that evil judge."

"This is *not* about your father. You take the museum."

Incredulous, Parker gaped at her. "My mom works there!"

"I know your mom works there. That's why we gave it to you. You won't even have to do anything—just ask your mom about stuff."

"No. No way I'm working with her."

"Oh, fine then, Parker. Just fine. You can take Grace Church."

"Hell, no!"

"Just give him the courthouse," Roo spoke up. "Maybe that curse'll rub off on him and he'll hang himself."

"Then *I'll* do the museum." Ashley's sigh was exasperated. "Roo wants the doctor's house. And the library–funeral parlor."

Glancing at Ashley, Parker feigned amazement. "Don't you ever find this disturbing? That your sister's so obsessed with dead things?"

"Why should it?" Roo threw back at him. "She goes out with *you*, doesn't she?"

Ashley doggedly kept on. "Gage said he'd do Grace Church."

"Way to go, Gage!" Parker clapped Gage hard on the shoulder. "Who's Grace Church?"

"Parker Wilmington, nobody here thinks you're funny."

"Come on, Ash, admit it. Everybody here thinks I'm *kind* of funny—"

"Etienne's going to find out stuff about voodoo. Oh, and Roo and I are going to research that little boy who died at the feed store. And Miranda gets Magnolia Gallery—but of course we'll all help her with that. And . . . and I guess that's about it."

"Damn." Parker did his best to sound disappointed. "I was hoping for a whole lot more."

Nodding sympathetically, Roo swept him with solemn eyes. "How sad. That's exactly what Ashley always says about you."

"Oh, except for this other idea I had." Ashley glanced hopefully around the group. "Instead of calling it Ghost Walk, why don't we call it something else?"

"*Great* idea." Parker was adamant. "Why don't we call it *off*?"

"How about"—Ashley paused dramatically, her eyes sparkling—"Walk of the Spirits?"

As everyone traded glances, Gage repeated it several times out loud. "Yeah. I like it."

"Me, too," Miranda spoke up. "I think it's good."

"I think it's romantic," Ashley sighed. "Walk of the Spirits . . . don't you think it's wonderfully romantic?"

"I think it's wonderfully . . . you." Etienne patted Ashley's shoulder. "But could we move a little faster here? I got me a lotta work to do this evening."

"That's okay, this is just our first outline. We still have to refine it. And we still have a lot more research to do."

Gage nodded. "Then we have to write up a script for the tour. And everything has to be timed. And—"

"Enough torture." Parker glowered at each of them. "I get the idea."

"But hey, y'all." Ashley fairly glowed with pride. "The important thing is that Miss Dupree loves our project even more now. Did you see the look on her face when she was reading our outline? I've never seen her that excited about any assignment before, have you?"

"I've never seen her excited about anything." Parker exchanged guy looks with Etienne. "She needs to get laid."

"You know, at some point, we really need to do a trial run of this thing," Gage advised, ignoring Parker. "Seeing it in daylight is totally different than seeing it at night. If we're gonna get the full effect, we need to walk it after dark."

"He's right," Ashley agreed. "Just . . . not tonight."

"How come not—" Parker began, then winced as Ashley squeezed his arm. Noting her glance toward Miranda, he was instantly contrite. "Oh. Sorry. I forgot about the wake."

Miranda was quick to reassure him. "If I didn't have to be there, I wouldn't go either."

They'd reached the Historical Society. Before anyone could go inside, Parker started backing away.

"Oh, for heaven's sake," Ashley scolded him. "It won't kill you to see your mother."

"But I haven't seen her in weeks, so the shock really *could* kill me." He paused on the curb, grin widening. "Besides, I wouldn't even know what she looks like. And besides that, somebody still needs to find out if we can take tours inside some of these businesses. So I volunteer."

"Right," Gage answered. "Like you're suddenly so interested."

"Hey, never let it be said that I'm not a team player!"

"A *cowardly* team player!" Ashley shot back.

As Parker sauntered away, Roo nudged Miranda. "See what I mean?"

They'd barely walked through the door when a tall, willowy blond woman glided toward them. Her hair was swept back into a diamond clip, she had Parker's eyes, and her tailored suit was unmistakably designer label. She was lovely and elegant and smelled faintly of expensive perfume.

"Why, hello, Ashley darlin'!" Mrs. Wilmington caught Ashley in a carefully distanced hug. "I see the whole group is here."

Whole group? Miranda felt a twinge of defensiveness. *Parker's not here.* She studied the woman more closely. Mrs. Wilmington was staring at Roo, and not quite managing to hide her distaste. Roo looked smugly victorious.

"And you must be Miranda." Parker's mother offered a welcoming handshake. "Well, aren't you just the sweetest thing."

Embarrassed, Miranda was all too aware of Roo and Ashley hiding smiles, while Gage and Etienne seemed to find the whole thing silently hilarious. Mrs. Wilmington's handshake was limp.

"My, my, you look so much like your granddaddy," the woman observed.

"Dead?" Roo mumbled, while Gage elbowed her in the side.

Mrs. Wilmington didn't notice. "He was a very special person, your granddaddy. He and I were close friends for a long, long time."

"Run for your life," Roo hissed in Miranda's ear. "She's after something."

"Parker told me about the project y'all are working on, and that you'd probably be stopping by." Mrs. Wilmington made an all-inclusive gesture of the room. "And I think it's just wonderful. Whatever it takes to get our young people interested in their community—I fully support it!"

She paused, fingering the strand of pearls around her neck. Her frown was brief, but compassionate.

"I'm so sorry to hear about your granddaddy, Miranda," she said. "Really, it's such a shame."

Miranda managed an awkward nod. "Thank you for the food and flowers, Mrs. Wilmington."

"You are most welcome. *Most* welcome. Now. How might I help you ladies and gentlemen today?"

To Miranda's relief, Gage stepped forward. "We were wondering if you knew anything about an old opera house. We think it used to be where the Magnolia Gallery is."

"Opera house . . . opera house." The woman's face sank into deep thought. "You must mean the Rose Opera House."

As Gage nodded, Mrs. Wilmington's voice grew nostalgic and sad.

"The Rose was almost completely destroyed by fire around . . . 1863? Well, very near the middle of the war. A small portion of the remaining building *was* salvaged, however. And many years later that became part of a brand-new gallery."

Catching Miranda's eye, Gage smiled encouragement. Parker's mother gestured them all toward a doorway.

"Come along in here," she instructed. "Let me just see what we've got on that subject."

They followed her into an adjoining room—part library, part office—where she quickly scanned several tall bookcases, then consulted the computer on her immaculate desk. After studying the screen for several moments, she turned to them again, adjusting small, dainty reading glasses on the bridge of her perfect nose job.

"Built in 1830 . . . let's see now . . . and my, yes, just as I suspected. Quite the hub of cultured society."

"Oh," Ashley sighed. "How romantic."

"There are several photos in these files. I can print them out for you, if you like."

Gage glanced at the others. "Thanks. That'd be great."

While the information was being processed, Parker's mother spoke the rest from memory. "Only the rich and titled could afford such luxuries, you understand. The operas—and plays—usually came here from New Orleans. In fact, any traveling shows passing near or through St. Yvette were always welcome. But there were local events, too, and local talent. Theater troupes and ballet, special events and extravaganzas."

Strolling behind Mrs. Wilmington, Roo made a face. "*Extravaganzas?*" she mouthed silently.

"You said aristocrats were the main audience." Arms folded over his chest, Etienne angled himself back against the wall. "Who exactly would that've been?"

"Well, the upper class, obviously. The ones who held all the power. Plantation owners . . . doctors . . . lawyers . . . wealthy merchants, just to name a select few. And, during the Civil War, high-ranking Confederate officers, of course. Until the Union army laid siege to the town."

Mrs. Wilmington removed her glasses and toyed with one pearl earring. Ashley stared longingly at the jewelry.

"Normally, there would be quite lavish parties at the opera house after the performances. Some of the performers were regarded as royalty—they were the famous celebrities of their day."

Roo was not impressed. "How famous? Like rock stars?"

Ashley gave her a lethal frown.

"They were honored and esteemed wherever they went." Mrs. Wilmington sounded deeply insulted. "They came here to St. Yvette not only from New Orleans, but from every major city in the United States. And some actually traveled from Vienna and Paris and London."

As the printer churned out copies, Etienne picked one up and began studying it. He motioned Miranda over so the two of them could examine it more closely. The photograph didn't seem particularly exceptional, Miranda decided—just like any other public building of that era, except on a much grander scale. Wide, tall columns; wide, shallow steps rising to the entrance; wide, massive doors; a wide, curved drive.

"Notice the architecture," Mrs. Wilmington said proudly, peering over their shoulders. "The driveway was specifically designed for horse-drawn carriages. So ladies and gentlemen could alight close to the building, without mussing their clothes."

"*Alight?*" Roo mouthed again to Miranda. "*Mussing their clothes?*"

Ashley's face took on a dreamy expression. "All those hoop skirts and fans . . . I just love hoop skirts and fans."

Trying to view the photo, Roo crowded in next to Mrs. Wilmington. The woman discreetly cringed and moved away.

"Can I see one of those?" Gage asked, coming over to join them. He retrieved another printout, then leaned in close to Miranda, comparing both photographs side by side. The photo he held had been taken on the night of a performance—the building crowded with people, the driveway lined with carriages.

The entrance overflowed with flowers.

Miranda made a small, choked sound in her throat. Curious, Ashley and Mrs. Wilmington walked up behind her while the others exchanged lowered glances.

"Ah, yes," Mrs. Wilmington said, apparently recognizing the picture. "All the roses. Aren't they lovely?"

With a gentle tug, Gage coaxed the paper from Miranda's hand. She didn't even realize she'd grabbed it away from him.

"What about the roses?" Gage's tone was casual, but Miranda could hear an underlying hint of excitement. "There're so many of them."

"And hundreds more you can't even see here," Parker's mother informed him. "Red roses had a special significance at the opera house."

Miranda had begun to shiver. From some distant place, she was vaguely aware of Gage's hand on her back.

"And," the woman added, "when red roses lined the driveway and spilled from every door and window of the opera house, it always meant that Mademoiselle DuVrey was performing that night."

"And why was that?" Roo stared pensively into Mrs. Wilmington's enraptured face. "Did she have body odor or offensive personal habits?"

Gage choked down a laugh. Ashley looked horrified. Etienne shifted from one foot to the other and mumbled under his breath. Mrs. Wilmington maintained her dignity.

"Through all these years, we've found precious little information about Mademoiselle DuVrey. We do know that she was originally from New Orleans, and that she was considered somewhat of a heroine by the Confederate soldiers. Apparently, she was so passionate about the southern cause, she frequently insisted on crossing enemy lines just to visit our camps and rally our troops. One can only assume she had *no* trouble acquiring escorts." Parker's mother gave a suggestive little smile. "But as for details of her personal life? Only that she was stunningly beautiful and had the voice of an angel."

"I bet men admired and adored her." Ashley's sigh was a little more yearning this time. Mrs. Wilmington seemed equally smitten.

"Yes, I'm sure of it. Whenever she performed at the Rose, it was to sellout crowds, standing room only. And *she* was the one who always insisted the opera house be filled with red roses."

Miranda realized the others had surrounded her now, all of

them curious and expectant, waiting for Mrs. Wilmington to continue. The woman's expression went thoughtful.

"It was her signature, really. You know, many people thought the opera house was named simply for all the flowers. But, actually, the Rose was rather like a nickname of the utmost respect. From Mademoiselle DuVrey's stage name. Ellena Rose."

18

Someone was squeezing her hand. No, *both* hands, Miranda realized—Gage on one side, Etienne on the other. Roo was staring at Ashley. Ashley was staring at Gage. Gage was staring at Etienne over Miranda's shoulder.

It was Etienne who finally broke the startled silence. "You wouldn't have any pictures of her, would you?"

"Of Mademoiselle DuVrey?" Mrs. Wilmington shook her head. "None here in the museum—well, at least no actual photographs. Apparently, they're quite hard to find, if any even exist. Some written accounts say that she was quite phobic about having her picture taken or even her portrait done. But there *are* several newspaper articles that mention her—and I do seem to recall an old playbill. In fact, there might even be a small caricature of her face on that. You'll find everything in our display featuring the arts."

Etienne jerked his chin toward the door. Without a word, they all walked back into the main room.

"Miranda, dear, I guess you know that your granddaddy is—was—an avid collector of Confederate memorabilia."

"Yes, he was." Images of all her grandpa's things came back to her. *The Civil War shrine.* "I think he really liked collecting things." *Profound statement, Miranda. Well, at least that's* one *thing about him you know for sure.*

Mrs. Wilmington seemed intrigued by the subject. "Oh yes, he was quite obsessed with it. It's not that difficult to find artifacts in this area—folks are always discovering buttons and bullets and old coins. But your granddaddy found some real treasures. In fact, a lot of what you see here in the museum is actually on loan from him."

"Told you. Here it comes." Muttering under her breath, Roo nudged Miranda. The warning escaped Mrs. Wilmington's notice.

"I can't help but wonder what his estate will decide to do with all these lovely things. It would be such a shame for them to end up in somebody's attic, where they can't be fully appreciated." The woman paused, her brow furrowing. "I don't suppose you know what *other* interesting things he might have kept at home?"

Roo seemed dangerously on the verge of responding when Gage quickly steered her away. As Miranda followed them, she could hear their muffled conversation.

"Don't even think about it." *Gage.*

"What?" *Roo.*

"Don't 'what' me. I know that look."

"Did you hear what she said to Miranda?"

"I heard."

"She's such a—"

"Dammit, Roo, shut up."

Mrs. Wilmington was still talking, but Miranda had tuned her out. *"Take it . . . the rose . . ." The Rose Opera House . . . roses spilling everywhere . . . Ellena Rose. So Nathan was talking about a place* and *a person. He wanted to get a message to Miss Ellena—Mademoiselle DuVrey—at the opera house.*

Thoughts and questions tumbled wildly through Miranda's brain. *But what's the message? And how am I supposed to deliver it to someone who lived a century ago?*

"Now, where did we move that display?" Mrs. Wilmington's voice drifted back to her. "We rotate the exhibits in here every six months, you know—there are *so* many things of interest, and we simply don't have the space."

Miranda tried to catch Etienne's attention. He was standing uncomfortably with Roo and Gage, while Mrs. Wilmington went on and on about charitable donations. Gage had Roo's shoulder firmly in his grasp—each time she tried to ease away, he held on tighter. Miranda felt as if the walls were closing in. She needed to get some air. She needed—

"Miranda, you were right!" With a conspiratorial whisper, Ashley tugged at her arm. "It's amazing! You were right about all of it!"

"Of course she was," Etienne mumbled, giving Ashley a wink. He'd finally managed to slip away from Mrs. Wilmington's lecture. Now, as a telephone rang and the woman hurried to answer it, Roo and Gage quickly followed him.

"Miranda was right, y'all!" Ashley said again, but Miranda didn't share the excitement.

"Okay, so we have a name. But how will I figure out the rest?"

"With time," Etienne reminded her. "It was the same way for

Jonas, yeah? He told me how frustrated he'd be, thinking he had something figured out, then having to do it all over again. But with time—and practice—he got more feelings about it, stronger feelings about it. With time, he just started trusting that he *knew*."

Before the discussion could go further, Mrs. Wilmington returned from her office. She directed them over to some framed documents on the wall, where they all proceeded to crowd in.

"Here are the articles—reviews mostly, nothing really personal—and here's the playbill. Ah yes, with this very tiny sketch of Mademoiselle DuVrey, which I'm sure is *quite* unflattering and does her absolutely *no* justice whatsoever. Plus, there are a few more photographs of the opera house. No interior shots, unfortunately."

"What about the fire?" Etienne asked. "You said the opera house burned during the war?"

"Yes, but not from any battle. I don't think anybody ever knew for certain what started that fire. Oh, there were speculations, of course—jealous actors, spurned lovers, disgruntled employees, drunken soldiers—all the way to a carelessly discarded cigar or an accidentally overturned lamp. Luckily, there wasn't a performance that night, so no audience was present. But there *were* some rehearsals going on."

Miranda was only half listening. Intent on the playbill, she gazed at the crude sketch of Ellena Rose that appeared alongside the diva's name. *Fair skin. You had very fair skin . . .*

Puzzled, she tried to pull back but couldn't. She realized the air had grown stuffy, and the conversation around her had become a low, indistinguishable hum. She couldn't take her eyes off Ellena Rose's face. *Fair skin . . . red hair . . . green eyes—no. One blue and one green . . . entrancing and irresistible . . .*

"No performance?" Miranda snapped back to the present. Her own voice was speaking out loud, and she was completely coherent, fully aware that no time had passed at all. "So then no one was hurt?"

For a brief second, Mrs. Wilmington seemed flustered. Then, with an apologetic laugh, she said, "My goodness, I'm getting ahead of myself. Yes, the opera house was closed to the public that night—but Mademoiselle DuVrey was in her dressing room." As if on cue, the woman's face went grief-stricken. "Poor thing. So young. Such a tragedy."

"She *died*?" Though the others glanced at one another in surprise, Ashley was close to tears.

"Heartbreaking, isn't it? A young woman like that, with everything to live for . . . the whole world at her feet . . . her whole life ahead—"

"Her whole story dragged out," Roo mumbled, before Gage could stop her.

Mrs. Wilmington gravely proceeded. "Apparently, the fire spread very quickly; there was total confusion and panic. By the time someone went searching for Mademoiselle DuVrey, it was already too late. She was trapped in her dressing room that terrible night. She perished in the flames."

"Burned?" Roo's dark-ringed stare was genuinely curious. "Or smoke inhalation?"

Mrs. Wilmington shuddered. "Her body was recovered the next day."

"And everybody was sure it was just an accident?" Gage asked.

"That's what history tells us."

"But history's not always right," Etienne spoke up. "A lotta history gets changed just through telling about it, yeah?"

After a brief hesitation, the woman's voice grew hard. "Times change very little. Tragedies occur—in many ways. Some people are simply self-destructive. Some people have everything they could ever want, and everything to live for, and they still throw it all away."

An uncomfortable silence filled the room. Miranda suspected that Mrs. Wilmington was referring to Parker, and from the others' strained expressions, they apparently thought so, too.

"So how come people around here don't know about the opera house?" Etienne smoothly changed the subject. "Me, I've lived here my whole life, and I never heard anybody talking about it."

"It's not marked either," Gage added, "like a lot of our other historic places are."

Mrs. Wilmington's nod was understanding. "I think it's mainly because the original building—or should I say, *most* of the original building—isn't there anymore. Once it burned, it stayed in ruins till long after the war. We have no way of knowing how much of it was left, or what parts of it were recovered and reconstructed into the gallery. I suppose it's unrealistic to hope that anything should last forever. But I fear one of these days, the Rose won't even be a memory."

"That's so sad." Again Ashley fought back tears. "Poor Ellena Rose. Nobody should ever be forgotten like that."

"But she hasn't been forgotten," Miranda whispered.

She realized Etienne was watching her, standing close, hearing every word. She looked up at him, her face solemn.

"Nathan *never* forgot Ellena Rose. That's why he's still here."

"I'm sorry, Miranda." Mrs. Wilmington smiled politely. "Were you asking a question?"

"We should probably be going," Etienne said.

Ashley, however, couldn't resist one last look at the photographs on the wall. "The opera house was such a beautiful building. Wouldn't you just love to hear all the stories it could tell?"

Parker's mother seemed amused. "Not all of them respectable, I imagine."

"Why is that?"

"Ashley?" Gage prompted, but Mrs. Wilmington was again in her element.

"Leading ladies often entertained suitors in their dressing rooms. People were expected to be discreet and look the other way."

"I bet she entertained lots of men," Ashley decided. "I bet she had lots of lovers."

Roo clenched her teeth. "Ash. *Come on!*"

"No, wait a minute, this is so interesting. I want to hear it."

"Yes, no doubt many lovers," Mrs. Wilmington picked right up.

"Women like her would have been constantly—and ardently—pursued."

While their discussion continued, Miranda began edging toward the door. A strange restlessness had settled over her, as though the room were suddenly too small, as though some sense of urgency were trying to get her attention. Her thoughts spun, connected by the most fragile of threads—she needed to untangle them. Now. Now, before they faded and disappeared, like the Rose Opera House.

Outside, the blazing heat was merciless. She leaned into the brick wall of the building and closed her eyes against the sun, too distracted to realize Etienne had followed her.

"Hey, *cher*, you okay?"

Startled, she took a second to hone in on his face. "It's there, Etienne. Answers . . . reasons . . . everything's there. Nathan, Miss Ellena, the message—all I have to do is put the pieces together and make them fit. I just don't know how."

She could see her frustration reflected in his eyes. *Or is that his own frustration?* She couldn't be sure, and when she looked again, it was gone.

"I don't know how," she repeated irritably.

"You don't *have* to know that now. You don't have to *do* that now." Etienne's gaze was steady, his voice calm. "You have the wake tonight and the funeral tomorrow. That's enough to handle."

"I had another vision. In the museum. When I looked at that playbill."

"So that's why you came out here." His features softened.

He lifted one hand toward her face, then drew back again as the front door burst open. Almost guiltily, Miranda stepped away to make room for the others on the sidewalk.

"Well, I am just *so* happy y'all stopped by today," Mrs. Wilmington gushed, though Ashley seemed to be the only one listening. "And be sure to let me know if there's *anything* else I can help with. Anything at all."

Gage and Etienne were having their own conversation at the curb. Roo was yawning. Impatient to get home, Miranda started pacing back and forth, past the front window of the museum.

"Oh my God."

It was only a glance, but it was enough to stop her. To freeze her there with both hands on the windowpane while the others curiously squeezed around.

"What is it?" Gage was there first, trying to follow the direction of her shocked eyes. "What are you looking at?"

"Him," Miranda whispered.

Her finger shook as she pointed to the photograph. An old, yellowed photograph of Rebel soldiers.

He was standing in the very back row, crowded in among many others, but proudly holding the reins of two magnificent horses. His gray uniform hung too loose on his thin frame; his face was just visible beneath the lowered brim of his cap. And though the quality of the photograph was poor—much of it faded to near obscurity—Miranda would have recognized him anywhere.

The Gray Soldier. Nathan.

He was strikingly handsome—nothing like the grim, haunted

specter of her visions. And yet the eyes were the same—she could see that now—and the pale hair was the same, and the lips, relaxed in an easy smile, were definitely the same lips that had spoken to her.

"Him," she murmured again.

Her pointed finger was still trembling. Gage's fingers closed around it and coaxed it down.

So young, so determined, all those soldiers. So strong and full of life. No thoughts of fear there, no hesitation; no thoughts of dying or losing the war. So certain of a quick return to homes and loved ones and the world they'd always known.

Eyes misting, Miranda focused on that one familiar face. *He looks happy.* Then, easing her hand from Gage, she touched the windowpane once more.

"Mrs. Wilmington, who is this?"

Readjusting her glasses, the woman peered over Miranda's shoulder. "Who? This man here?"

"Yes, him."

"Goodness, I have no idea. Some poor Rebel soldier, obviously."

"Do you know where this was taken?"

"Hmmm . . . well . . . it *might* have been one of these old houses on the Brickway. Or close to here, at any rate. So many of them look alike, you know. And unfortunately, some were torn down before we could save them."

But Miranda was scarcely listening. She caught her breath and struggled to choke out the words.

"That's our house. Hayes House."

"You're kidding." Gage glanced from her to the photograph. "Are you sure?"

"I'm sure. I mean . . . I'm pretty sure—"

"I don't think so, Miranda." Ashley sounded sorry for disagreeing. "That doesn't even *look* like your house."

Noting Etienne's pensive stare, Roo gave him a shrug.

"That's Hayes House," Miranda said firmly.

True, it wasn't the *exact* Hayes House of today. A different color, different windows, a slightly different shape. It looked smaller, and stood at the end of a dirt road, the roofs of several outbuildings barely visible in back. There was no wall behind it bordering a park, not as many trees, no landscaped gardens. But she knew it was Hayes House just the same.

"How can you tell?" Gage asked her.

I feel it. I know.

"This picture is from your grandfather's collection," Mrs. Wilmington offered helpfully. "He kept excellent records—he documented everything. The photograph should be fairly easy to trace."

Though Roo arched a look at Miranda, none of them spoke. Only Mrs. Wilmington, who commented again on the picture.

"I especially love the officers' uniforms, don't you? So sophisticated, so noble. And this one officer here . . ."

Miranda hadn't paid any attention to the man in front. Tall and distinguished, but with his hat tilted rakishly, he had dark hair, a dark goatee, and a long dark mustache, impeccably trimmed.

"This was Travis Raleigh Fontaine," Mrs. Wilmington finished.

"He was a very well-known, high-ranking Confederate officer. Quite the ladies' man of his day. But you can tell *that* just by looking at him."

Trying to be inconspicuous, Miranda gestured to Etienne. Her restlessness was getting worse, tiny pins and needles all over her body, but there was something about this photograph—*something important!*—something else she couldn't quite figure out . . .

"Notice his sash." Mrs. Wilmington was clearly enamored. "The cut of his clothes, the shine on his boots. And, of course, a true southern gentleman was never fully dressed without his pocket watch."

Rolling her eyes, Roo tugged on the back of Gage's shirt. "Save me," she muttered. "I can't take any more."

Gage batted her hand away. Roo tugged more determinedly on his back pocket.

"You can actually see the chain here." Parker's mother tapped the window, demanding their attention. "Even in black and white, that chain seems to glitter. Solid gold, you know."

Leaning forward, Ashley strained to see. "It really *does* glitter! Oh, I think men with pocket watches were so handsome."

"Distinguished, without a doubt. A pocket watch and chain were as unique as the man who owned them. Take watch chains, for example. There were various lengths depending on where the watch was to be worn. In a vest pocket, perhaps. Or in the pocket of one's trousers. There were even shorter chains, which attached the watch to a small ornament called a fob—and which in turn anchored the watch to a side pocket. But no matter its length, a chain assured that the watch was easy to handle and didn't get lost."

Something . . . Miranda rubbed at her temples. *Something . . . what is it? It's there . . . answers . . . if only—*

"Were all chains fancy like this one?" Ashley asked.

Mrs. Wilmington was delighted to elaborate. "Oh no, they could be made of many different materials."

Etienne's body tensed. Miranda felt the quick catch of his muscles . . . the slide of his hands up her back . . . as he slowly gripped her shoulders. And she knew the realization had struck both of them at the exact same time.

"They could be gold-filled or platinum," Mrs. Wilmington rattled on. "Or expensive leather, or studded with precious stones. But some were much plainer—a ribbon, or a common strap. Even string. Oh, and some women even wove them out of their hair."

The silence was sudden and stifling. Five bodies held together by an undercurrent of shock.

Mrs. Wilmington was clueless about the response she'd just caused. She tapped again on the window glass.

"Yes, indeed," she said, "that was the truest devotion. To have a watch chain woven from your sweetheart's hair."

19

"LET'S SEE THAT THING AGAIN," Gage said, reaching toward Etienne. Obligingly, Etienne handed him the braid.

The six of them were on the veranda of Hayes House, drinking lemonade. Ashley had called Parker on his cell phone, and he'd met them there within minutes. Now he and Ashley shared the porch swing, while Gage and Etienne slouched in wicker chairs. Roo sat cross-legged on the floor, pressing a frosty glass to one cheek. And Miranda sat beside Roo, leaning back against the wall, with her eyes wearily shut.

"People are still bringing food," Ashley whispered while more visitors came up the walk. "I feel like we shouldn't be here."

"I want you here," Miranda assured her. "Just let them step around us."

They all grew quiet as more people walked past, as solemn looks and sympathetic smiles and comforting words were offered. Without bothering to open her eyes, Miranda nodded and mumbled politely in response to each comment. She'd probably hear about it later from Mom. About how rude people thought that niece of Aunt Teeta's was. Right now she couldn't care less.

"It sure looks like human hair." Gage marveled, turning it over in his palm. "It sure *feels* like human hair. Sort of."

"It's old. And who the hell knows where it's been all these years." Etienne took a long swallow of his drink. The front of his T-shirt was damp with sweat, and he'd carelessly shoved his hair back from his forehead.

"I can't believe I didn't make the connection." Seriously put out with herself, Miranda groaned. "I saw some watch chains in my grandpa's room. I just didn't know what they were."

Gage handed the braid back to Etienne. "Well, whoever's hair this was must have been a redhead."

"Ellena Rose," Miranda said. "She was a redhead."

There was a brief pause as everyone traded glances. Then Ashley scooted to the edge of the swing.

"Miranda, how do you know that?"

"I just . . . the playbill."

Parker gave a derisive snort.

"Wow. It wasn't even a photo of Ellena Rose." Roo set down her lemonade and lit up a cigarette. "So you got her hair color from just a black-and-white sketch?"

"Yes. She had red hair and different colored eyes—one green and one blue."

"Maybe she was wearing contacts," Ashley suggested. Five stares aimed in her direction. Her smile began to fade. "She was a celebrity. Celebrities wear contacts to match their clothes."

"You know, Ash," Roo stated, "even after all these years, your keen powers of perception continue to amaze me."

Etienne gamely switched the subject. "That picture of the soldiers? Miranda's right. I'm sure that's Hayes House in the background."

Without a word, everyone looked warily toward the front door, as if half expecting the house to come alive.

"Why didn't you say something before?" Miranda glared at him.

"'Cause I needed to think about it. And"—he hesitated, almost sheepish—"I didn't want you freaking out any more than you were already."

"I'm more freaked out that you didn't say anything."

"Sorry. But it *is* the same house—the way it was originally."

Now it was Parker who groaned. "Oh, don't tell me. The house contacted you. You talk to dead houses."

"The thing is," Etienne continued, unfazed, "I've worked plenty construction, and I've done plenty work on *this* house—I know good renovation when I see it."

Roo cast Miranda a bland look. "Construction sites are popular in this town. A chance to see Etienne Boucher without his shirt on. Very hot."

The others could hardly keep from laughing. As one more sad-faced visitor approached the house, they all tried to compose themselves.

What's wrong with me? I shouldn't be joking at a time like this. Miranda felt both guilt and defiance. *What did Etienne say? About people laughing the hardest when they're scared and don't want to show it?*

"Your *grand-père's* things." Focusing on Miranda, Etienne steered the conversation back again. "You're gonna have to go through them, yeah? See what else you can find out?"

"I can't do that."

"Why not?"

"I can't just tell Aunt Teeta I want to go through his things."

"You're his granddaughter. Just say you want to know more about him. It's true."

"Just say it's for our project," Ashley said helpfully. "Which is also true."

"If he documented anything about that photograph, it could really help us."

"I didn't see any files in his room," Miranda added. "And I didn't see any papers in there either."

Etienne gave a distracted nod. "He didn't keep things like that in his room. He kept them in the attic."

"Well, if you know so much about them, why don't *you* go through his things?"

"Look," Gage broke in, "we can *all* go through his things. We can *all* help."

"Oooo, I love attics." Ashley gave a little squirm of anticipation. "Maybe your grandpa has some old trunks up there, do you think? Like attics in the movies? With clothes and old hats and those dressmaker dummies?"

Roo drew on her cigarette. "You're looking for dummies? Don't tempt me, Ash."

"Well, as tempting as it is to continue this fascinating and stimulating discussion"—Parker grimaced—"I've got to get home." Standing, he pulled Ashley up with him. "I guess we'll see y'all later?"

As the others got to their feet, Ashley gave Miranda a tight hug. "We're coming tonight. You know, to the wake."

Miranda, once more, was touched. "Look, you guys, I appreciate it—really. But you don't have to. It's going to be so depressing."

"We're coming," Roo said.

"Yeah, Roo likes depressing," Parker insisted. "She'll feel right at home."

"Parker, that's so rude," Ashley scolded him. "This isn't anything to joke about."

"Right. Sorry."

The last to leave, Gage paused on the top step to look back at her. "We'll be there."

An evening had never felt so endless.

As a steady stream of people—all friends of Aunt Teeta; the whole town, it seemed—came and went from the funeral home, Miranda was forced to stand and shake hands, endure countless introductions, and say "thank you" till she wanted to scream. She couldn't concentrate on the wake or anything else around her. Clues kept flitting through her mind—unknown connections between a soldier and an opera singer, a watch chain, a fire, and Hayes House.

"Oh, Miranda, are you doing okay?"

Deep in thought, Miranda was startled by Ashley's hug. She hadn't noticed the group coming in, but now she saw them talking quietly to Aunt Teeta in one corner of the room. They all looked as strained as she felt. Especially Etienne.

Despite her own misery, Miranda's heart went out to him. She still didn't understand the closeness he and her grandfather had shared, but it was obvious Etienne was hurting. She watched his gaze shift slowly, reluctantly, toward the casket. His jaw was rigid, his features like stone.

"Is Etienne—" she began, but Ashley was already shaking her head.

"He's taking it really hard, I think. But he doesn't want anybody to know it."

Before Miranda could respond, the others were there, all offering sympathetic hugs. When it was Etienne's turn, his hug was tense and brief.

Feeling dangerously emotional, Miranda tried to lighten the mood. She scanned Parker, Gage, and Etienne with a critical eye.

"Look at you guys," she said at last. "I didn't even recognize you. Y'all clean up real good, as Aunt Teeta would say."

Parker grinned. Gage and Etienne seemed vaguely embarrassed. Amused, Roo and Ashley deliberately looked the boys up and down.

Leaving Miranda to her family duties, the rest of them began drifting away, recognizing friends and neighbors in the crowd, making rounds to say hello. Miranda was relieved when Mom told her to get some air. The place was close and stuffy and reeked of lilies, and as she made her way through the many visitors, it suddenly dawned on her how haggard her mother looked.

She couldn't help feeling a twinge of guilt. Mom, as usual, had had to take care of all the burdensome details—wake, funeral, burial, eulogy—and had already made lists of even more things that would need attention afterward. Papers and various legal documents, bank boxes, the will, and Grandpa's possessions—the sheer thought of what Mom would have to deal with was staggering. Miranda made a firm mental note to help her out more and complain less.

Noting that everyone was engaged in conversation, she slipped out the front door. A few strangers lingered on the walkway, chatting quietly, but, to her surprise, she spotted Parker at the far end of the porch. He was alone, bent forward with his arms crossed on the railing, staring up at the sky.

"Parker, what are you doing out here all by yourself?"

He didn't seem particularly surprised by the interruption—just turned his head to look at her. No cocky grin now, no smart-ass jokes. Just a pensive face and a nice smile.

"Hey," he said.

Had he been drinking? Miranda thought she could smell a faint trace of liquor on his breath, but she didn't see any evidence. Maybe he was hiding it—in his car or in a suit pocket.

Keeping a friendly tone, she tried again. "What happened? Did Ashley kick you out?"

"Actually"—his smile tightened—"I'm not very good at these things."

"Me neither. You want to know something?"

"Sure."

"I keep wondering if all these people are just here out of curiosity. Like this is a sideshow—step right up, come see crazy old Jonas Hayes."

Parker shrugged. "Some of them, I guess. He *is* kind of a legend in this town."

"I'm glad it's a closed casket. I don't want everyone staring at him."

"People have always stared at him."

Though it wasn't said unkindly, Miranda frowned. "But maybe if people had really gotten to know him, they wouldn't have thought he was crazy."

"Maybe. But you're talking about St. Yvette. Most people his age who lived here are dead now. A lot of people your mom's age have either moved *away* from here or moved *to* here from someplace else. And with our generation, we hardly ever saw him at all. So most of what people know about Jonas Hayes is probably from stories they've heard."

"But stories get changed through the years. So who knows what's even true?"

"I guess it depends on the story," Parker said quietly. "Don't tell me you've never heard any of them."

"Not really." Sure, Mom had shared that one episode with her, but ever since then Miranda had longed to know so much more. "I mean, it's not like I've never asked my mom about it. But somehow it just never seems to be the right time."

"You get that, too, huh? Always something better to do than

sit down and talk with your kid. Oh, unless it's to criticize, of course."

Miranda heard the bitterness in his tone. She thought of all the arguments she'd had with her own mother, and she sympathized.

"I feel that way sometimes," she admitted.

But Parker had returned to their former topic. "I can tell you something about your grandfather. Well, something my mom remembers. I've heard her talk about it."

"And it's really true?"

"She says it is." Sighing, he wheeled around and propped back on his elbows, stretching his legs out in front of him. "A little girl disappeared, and your grandfather told them where to find her."

"That's all? That's not much of a story."

"Okay. Did I mention that the little girl *told* him where to find her? And that she happened to be *dead* at the time?"

Miranda felt the hairs lift at the back of her neck. "Go on."

"They searched for this kid for weeks. She was like, five or six years old. The whole town was out looking for her. And then Jonas Hayes walks into the police station one night and says he knows where she is."

Just like the other time Mom told me about. Swallowing hard, Miranda leaned against the railing beside Parker. "And *did* he know?"

"He led them straight to her. They found her body stuffed inside an old tomb near the Falls."

"So . . . she really was—"

"Dead. Strangled. Just . . . you know . . . a little kid." Parker's voice lowered harshly. "The killer ended up being some relative—some cousin or something. The guy was so freaked out that they found the body, he confessed in a note and then shot himself."

Miranda hesitated, yet she had to ask. "But before they found the note, did the police ever think my grandpa did it?"

"Hmmm . . . let's see." Parker began counting on his fingers. "First, he'd been caretaker at the Falls for years. Second, the tomb where they found the girl's body was way back in those woods, really hard to get to. Third, the Falls had already been searched, but nobody found anything. And fourth, he told the cops that the girl—the *dead* girl—had asked him to come and get her." Turning slightly, Parker seemed amused. "Hell, no. No suspicions there."

For a split second the night seemed to recede around her, stars spinning out in all directions. Miranda met Parker's stare full on.

"Parker, he wasn't crazy."

"Excuse me? Did you happen to notice him scaring the crap out of us the other day?"

"He *wasn't*," she insisted. "And he really *could* communicate with spirits."

"Hey, I don't know, okay?" Distractedly, Parker ran one hand down the front of his jacket. For the first time Miranda noticed the slight bulge from an inside pocket. A flask? She stared at the jacket. Then she stared at Parker. Noting her scrutiny, he gave a wan smile.

"Yes. To answer your question, yes, I have. But just a little."

"Parker—"

"Don't start. I get enough of that from Ashley."

"Only because she cares about you. She doesn't want to see you hurt yourself."

The bitterness reached out from his voice . . . spread across his face. The smile disappeared. "Maybe I *want* to hurt myself."

"But *why*? You have . . . you have so much—"

"What? Potential? All that wonderful, perfect potential I'm expected to fulfill?"

Miranda softened. "I wasn't going to say that. I was going to say you have *so much.* That's just it. You have everything."

"Maybe I don't *want* everything. Maybe I want something else *besides* everything."

"Then what is it, Parker? What is it you really want?"

Silence fell between them. As Parker gazed out into the night, Miranda noticed the tension in his shoulders, the tightening of his jaw.

"Etienne told me how your grandfather loved you," Parker murmured. "Jonas Hayes, the lunatic—how he loved you so much and felt like he knew you, even though he'd never met you before now."

Miranda couldn't speak. She watched Parker's expression go darker.

"Weird, huh. Everybody thinks *my* mom and dad are perfect. But you know what? They don't even know me. I've lived with them my whole life, and they've *never* known me."

He looked at her then, and for one brief second there was such sadness in his eyes. A glimpse of truth that was raw and aching and vulnerable. "You're a nice girl, Miranda. I'm glad your grandfather loved you so much."

As though suddenly self-conscious, he drew back from her. The bare emotions vanished; the old carefree facade took their place. When Ashley walked out on the porch, Parker gave a loud, shrill whistle that echoed clear across the parking lot.

"Parker Wilmington!" Ashley hissed. Trying to ignore the offended stares of onlookers, she marched over and planted her feet angrily in front of him. "What on earth has gotten into you? I am *so* sorry, Miranda."

Parker grinned. He lunged for Ashley, grabbed her around the waist, and pulled her close. "I'm leaving. You staying or going?"

"Go," Miranda insisted. "This thing's almost over. There's no reason for you guys to hang around."

Ashley didn't seem convinced. "Are you sure? The others are leaving, too, but I can stay. I can always walk home—"

"No walking home," Parker ordered.

"I can always get a ride later with Etienne—"

"No riding with Etienne!" Parker's hands went up in despair. "Dammit, I'll be competing with that guy for the rest of my life!"

"*And* Gage, don't forget," Ashley teased.

"*And* Gage." Wrapping her in a hug, Parker steered Ashley toward the steps. "I'll be competing with Etienne *and* Gage for the rest of my life!"

Ashley gave Miranda a see-what-I-put-up-with sigh. Hiding her concern, Miranda watched the two of them get into Parker's car and drive away.

By nine-thirty, the dreaded ordeal was over. As Miranda watched the final visitors leave, her mother and Aunt Teeta went off with the funeral director to discuss last-minute details for tomorrow's service. A welcome silence descended around her, along with a crushing wave of exhaustion. She felt numb and totally drained. And standing there in that sudden quiet of the viewing room, she realized that she and her grandfather were alone together for the last time.

It wasn't supposed to be like this, Grandpa. We were supposed to get to know each other and be happy. You and Mom were supposed to make up. And you were supposed to live for years and years and years, and always be there when we needed you . . .

Bitter tears blinded her. Grief and regrets tore at her heart, the ache almost unbearable. She hadn't expected to feel so much—not this depth of emotion, certainly not this depth of pain—but even more than that, not this fierce and burning anger. *You weren't supposed to do this, Grandpa—you weren't supposed to leave me.*

With no distractions now, she let herself focus on the casket. It rested there at the front of the room, covered by a spray of roses, flanked by plants and flower arrangements, serene and dignified beneath carefully dimmed lights. Nothing had really changed in here, Miranda reminded herself, nothing except the subdued chatter and crowds of people, yet the room was different somehow. Definitely and somberly different. This was death. This silence was death . . . these shadows were death. And this aloneness—this coffin abandoned when everyone else went home tonight—this terrible aloneness was also death.

Miranda thought of her father.

And she thought of the Gray Soldier.

That haunted, hopeless face of his; that desperate, endless wandering.

Because he's searching for something, for someone . . .

Because he's alone.

All at once the awareness was too much for her. All at once she wanted to go to her grandfather, to see him, hold his hand, hear his voice. *Tell me what to do, Grandpa. If this had to happen to me, why couldn't you have stayed here to tell me what to do!*

She started toward the casket when something stopped her. Some slight noise just outside the door, a footfall so soft, she wasn't certain if she'd actually heard it or only sensed it. Panic stabbed through her—fears of restless phantoms—and, though she told herself she was being irrational, she ducked down behind a chair and held her breath.

The footsteps entered . . . paused . . . and passed her by. Summoning all her courage, she forced herself to look out around the chair.

Etienne.

He was standing alone beside the casket. Just standing there with his arms at his sides and his head bowed. The tension that had gripped him earlier was gone; now his shoulders sagged, and his whole body seemed tired. As Miranda watched from her hidden place, her heart cried.

"Jonas," he whispered. Again, a sound so soft, Miranda wondered if he'd even spoken aloud. "I had to come one more time, yeah? Say good-bye . . . say thank you . . ."

Etienne's voice broke. Stepping slowly forward, he slid his

hands across the top of the casket and rested his face against the polished wood. The words he murmured were hushed and foreign and filled with pain. His body shook with silent tears.

"Our secret," he choked then, drawing a deep, unsteady breath. "You saved me, Jonas. I'll keep our pact, I swear. I'll never tell . . . I'll never forget."

A muffled sob escaped him. And then, everything went completely still, as though the aftermath of his sorrow had spread a gentle calm throughout the room. Overcome by what she'd just witnessed, Miranda could scarcely keep her own emotions under control. She sank lower out of sight, and when she looked again, Etienne was gone.

Oh, Etienne . . . I'm so sorry . . .

More determinedly this time, she walked to the casket. She straightened the roses on top, and ran her fingertips lightly over the lid. She could feel wet streaks there from Etienne's tears, but after a brief hesitation, she left them where they were.

What is it, Grandpa? The pact you and Etienne made? The secret you two kept? And what did you save him from? For it was clear to her now that whatever connection her grandfather and Etienne shared went far deeper and was far more important than she'd imagined.

Closing her eyes, Miranda conjured up her grandfather's face, the kindly face from her cherished photograph. *I need you, Grandpa. I've always needed you. Only now I need you more than ever, and it's too late.*

She realized then that she was waiting for him to answer—

expecting him to answer as she strained her ears so desperately through the silence, as her thoughts groped so pleadingly in every direction. *Wanting* him to speak to her, but terrified as well; craving something that only he could give her—peace, closure, a gentle word of confirmation—yet, at the same time, *willing* him to prove her wrong.

"Miranda? Honey, let's go home."

Whirling around, Miranda saw her mother and Aunt Teeta in the doorway. As Teeta began to cry, Mom automatically braced her in a hug.

"I'm being silly." Aunt Teeta tried to smile through the tears. "I just hate leaving Daddy behind like this. I hate to think of him being here, all alone in the dark."

"But he's not really here." Though Mom's voice was strong, Miranda heard a tremor below the surface. "You and I both know he's finally at peace. He's gone on to a better place. Where it's never dark, and there's Mother and lots of other people who love him."

Aunt Teeta listened and seemed comforted. With one arm pressed firmly against Teeta's back, Mom steered her toward the front door. "Miranda, are you coming?"

"Another minute, Mom."

"Sure, honey, take your time. We'll be in the car."

Miranda waited till they'd walked away, till they'd spoken quietly with the funeral director, who glanced back at her with an understanding nod, showed the two women out, and politely disappeared. Once more she turned to the casket. Her breath was coming faster, and her heart gave a curious flutter in her chest.

"This is what you meant, isn't it, Grandpa?" she whispered. "What Mom just said—*this* is what it's all about . . ."

Images rushed back at her—vivid scenes and conversations, words and pictures overlapping and blocking out everything else.

She shut her eyes tightly to ward them off, but they grew only more insistent. *Grandpa at the Falls . . . Grandpa so sick in his room . . . the Gray Soldier standing by my bed—"Listen . . . help them . . . don't turn them away."*

"Oh, Grandpa . . ."

"Listen, Miranda . . . watch . . ."

"Grandpa?"

She knew it was him. Here in this empty viewing room, in this deserted funeral parlor, in this vast and eternal silence of death, she knew his voice, and she felt the gentleness of his smile.

"Listen, Miranda . . . watch . . ."

"I hear you," she whispered. "And you *are* in a better place, aren't you? You're *not* alone, just like Mom said. But all those others—" She broke off tearfully, then drew a deep breath. "All those others who can't find what you've found—peace, and someone to love them, and a place to go home to, and how to get there . . ."

How to get there . . .

The air stirred softly behind her. For a split second, Miranda could almost swear that a hand had touched her shoulder, coaxing the next solemn words from her mouth.

"It's *me*, Grandpa. *I'm* how they'll get there."

20

"HONEY, you don't have to be at the funeral tomorrow, you know."

Back at the house again, Miranda and her mother had taken refuge in the kitchen. While her mom sorted listlessly through all the food, Miranda sat at the table, cradling her head on folded arms.

"I know. But I want to be there for you and Aunt Teeta. And Grandpa."

Mom smiled at that. "Your aunt Teeta's better, she really is. She just needed to get her grief out of the way."

Get her grief out of the way. Is that even possible? Can you ever really get it out of the way, or does it just hide someplace deep inside you, ready to crawl out again when you least expect it?

"Mom, do you think Aunt Teeta would mind if I went through some of Grandpa's things in the attic?"

Mom looked surprised. "Goodness, why in the world would you want to go through that old stuff?"

"Mrs. Wilmington at the museum said he kept really good records of everything he collected. We thought we might find something to help with our project."

"Of course I don't mind!" Aunt Teeta appeared in the doorway, wrapped in her chenille bathrobe, with kitty slippers on her feet. She seemed almost her jolly self again, though her face still looked tired. "You just help yourself to whatever you need up there. I'll probably end up donating all that stuff to the museum. I don't want anything old or depressing in this house anymore."

Mom looked amused. "You wouldn't be talking about Daddy, would you?"

"Well . . ." Reaching for the teakettle, Aunt Teeta couldn't help chuckling. "He *was* pretty old and depressing, bless his heart. But I'm going to miss him all the same."

Mom didn't respond to that. Miranda reached out and touched her mother's hand.

"All your friends are welcome here, darlin'," Aunt Teeta asssured her niece. "It'll be good to have young people in the house. It needs some laughter and enthusiasm and fresh ideas."

"You'll love Ashley, then," Miranda told her. "I wish I had her enthusiasm."

"I wish you had Etienne Boucher. But that Gage is awful cute, too." Winking, Aunt Teeta picked up her mug of mint tea and started for the stairs. "I'm off to bed, dear ones. Sleep tight."

Mom gave Miranda a teasing look. "What's all this about Etienne Boucher? Teeta seems awfully determined to get you two together."

"He's just a guy at school. In my study group. It's nothing." Then, as Mom lifted an eyebrow, Miranda added, "He's the guy who fixed our air conditioner."

"I like him already. Who's Gage?"

"His cousin. And I'm not getting together with anyone."

"You don't have to convince *me*, honey." She pointed to the counter covered with leftovers. "Potato casserole?"

In spite of herself, Miranda couldn't help but laugh. "No potato casserole."

"Ham? Jell-O salad?"

"No, I just want—" *I just want to talk to you about what's going on in my life. About Grandpa. About the things he needs me to do, now that he's gone.*

But of course she couldn't. Not now . . . probably not ever. Not after all the baggage left over from Mom's childhood, not with all the burdens on Mom's shoulders. For the first time it was beginning to dawn on Miranda what her grandfather had meant, how alone she would be with this gift she'd never asked for or expected.

"Baked beans?" Mom was staring at her. "Buttermilk pie?"

Again Miranda laughed. "No food. Just sleep. See you in the morning."

Wearily she made her way to the third floor, changed into pajamas, and climbed into bed—but she couldn't shut off her mind. Along with all the questions, there was now a new and very real sense of responsibility that she found both disturbing and comforting. *What do I do? How will I know? And how should I do it?* Oddly enough, when the screams came that night, they seemed more sad to her than frightening. And when she finally dozed off, it wasn't a cry that woke her, but the soft sound of a footstep.

"Psst. You awake, *cher*?"

Miranda fought her way up from sleep. "I am now." Annoyance gave way to relief. She wondered why she wasn't more startled; it was almost as if she'd expected Etienne to show up. "What do you think you're doing?"

"Well, you musta been wishing for me, yeah?" he teased. "'Cause here I am."

Switching on the lamp, Miranda solemnly patted the edge of the bed. "Sit down. We need to talk."

"Awww, don't be mad now. I just—"

"I know. You wanted to check on me. And I'm glad—I'm glad you came."

"Good. 'Cause I also wanted to leave you this." Holding out his hand, he showed her the braided watch chain. "Look, I know how you feel about it, but I really think you should be keeping it with you. Just in case you pick up on something, yeah?"

Miranda instantly recoiled. *But this is part of it. This is part of what I have to do.* Taking a deep breath, she pointed reluctantly to the dresser.

"Put it in the drawer. I don't want to look at it." As Etienne did so, her voice tightened. "Something happened tonight, Etienne. And I need to tell you."

Pausing a moment, he scanned her face with narrowed eyes. Then he lowered himself beside her.

"Something's changed, hasn't it, *cher*?" he murmured.

"Yes."

"And you've changed with it."

And then she told him. About her feelings at the funeral

home, her sadness and sense of loss, her sudden and overwhelming revelation of purpose, and hearing her grandfather's voice. Everything but having hidden and watched and eavesdropped on his own personal sorrow. When she'd gotten it all out, neither of them spoke. He'd moved closer to her, and, for the moment, it made her feel safe.

"You know what I keep wondering?" Miranda's tone went even more serious. "I keep wondering if all those spirits think *I'm* the one who's lost."

That not-quite-smile brushed his lips. "We're all a little lost. We're all trying to find something."

Miranda considered this. "I know you and Grandpa tried to tell me before. About my gift . . . and how I can do so much good with it. But tonight—for the first time—it was *real* to me. Like I finally *got* it. Like it finally all made sense."

"Sometimes we can be hearing the same stuff over and over again, yeah? And we know it's true, we know it *there*"—Etienne lightly tapped her forehead—"but what matters is when we finally know it *here*." As he touched his heart, she couldn't help giving a wan smile.

"The weird thing is . . . I'm okay with it. I mean, I'm still sort of scared . . . but I'm okay."

"You've always been okay, *cher*. Way more than okay."

As her cheeks flushed, she hoped he hadn't noticed. "How am I ever going to know all the stuff I need to know? I mean, I need to learn *everything*."

"Tonight?" Etienne kept a perfectly straight face. "I'm not sure I'm up to it."

Miranda's stare was deliberately reproachful. "This is about Nathan. He needs me. *Now*."

Groaning softly, Etienne lay back, pillowing his arms beneath his head. "I can see I'm gonna have to be humoring you. So what do you wanna talk about?"

"Why spirits stay earthbound."

"For a lotta reasons. Attachments. To certain people. Or places. Or things they can't let go of."

"Because they're sad. Or angry."

"Maybe they want revenge."

"Or they have unfinished business. Or they're afraid to leave, because it's familiar and they were happy."

"Or maybe 'cause they don't know they're dead."

"It makes sense, doesn't it?" Tucking her hair behind her ears, Miranda stared into the shadows. "Like in war. All those soldiers who never expected to die. All of them caught up in such intense emotions."

"Fear. Grief."

"Most of them probably died so fast, there wasn't time to think. There wasn't time to realize what happened to them." Her face grew pensive. She recalled what Mom had said about Dad. "What would that be like: Here one second, and gone the next? Would you feel surprise? Shock? How long would it take you to know you'd actually died?"

"Your *grand-père*, he said their concept of time's not the same as ours. Maybe to them, a century's the same as a day. Maybe to them, time doesn't exist at all. And they have to keep doing the same things over and over again. And nothing ever changes, nothing ever gets fixed."

Miranda thought back. In her mind she could see Nathan's ravaged face; she could see the hopelessness in his eyes.

"I don't know how any of these spirits—or the people they once were—can survive the pain they're in."

"You'd be surprised what people can survive," Etienne murmured. "When they have to."

Something about the way he said it caught at her heart. She lowered her pillow and started to reach for him, but he was already off the bed, moving swiftly and silently toward the dark, open doorway to the sunporch.

"Etienne, what—"

"Ssh," he hissed at her. "Something's out there."

21

Miranda froze where she sat. As Etienne slid into the shadows beside the door, she caught the quick movement of his left hand—the glint of something sharp.

"Well." Parker grinned, creeping slowly across the threshold. "This is cozy!"

A stream of undecipherable words burst from Etienne's mouth. Parker immediately looked offended.

"Hey, I don't have a clue what you just said to me, but it wasn't very polite."

"Good way to get yourself killed," Etienne muttered.

Parker stared at him, incredulous. "Is that your *knife*? You were actually going to *stab* me?"

"Knife?" Miranda echoed. Startled, she craned her neck for a better view, but as suddenly as it had appeared, Etienne's knife had vanished.

"I told you not to sneak up on him. You know he always has that hunting knife when he's not in school." Behind Parker, Roo poked her head in. "Hey, mind if we join you?"

As Parker, Roo, Ashley, and Gage crowded into the room, Etienne threw up his hands, turned his back, and continued his muttering. Miranda could only stare in disbelief. Roo was barefoot, wearing baggy pajama bottoms and a St. Yvette High jersey; Ashley had on a long robe and tennis shoes. Both girls were carrying food, and Parker and Gage held flashlights, which they'd switched off.

"Sleepover!" Ashley giggled while Parker pressed a finger to her lips.

"Ssh! This is a covert operation! You want to wake everybody up?"

Miranda didn't know whether to laugh or be upset. For the time being, her discussion with Etienne was on hold. "*What* is going on?"

"Etienne told Gage he might stop by here tonight." Parker's grin widened. "We're not interrupting anything, are we?"

Etienne frowned at his cousin. Gage returned it with an innocent shrug.

"That's right," Ashley picked up. "So we figured, why should y'all have all the fun?"

"Ashley brought chips," Roo added, then brandished a greasy paper bag. "I made popcorn."

Leaning toward Gage, Parker mumbled, "She can't ruin popcorn, can she?"

"I wouldn't bet on it," Gage mumbled back.

Miranda was still trying to process the intrusion. "Just tell me one thing—how do you guys get away with sneaking out at night? My mom would have a fit!"

"Right." Parker's grin turned scornful. "Like *my* mom and dad ever know if I'm there or not."

Ashley was totally unconcerned. "Oh, we just tell them we're going to the tree house. They never check on us there."

"What's the tree house?" Miranda wanted to know.

"Well, when we were little, Gage's daddy built a tree house for the three of us in his backyard. We used to have a secret club. And we'd play over there, and hide from people, and pretend we were knights in a castle."

"Gage and I were knights," Roo corrected her. "*You* always had to be rescued."

"Well, I liked the way Gage threw me over his shoulder and carried me down from the tower."

"Gage did that?" Clasping his hands over his heart, Parker sighed. "My hero."

Gage ignored him.

"We used to camp out in that tree house at night." Ashley nibbled a potato chip. "In fact, we *still* like sleeping together over there."

Parker wiggled his eyebrows and gave Miranda a stage whisper. "Very kinky."

"Oh, for heaven's sake, Parker—not *that* kind of sleeping together." Ashley paused for a second. "It *is* just Gage, after all."

Gage stared at her. "What's *that* supposed to mean?"

"Oh, nothing." Ashley plopped down on the bed next to Miranda. "Just that we love and respect you so much, we wouldn't *dream* of taking advantage of you."

"Sometimes *I* dream of you two taking advantage of him," Parker said seriously. "It's one of my favorite fantasies."

Gage tried unsuccessfully not to look embarrassed. "You need a life."

"So what's on the agenda for tonight?" Ashley asked.

Miranda couldn't keep from laughing. Although she and Marge and Joanie had done lots of spur-of-the-moment things together back in Florida, nothing could compare to the surprises from this crazy bunch. She realized she was starting to get used to—and even enjoy—these unexpected adventures.

"Popcorn, anybody?" Roo opened the paper bag and held it out.

Parker immediately backed away. "Uh . . . I pass."

"Y'all keep it quiet," Etienne warned.

He'd positioned himself near the door of the sunporch, while Parker sat beside Ashley, and Gage claimed the rocking chair. Roo sank cross-legged to the floor near Etienne's feet, her back propped on a pillow that Miranda tossed down to her. They could all hear the TV blaring and Aunt Teeta snoring from the rooms below.

"Well, as long as we're all here," Miranda began, while Parker let out a prolonged groan.

"Uh-oh. I sense drama."

"Impossible," Roo said offhandedly. "You *have* no sense."

"This might be a good time to talk about our project?" Miranda continued. "How's the research going?"

"Oh! Me first!" Waving her arm, Ashley gave an excited little squirm. "You know how the museum and those shops on both sides of it are all attached to each other? Well, Parker's mom said they all used to be just one big building!"

The others waited. When Ashley merely sat there beaming at them, Parker drew back in exaggerated surprise.

"Wow! That's really fascinating, Ash!"

"No, that's not the fascinating part." Ashley looked slightly offended. "I haven't gotten to that yet."

"Then hurry and *get* to that part. The suspense is killing us."

"The building used to be a club. Like a private gentlemen's club. Except upstairs, that's where they'd meet their mistresses."

Parker smacked a hand to his forehead. "Hookers! Damn! And I took the courthouse!"

"*Not* prostitutes." Another offended look from Ashley. "*Mistresses.* It's not just about sex, you know. There's a very big difference."

"Is that the sad part?" Parker asked.

Ashley continued, undaunted. "I found out there was a murder in one of those upstairs rooms. That when a very rich plantation owner wanted to end the relationship with his mistress, she stabbed him to death. In bed."

Calmly munching her popcorn, Roo gave a supportive thumbs-up.

"And the drugstore next door to the museum? People who work there say they've heard *moaning* at night in one of those storage rooms on the second floor."

The boys traded glances.

"And this moaning," Parker said, straight-faced, "did it come *before* or *after* the guy was stabbed?"

"*Anyway*," Ashley concluded," that's what I've got so far."

Noting her sister's outstretched hand, Roo obligingly relinquished the popcorn. "Did y'all know that furniture makers ran some of the first funeral homes? Because they were the ones who built the coffins?"

"Fascinating." Parker was all dignified solemnity. "And such a grave undertaking." He ducked as Ashley's popcorn sailed at his head.

"I know embalming really got its start during the Civil War," Gage spoke up. "With all those dead soldiers sent home to their families, the bodies had to be preserved."

Nodding, Roo stretched out her legs, frowned at her toes, then sat cross-legged again. "So my two buildings are the funeral parlor and the doctor's house. But when I started finding stuff on Dr. Fuller, I started finding stuff about an epidemic, too. I mean, they *called* it an epidemic, but nobody knew what was causing it."

"And when was this?"

"Around nineteen hundred. The statistics were unbelievable, so many people died. And lots of them were children."

Parker automatically grabbed a tissue off the nightstand and gave it to Ashley.

"Did they ever figure it out?" Gage asked.

"Not really. The research kept saying how Dr. Fuller was so dedicated, he had all those patients to take care of, he was trying to identify the epidemic, he was trying to find a cure. But so many patients kept dying, the funeral parlor could hardly keep up. There were funerals going on practically all the time."

"So did the doctor end up dying?" With a sad sigh, Ashley rested her head on Parker's shoulder. "And did the undertaker end up dying? Whatever that disease was, it must have been really contagious."

"That's what I thought, too. But Dr. Fuller and Mr. McGrail

lived to be very old men. Which leads me to a theory." Roo paused, one eyebrow raised. "What if my buildings had this really sinister connection? Dr. Fuller poisoned his patients, Mr. McGrail did the funerals, then the two of them split the profits?"

"I bet you're right." Ashley's sadness gave way to indignation. "That totally creeps me out."

Roo looked mildly gratified. "So what about your voodoo, Boucher?"

Arms folded over his chest, Etienne leaned lazily against the wall. "Mama, she had me go talk to my *tante* Bernadette—she's my *grand-mère*'s sister. And she's about a hundred years old."

"She's great." Gage laughed softly. "She tells the best stories."

"Yeah, well, she remembers some of that voodoo around here. In fact, she *saw* some of those wild parties going on back in the bayou. And that house on the west side of the Brickway, where the antique shop is now? There was a cook who worked there way back then—an old lady named Dominique, all heavy into voodoo. She had herself a secret place in the attic, and some pretty high-class clients sneaking over there to see her. My *tante* Bernadette, she says you never wanted to eat any of Dominique's cooking—you never knew what kinda spell she might be putting on you."

"Oooh." Ashley gave a delicious shiver. "This is going to be the *best* tour! Gage, you go next."

"No problems researching the church," Gage replied. "They keep records of just about everything. There's almost *too* much information—it's hard to narrow it all down. But I'm sort of leaning toward these old manuscripts Father Paul told me about.

They were handwritten by French monks and brought over here by some of the earliest missionaries. Could be some good stuff in those."

Roo took the potato chip bag from Miranda and passed it on. "Okay, Parker. Enrapture us once again with your dullness."

"You mean, my evil courthouse." Giving a mock shudder, Parker lounged comfortably back on the bed. "Evil judge. Unfair convictions. Botched hangings. Judge swings from rafters and dies a slow, painful death. Judge gets exactly what he deserves. Nothing we don't already know."

Ashley was clearly annoyed. "That's it?"

"What else do you want?"

"Some historical facts would be nice."

"Like what?"

"Well, tell us something about the prisoners. What kinds of crimes did they commit?"

"I don't know anything about the prisoners. Why would I need to know that?"

"Parker!"

"Come on, crime is crime. You got murder. Stealing. Murder. Treason. Murder. Oh, and did I mention murder?"

"That's incredibly historical." Roo's stare was bland. "And incredibly descriptive. Wow. I feel like I was there."

Parker grimaced. "Okay, fine. Let me run through the prisoners for you. Murderers. Thieves. Murderers. Spies. Murderers. Oh, and did I happen to mention killers, too?"

Frowning, Ashley shook her finger at him. "I will say this one more time. If you mess up our project—"

"Miranda!" Parker broke in quickly. "Update us on your dashing, see-through soldier!"

"Parker Wilmington, shame on you. Don't call him that. And Miranda has enough on her shoulders right now without you being so insensitive."

"I'm not being insensitive. All I said was—"

"Actually," Miranda interrupted, "I *have* been thinking about Nathan. And I've had some ideas."

She was the sole focus of attention now. As the room grew expectantly quiet, she tried to organize all the thoughts scrambling in her brain.

"I keep thinking about what he said." Miranda addressed the five rapt faces. "'No, you're wrong' and 'I swear to you, for the love of God' and 'I'm the one you want, only me.' Like he was really trying to convince someone. Like he really wanted someone to believe him."

"You!" Ashley exclaimed. "He wanted *you* to believe him!"

"No, I don't think so. It wasn't like in the park—I *knew* he was talking to me then. But those other times, he was definitely talking to someone else—and I was only hearing *his* side of the conversation."

"So what does that have to do with what happened in the park?"

"That's my point. I think it has *everything* to do with what happened in the park."

In possession of her popcorn once more, Roo dug absentmindedly through the bag. "Sounds to me like he's confessing."

"Or defending someone?" A frown settled between Miranda's brows.

"More than that," Etienne offered. "Protecting somebody."

"And maybe taking the blame for something he didn't really do."

Shrugging, Gage slowly swept his hair back from his forehead. "Sacrificing himself?"

Roo nodded. "Yeah. To defend and protect and save somebody else."

"He was suffering," Miranda recalled, while Parker promptly rolled his eyes.

"Not such a stretch, O Psychic One. The guy *did* have a bullet hole in him."

Miranda disregarded the comment. "No . . . before that, I mean. Some kind of punishment. His throat was raw, and his lips were all cracked. He could taste his own blood. And he really needed water."

"Bar fight and hangover. Mystery solved."

"I think he was being tortured."

"By who?" As Ashley gasped in horror, Etienne began pacing the length of the room.

"Prisoner of war?" he mumbled. "Makes sense."

"It does," Miranda agreed. "Maybe he had important information the Yankees wanted. And he wouldn't talk—he wouldn't betray the Confederacy."

"The Union army *did take* St. Yvette," Gage reasoned. "And there's documented accounts of how bad some prisoners were treated."

For a brief moment, Miranda looked down and clenched her pillow tighter. *Yes . . . yes . . . I've heard how they were treated . . . I've heard their cries, their screams . . .*

"Oh, poor Nathan." Ashley's voice caught. "I can't stand to think of people being mean to him."

Parker clutched his head with both hands. "For Christ's sake, Ashley. You're doing it again. You're talking about that imaginary guy like he's real."

"Of course he's real. Miranda saw him. And we all saw the braid he gave her."

"So he was tortured and then killed?" Still pacing, Etienne glanced at Miranda. She'd sunk deep into thought, unaware the room had grown quiet. "Miranda?"

Something . . . something . . . not quite right . . . As Miranda slowly raised her eyes to Etienne's, he came to a stop. "I don't know. I'm not sure."

"What about?"

"The way we're putting it together."

"Well, Miss Ellena has to come in there somewhere." Gage tried to be helpful. "We know she and Nathan had some kind of connection. And he did want you to get a message to her—"

"But I still feel like we're missing something."

Parker's scowl swept the faces around him. "Yeah, your minds. Your sanity. Should I go on?"

"Yes, go on," Roo said dryly. "Go right on out that door."

"Actually, we should *all* be going out that door." Checking his watch, Gage immediately stood up. "It's getting late. And tomorrow . . ."

None of them mentioned the funeral. Even after everyone had left, Miranda tried not to think about what the next day might bring.

Something more . . . something I'm not quite getting . . .

But it was there. She knew it was there, so close, just beyond her grasp.

Something important . . .

Something unexpected . . .

A tragic secret only she could discover.

22

The next morning couldn't have been more dreary.

The sky was overcast, the air thick with the promise of rain. A hot, restless wind scattered broken leaves and crushed petals around the casket. Thunder growled low in the distance, and the mourners looked as wilted as the flowers.

Perfect, Miranda thought glumly as she and Mom and Aunt Teeta sat beneath the canopy beside the gravesite. *Perfect weather for a funeral.*

But her new friends had come, just as they'd promised. She spotted them standing respectfully toward the back of the huge crowd, and she wondered why she suddenly felt sentimental, watching them. She'd known them only a few days, yet it seemed a lifetime. Already—for so many reasons—she felt closer to them than she ever had to Marge and Joanie.

With the service ending and people drifting away, she longed to escape—with Parker and Ashley, Roo and Gage and Etienne—back to school, back to noise and laughter and chaos. As the group approached, she was overcome with emotions. When Etienne laid a flower on her grandfather's casket, she nearly broke down.

"Hey," Gage whispered, wrapping her in a hug. His eyes were

so gentle, so compassionate. He slid his fingers beneath her chin and tilted her face toward his. "It'll all be okay. You'll see."

She knew the others were watching. Embarrassed, she lowered her head, but Gage's arm was still around her, keeping her close. Even Etienne's face had a certain tenderness about it; he seemed glad that Gage was consoling her.

It struck her, then, the irony of her grandfather's passing. The end of one chapter, the start of another. Jonas Hayes had fulfilled his legacy; now he'd passed the torch on to her. And Miranda's new life was not merely with the living now . . . but with the dead, as well.

"We'll see you later," Gage whispered. Releasing her, he stepped away and smiled, showing a dimple in one cheek.

Miranda smiled back. "Thanks so much, you guys. Thanks for helping me get through this."

"Always," Ashley replied, and waved to her while they headed for Parker's car.

Miranda was exhausted by afternoon.

She'd hoped that after the funeral, the constant flow of visitors might stop—but it seemed to get only worse. More food kept arriving, and more people filled the house, spilling out onto the veranda, the front and back lawns. But Miranda had had her fill of death. All she wanted now was to get away from everyone and everything, and with so many distractions, she figured no one would miss her.

Slipping up to her room, she closed the door, changed her

clothes, and stretched out across the bed. She hadn't planned on falling asleep, but when she lifted her head from the pillows, it was almost six o'clock.

Their company had gone. When Miranda went to the living room, she found Aunt Teeta snoring in the recliner and Mom asleep on the couch, the TV shut off. *Why don't you sleep in a bed anymore, Mom? Do these walls and closed doors scare you? Old, dark memories of this house? But the past is over; you and Aunt Teeta and I are together. Things will be better for you now.*

Starting upstairs again, she suddenly remembered the attic. This was a perfect time to look through some more of her grandpa's things, to see if she could find any information on St. Yvette or that old photograph of the Gray Soldier. After a brief search, she located the attic door and made her way up a narrow flight of steps to a landing.

It opened onto a large, low-ceilinged space—the very kind Ashley would love. Stale and musty and swelteringly hot. Mysterious beneath deep shadows and heavy layers of dust. Bathed in a jaundiced glow from the old, yellowed shades at the windows. There was even a dressmaker's dummy.

Miranda picked her way cautiously through a maze of boxes, bags, trunks, and suitcases; piles of outdated magazines and newspapers; rusty file cabinets; wooden crates; claw-legged furniture draped with dirty sheets; paintings and portraits shoved back into corners. But Mrs. Wilmington had been right about one thing—nearly every item was labeled with a concise, handwritten description. Intrigued, Miranda raised a window shade, pulled one of the cartons into a shaft of dim light, and sat down to explore its contents.

Here was photo after photo of southerners posed in their best finery; plantations and gardens; quaint shops and markets and modest antebellum homes; an eclectic assortment of buildings. But there were many other pictures, as well—the grim realities of war. Maimed and mangled soldiers, ravaged by disease, wrapped in dirty bandages. Row after row of corpses—unknown, unidentified, unclaimed. Amputations, grim surgeons at work, field hospitals, embalmings. Stockades and armed guards; weary prisoners, sunken-eyed, emaciated skeletons in filthy, ragged clothes . . .

Miranda frowned. It was getting hard to breathe with all this dust. Distractedly, she ran a hand back through her hair; cobwebs clung to her fingers, and she choked back a sneeze. *Something . . . something . . .* Shadows were beginning to lengthen through the uncovered window and around the grimy edges of the window shades. *Damn—what* is *it? What's* missing*?* She didn't want to be up here anymore, yet she couldn't shake the feeling that whatever she was looking for was beckoning again, practically within reach. Here somewhere, hidden among all these old things. *Why can't I figure it out?*

Frustrated, she gathered up the photographs and crammed them back in the box. No pictures of Nathan. No pictures of Ellena Rose. No pictures of Hayes House the way it used to be. Just that nagging sense of being so close, *so close,* to some sort of answer . . .

Without warning, her whole body went rigid. She could swear she'd seen a movement just then, from the corner of her eye. An ever-so-subtle movement near one of the windows, where dust motes hovered in the air like waves of heat over a summer road. For a second she could even swear those ripples of dust had taken on human form . . .

"It *is* you, isn't it?" she murmured. "What do you want?"

But he didn't speak aloud this time. His mouth hung open in a silent plea, his stare was without hope. And as one empty hand reached out to her, she heard the anguished crying from his heart. "*Take it . . . the rose . . . help me . . .*"

Miranda shut her eyes. Slowly, cautiously, she focused on his presence, his nearness, his tenuous reality. Pain flowed out from him in waves. She was aware of her own senses sharpening, just as they had at the gallery that day—curious, open, accepting. *You know, don't you? You know I'm trying to help you.*

A current passed between them.

An understanding so powerful, it took her breath away.

She opened her eyes to look at him again, but he was gone.

You came to me in the park because that was your battlefield . . .

Trembling, she set down the box of photographs. She leaned heavily against the wall and gazed at the spot where Nathan's ghost had just disappeared, her thoughts still trying to follow him.

But the first time I heard your voice, I was in the apartment over the garage. And then you came to me in my bedroom. And now here to the attic . . .

Why here?

Miranda got quickly to her feet. Images and emotions swept through her, and she welcomed them, invited them. In her mind she could see the photograph—the one from the museum—Nathan and his comrades posed in front of a much older and much different Hayes House.

Hayes House . . .

It was more than just having your picture taken, wasn't it? There was something else that tied you to this house—a connection so much stronger than a photograph.

Scarcely able to contain her excitement, she headed for the stairs.

You spent time here. There were things you had to do: important things . . . hidden things . . . secret things . . .

Deep, dark, dangerous secrets . . .

And because of those secrets, you died.

23

Back in her room again, Miranda waited impatiently for Mom and Aunt Teeta to wake from their naps. When she finally heard signs of life downstairs, she found both of them busy in the kitchen—Mom washing dishes, Aunt Teeta fussing over several potted plants that had been delivered earlier. Miranda decided not to mention Hayes House in front of her mother. Instead, she waited till Aunt Teeta went out to the veranda, then sat down with her in the porch swing.

"Aunt Teeta, I was going through one of those boxes in the attic—"

"Oh, that's just fine, darlin'." Fanning herself with a magazine, Aunt Teeta scooted sideways to give Miranda more room. "Did you find anything y'all could use for your project?"

"There's so much up there. Did Grandpa really collect all that stuff?"

"Every bit of it. Treasure hunting—that's what he always called it—treasure hunting always made him so happy."

A smile lit Aunt Teeta's face, then began to fade. "Well . . . till near the end, anyway. He seemed different . . . not as enthused about it. Not as satisfied. And he was so tired."

Miranda thought of that day at the Falls . . . her grandfather's erratic behavior . . . the confessions he'd made. "Do you know why? I mean, did he ever give you any reasons?"

"He never talked about himself much. He suffered from these . . . dark moods from time to time. But this wasn't the same."

Dark moods. Miranda remembered that midnight discussion with Mom, those stories about Grandpa's moods. She decided to play innocent and let the remark pass.

"Maybe I should have paid more attention," her aunt reflected. "Made him rest more . . . forced him to take better care of himself . . ."

"From what I've heard about Grandpa, nobody could force him to do anything."

"Well, you're certainly right about that. And your mama's just like him, but don't you ever tell her I said that, 'cause I'll deny it till the day I die." Giving a conspiratorial wink, Aunt Teeta began to laugh—that deep, merry laugh that everyone loved. After a few seconds of uncontrolled hilarity, she caught her breath and dabbed at her eyes.

"Oh mercy, that felt good. And you know what, darlin'? *You* remind me of your grandpa, too. Funny—I can't quite put my finger on it, but it's there, all right. In a really *good* way."

As Aunt Teeta wrapped both arms around her, Miranda nestled into her hug. *I wish I could tell you, Aunt Teeta. I think you'd understand . . .*

But now was not the time. And when Aunt Teeta finally pulled away, her face had gone thoughtful once more.

"You know, honey, maybe after all these years, your grandpa's hobby just got to be too much for him. More work than fun. Maybe he should have given it up a long time ago."

But he couldn't, Aunt Teeta. And it did *get to be too much for him, but he* still *couldn't. Not till he found me.*

He was waiting for me. He'd always *been waiting for me.*

It was another realization that struck to the core of her being. Miranda fumbled to change the subject.

"Aunt Teeta, do you know if Hayes House was ever anything else?"

"What do you mean, darlin'?"

"Since it was first built, has it ever been anything else besides a house?"

Leaning her head back, Aunt Teeta wrinkled her brow in deep thought. "No, it was always just a house, as far as I know. But way back when, one of your grandmas *did* take in boarders here for a while. Especially during the Civil War, with so many people coming in and out of town and not enough places to put them up. It worked out good for everybody—she loved to cook, and I'm sure the extra money came in handy. And folks could board their horses, too, out in her barn."

"There was a barn?" Miranda's pulse quickened. *Nathan with those two beautiful horses . . .*

"Well, not since *I've* lived here, but I know I've seen a picture or two somewhere. A barn . . . or maybe stables. I can't imagine what happened to those old pictures, though. Your grandpa kept track of all that."

"But the barn—stables—were here?"

"Out back behind the house. Of course, the property was much bigger then. Hayes land has been sold off little by little through the years."

"Did any famous people ever stay at the boardinghouse?"

"Hmmm. *That* I couldn't tell you."

"Maybe there was a guest book? Or a ledger? Old receipts, things like that?"

"Oh, honey, if there were, then they'd be somewhere in all your grandpa's stuff. Either here or at the museum. I wouldn't have the slightest idea where to look."

Miranda couldn't recall seeing any of those items at the museum. But she hadn't really been looking for them—and hadn't Mrs. Wilmington said the exhibits were changed on a regular basis?

"Back then, it was common for travelers to stay over at plantations." Frowning, Aunt Teeta rolled up her magazine to swat at a mosquito. "Of course, the hotel was more convenient for business in town, but there were only so many rooms, and not everybody could afford the prices. Lots of times, local families handled the overflow. Good ole southern hospitality—I don't imagine they'd have turned anybody away."

Just what Mrs. Wilmington said. Miranda's thoughts were jumping again, bouncing from one possibility to another. "So someone famous *could* have stayed here."

Her persistence seemed to amuse Aunt Teeta. "Anybody *could* have stayed here. Or *eaten* here. Or *slept* here. Or kept their horses and *carriages* here. Goodness, is this all part of your research?"

"We need all the information we can get." Deliberately evasive, Miranda looked up to see her mother smiling at them from the doorway.

"I've got bacon and eggs," Mom announced. "For whoever's hungry."

The porch swing stopped. Aunt Teeta lifted her arms, a comical hallelujah.

"That's the best news I've heard all day! I'm so tired of funeral food, I could scream." Then, a little guiltily, she added, "Though the intentions *were* kind and generous."

As Aunt Teeta stood up, Miranda headed quickly for the front steps. "Go on and eat without me, you guys. I won't be long."

"Miranda?" Mom was surprised. "You didn't tell me you were meeting your friends tonight."

"I'm not meeting them. I just want to take a walk."

"Now? Alone? Honey, it's nearly dark—"

"Oh, let her go," Aunt Teeta scolded, motioning Miranda to make a run for it. "She'll be fine. It's perfectly safe around here."

"Yeah, Mom." Miranda couldn't resist. "It's a small town, remember?"

Mom knew when she'd lost the battle. "Two against one—that hardly seems fair."

Relieved, Miranda watched her mother and aunt close the screen door behind them. She was halfway down the steps when she heard the door creak open again, and Aunt Teeta's voice unexpectedly stopped her.

"I'm sorry, darlin'—but something just came to me."

Miranda turned around. Aunt Teeta was standing at the edge of the veranda, her expression vaguely distressed. While an uncomfortable silence stretched out between them, Miranda felt a stab of alarm.

"Aunt Teeta, what's wrong?"

Her aunt roused. She fixed Miranda with troubled eyes and spoke hesitantly. "I was thinking about our talk. When you asked me about your grandpa—why he was so different near the end. I said I didn't know, and that's true. Only . . ."

Miranda's heart gave a sudden lurch. "Only what?"

"He brought something home a few weeks back. Something he'd found on one of his treasure hunts. And after that . . . well, it might be my imagination, or it might be nothing at all. But that *really* affected him. Like he got restless and depressed at the same time. Researching for hours and hours, exploring till way past dark."

"What was it?" Miranda could hardly keep her voice level. "What did he bring home?"

"I have no idea. But he was truly obsessed with it."

"Do you know where it is? Did he store it somewhere?"

Her aunt gave a helpless shrug. "All I can say for sure is that he *wouldn't* have thrown it away. He never threw *anything* away."

"Then do you at least remember where he found it?"

"I'm pretty sure it was at the Falls. He went back there a lot after that." Aunt Teeta's expression grew sad. "And you know, when I think about it now, it was almost like he knew he was running out of time."

24

It's closer.

Whatever this is I'm supposed to find, whatever I'm meant to do, it's so much closer, I can feel *it.*

Moving along the Brickway, Miranda could still hear Aunt Teeta's words echoing through her head. She felt both stunned and excited; her thoughts and emotions were in complete turmoil. Pausing to catch her breath, she realized she'd been running.

Concentrate, Miranda. You have to concentrate.

But focusing right now was too much to demand of herself. And getting more answers seemed only to raise more questions.

What was it you found, Grandpa? Because that's when it started, wasn't it? That's when Nathan's spirit started contacting you.

It all made perfect sense—her grandfather's desperation, his frantic mumblings at the Falls that day. *That's where you found something important, some treasure the Gray Soldier was connected to. That's why you kept going back to the Falls. You were looking for clues. You were looking for a way to help him. Because you* did *know you weren't going to be here much longer.*

I won't let you down, Grandpa. Not you or *Nathan . . .*

It had started to rain. Not very heavily yet, more a warm,

clinging drizzle that thickened the air like fog and distorted everything around her. There weren't many people out this evening. Hazy light glowed from lampposts and houses and a few shop windows, but the sidewalks were mostly deserted. And yet . . .

There are things in this fog.

Many presences in this fog.

Miranda couldn't see them, but she knew they were there. All around her, very real and very close.

"Help us . . ."

"We're lost . . ."

"We want to go home . . ."

A clammy breeze trailed over her, as if ghostly fingers were plucking at her clothes, urging her to reach through the mist and into the past.

"You're the way, Miranda. You're the way between the living and the dead . . ."

Miranda stopped walking. Her hair and clothes were wet, and she didn't know where she was. She hadn't meant to stay out here this long, or to walk this far. But as she squinted through the rain, she saw the Magnolia Gallery looming high above her.

She was standing on the steps of the entrance. Her hands were pressed against one of the tall, round columns, and she could feel a warm rush starting through her, stirring her deepest instincts.

Take your time. Trust yourself.

She slipped into it so naturally, it was like breathing.

Suddenly she was there amid the muffled applause and conversation . . . the clinking of glasses . . . the flow of champagne.

She was drowning in the sweet scent of roses. She heard the sobbing—*"Nathan . . . oh, Nathan, why?"*—the swish and fall of the curtain onstage, and the silence, the terrible silence . . .

And footsteps. No . . . *heavier* than footsteps . . .

Boots. Strong and solid, a bold walk, a man's boots . . .

Something brushed past her in the fog.

A tall figure—a stranger—imposing and silent, his gray uniform woven from swirling mist . . . bringing bad news . . . bringing terrible news . . .

Miranda's senses kicked into high alert. She could feel danger emanating from that stealthy, solitary figure, washing over her like waves of a drowning tide. She could hear him muttering, words low and fierce, intense but hard to make out. An official tone, a tone of authority. And all the while, like sorrowful background music, came that constant, heartbroken sobbing, *"Nathan . . . why?"*

Miranda was trembling and invisible. She was a ghost in this specter's world, and his world was a cold, black night. He didn't see her, didn't know she was there, even though they were close enough to touch. She could smell his sweat, and the sweat of his horse, the duties and atrocities of war clinging to his body, the sad and angry tears dried upon his cheeks . . .

She watched him pause . . . examine a small glass bottle in his hand. And she could smell *that*, too, as faint as it was—bitter and swift and final—a smell of certain death.

Without warning, he turned around. Miranda could see him clearly now, and as she silently whispered his name, Travis Raleigh Fontaine slipped the vial of poison back into his pocket.

"A fair exchange, Ellena." His voice trembled . . . a voice of eternal torment, a voice from beyond the grave. "My mercy . . . for your betrayal."

There was one sharp hiss as he struck the match. One brief spark between his fingertips, before he flung it to the ground, before it burst into flames.

The tread of his boots faded. The glory of the opera house flickered once more, brightly, then disappeared. As Miranda sank to the gallery steps, the evening turned dark, and the drizzle became a downpour.

Oh, God . . . what really happened that awful night?

The spirit had gone, yet she still had an eerie feeling she wasn't alone. When she glanced over her shoulder and saw the dim glow of light floating toward her through the rain, she wondered hopefully if it might be her mother or Aunt Teeta, carrying a flashlight, coming to find her.

"Mom?"

But it wasn't Mom who stood before her, holding a lantern in one pale hand. With a hooded cloak of fog . . . long red hair tumbling down . . . bone-white face . . . eyes unearthly, shining tragic with tears.

"You were my life, Nathan," Ellena Rose whispered. *"And now you are my death."*

25

Miranda was back in her own world.

The only thing she could hear now was the pouring rain and her pounding heart. Ellena Rose had vanished, yet the lantern light remained, moving steadily closer.

"Hey, Miranda, is that you?"

"Roo?"

Surprised, Miranda saw that it really *was* a flashlight this time—no, *two* flashlights—and that Roo and Gage were hurrying up the steps to join her beneath the covered entrance of the gallery. Both of them were soaked. As they pinned her with the beams of their flashlights, she squinted and ducked her head.

"What are you guys doing here?"

Roo's reply was matter-of-fact. "Looking for you."

"You're kidding."

"We called your house." Gage smiled, shoving wet hair back from his eyes. "Just to see if you felt like getting out for a while. Your mom was really worried—she was about ready to search the town."

"When she told us how long you'd been gone, we thought maybe you'd walked over here," Roo added. "And we were wet anyway."

Gage passed Miranda his cell phone. "Hit redial. And tell your mom we'll bring you home after we get something to eat."

"Are you sure Etienne's picking us up?" Roo frowned at him. "I'm starving."

"You're always starving. And yes, I'm sure. I already called him."

"I don't see any extra umbrellas," Miranda teased, seeing no umbrellas at all.

Gage gave a long-suffering sigh. "Roo likes the rain. She likes walking in it. Playing in it. Sitting in it. Thinking in it—"

"It's a spiritual thing." Roo shrugged. "It makes me feel clean."

"So would taking a shower. Or me spraying you with a hose."

With a dismissive wave, Roo plopped down next to Miranda. She set aside the flashlight and started digging through the pockets of her overalls. "Damn. Most of my cigarettes got wet."

"Then this is a perfect time to quit." Sitting across from her, Gage grabbed for one of her pockets, but she twisted away.

"Leave those alone. They keep me calm."

"Right. Like you're so nervous all the time."

"See? They work."

"Call your mom, Miranda."

Miranda did so. After squaring things with her mother, she handed the phone back to Gage.

"So," Roo began nonchalantly. She struck a match, lit her cigarette, then flicked the match out into the rain. "Do we have to guess, or are you going to tell us what happened?"

Staring at Roo's match, Miranda couldn't help but shudder. "How'd you know something happened?"

"You have that look."

"Of wisdom?" Miranda tried to joke.

"Of wiped out."

"I am wiped out. And you're not going to believe what I just saw."

"Do we look like Parker? Hey, we believe in everything."

"I know how Ellena Rose really died."

Impressed, Roo took a drag on her cigarette. Gage offered an encouraging nod. And by the time Miranda related the details, both Roo and Gage were as enthralled as she was.

"So Travis did it," Gage murmured. "He poisoned her, then set the building on fire to hide the murder."

"A clandestine meeting." With a vague frown, Roo tapped off her ashes. "They make love, he pours the wine, and no more Ellena Rose."

But Miranda met Roo's frown with one of her own. "I don't think there was any romance that night. And I'm not so sure he hid the poison in wine . . . or in anything."

"Explain."

"From what Travis said . . . and the feeling I got when he said it . . . What if he wanted her to *know* he was poisoning her?"

"Double cruel."

Gage paused to mull this over. "If there were rehearsals going on that night, there must have been people around. Wouldn't she have called for help or fought back when he tried to poison her? She must have figured *somebody* would hear her and come to help."

"You're right," Miranda murmured. "I think she took the poison deliberately. And willingly."

Tossing her cigarette, Roo fixed Miranda with a level stare. "He definitely had something on her. Otherwise, she *would* have fought back. And whatever he threatened her with must have been pretty bad if she thought dying was better."

"Blackmail," Gage insisted. "Any ideas why?"

Frustrated, Miranda shook her head, but before she could answer, a horn honked from the curb.

"Hey!" Parker leaned out the passenger side of Etienne's truck. "Don't y'all have enough sense to come in out of the rain?"

Peering over his shoulder, Ashley waved at them. "Come on! Let's go to The Tavern!"

"We'll ride in the back!" Roo yelled.

Grumbling, Gage ushered the girls ahead of him. While Parker helped Miranda into the front seat, Gage boosted Roo onto the truck bed and climbed in after her. There weren't any close parking spaces when they got to the restaurant. By the time they made a mad dash for the door, the rest of them were as wet and bedraggled as Roo and Gage. They found a large table in the back—and their waitress, who spoke Cajun to Etienne, took their orders, then brought a roll of paper towels so they could all clean themselves up.

"Did Miranda tell you?" Flipping her bangs from her eyes, Roo stared at Etienne. He immediately looked suspicious.

"Tell me what?"

"I can't believe she didn't tell you, riding over here."

"Tell me *what*?"

"I thought girls told you everything. You must be losing some of that charm."

Before Etienne could manage a comeback, Miranda held up her hands for quiet. "I was waiting for all of us to be together."

Seeing she had everyone's undivided attention, she recounted her whole experience again, as well as her discussion with Roo and Gage. It didn't take long for a ripple of expectation to travel around the table—to everyone but Parker. He shook his head in disgust but stayed quiet.

"So Ellena's life for his mercy," Etienne mused. "That was Travis's exchange?"

"He said 'my mercy for your betrayal.'" Miranda knew the words by heart.

"Yeah, well, it musta been a pretty big betrayal if he thought poisoning her was merciful."

Thoughtfully, Gage leaned forward. "We know Travis was an officer—both from Miranda's vision and from the picture in the museum. And we also know from the picture that he and Nathan probably knew each other."

"Nathan was holding those horses," Ashley recalled. "Only . . . soldiers didn't ride horses, did they? Soldiers walked."

"But officers rode horses. So maybe—"

"He could have been in charge of them, right? Like a . . . some kind of vet? Or . . . or maybe he was like their horse trainer? Or a horse assistant?"

"Aide-de-camp?" Roo shrugged. "What if he was Travis's aide-de-camp?"

"Aid the what?"

"Aide-de-camp. It's like a personal assistant."

"Isn't that what I just said?" Confusion wrinkled Ashley's brow.

"If Nathan *was* Travis's aide-de-camp, he must have had special privileges," Gage pointed out. "A position like that meant lots of comforts a regular soldier wouldn't have. And he probably wouldn't have been sent to the front lines."

"Which makes it less likely he was killed in battle." Glancing at Parker, Roo couldn't help sounding smug. "And which also supports Miranda's theory about his being tortured and shot."

Though Parker rolled his eyes, Etienne nodded agreement. "Look, he'd probably have known a lot about Travis, yeah? Seen a lotta things going on . . . heard a lotta things being talked about—by Travis and the other officers."

"Official correspondence." Solemnly, Gage ran through the possibilities. "Battle plans. War strategies. All kinds of classified information."

As the food arrived, there was an impatient time-out. After mustard, ketchup, and hot sauce were hurriedly passed around, drinks refilled, and the first few satisfied bites taken, the group's discussion resumed in earnest.

"If Travis had access to classified information, maybe that's how he found out something about Ellena." Miranda's voice tightened with excitement. "And it was something so awful, something she felt so threatened by, she was willing to kill herself over it."

Parker shot each of the girls a mock scowl. "Women. What can I say? They can't be trusted. They end up breaking your heart. All of them are traitors."

"Oh my God," Miranda mumbled. "Parker . . . oh my God . . ."

Traitor.

It was only a word . . . but suddenly she knew.

"Parker, you are *brilliant*!"

Parker lifted clasped hands toward heaven. "It's a miracle! Somebody who finally recognizes my *genius*!"

"She was a spy!" Straightening in her seat, Miranda gripped the edge of the table, her eyes going wide. "Don't you see? That's why she drank the poison—she knew that if she didn't, she'd be hanged. Ellena Rose—Miss Ellena—she was a *Yankee spy*."

26

It was as if all the puzzle pieces were nearly in place. As though the whole picture were finally coming into focus, with details vivid and intact. As the noise of The Tavern continued around her, Miranda felt a swift and sudden detachment. In the space of a heartbeat, time stopped and slammed her into the past, where scenes and people and conversations raged like a hurricane through her senses. *Nathan . . . Ellena Rose . . . Travis Fontaine*—lives intertwined and shattered and forgotten . . .

Until here . . . until now . . .

Until Grandpa and me.

"That's got to be right," she heard Roo mumble. "Once they discovered she was a spy, she'd have been executed."

"And think of her career." Ashley sighed. "The scandal."

Etienne's tone was humorless. "Hell, in *this* town, the *locals* mighta strung her up. Me, I'd have taken that poison, too."

The mood around the table had gone somber, as though none of them really wanted to admit Miss Ellena's guilt. Even Parker seemed to be considering Miranda's theory.

Leaning back in his chair, Etienne stroked his fingers along his chin. "She coulda gotten secrets from anybody. Or passed secrets to anybody. Especially if she was somebody's mistress."

"Or *many* somebodys' mistress." Parker chuckled.

"It would have been so easy for her—men would have told her anything. They'd have given up secret information just like *that*." Snapping her fingers, Ashley coolly confronted Parker's indignation.

"Come on, give us guys a little credit. Why would any high-ranking officer share classified information with his little groupie, huh?"

"Because those high-ranking officers were men." Roo's stare was as condescending as her tone. "And men only think with their—"

"Downstairs brain," Ashley finished.

While the guys conceded with slight embarrassment, Roo and Miranda laughed. "Good one, Ash."

"Everything we know—or think we know—about Ellena Rose fits the spy profile." Etienne tried to steer the conversation back again. "Remember the part about her crossing enemy lines—how she never had any problems? And how she loved traveling through the South?"

"She probably had contacts all over the place," Gage reasoned. "Nobody would ever have suspected her."

"And even if they did, nobody else woulda believed it."

"Till Travis Fontaine." Reaching across Gage, Roo traded her empty glass for his half-full one. Gage stared into the empty glass and frowned.

"So Travis must have been one of her informants, except he didn't know it." Miranda picked up the probable scenario. "And when he found out, he felt betrayed for himself *and* the Confederate army."

"And he wouldn't have had a choice, really." Gage's expression was troubled. "He knew he'd have to turn her in. He knew she'd have to be executed . . ."

Nodding at Gage, Ashley lowered her voice. "So he gave *Ellena* the choice."

"Some choice." Parker grinned. "Either *I* kill you, or *you* kill you."

Despite Parker's twisted attempt at humor, a heavy silence settled over the group.

At last Etienne cleared his throat. "So Travis, I guess he musta loved her, yeah? To give her a way out like that?"

"I can't even imagine." Ashley fixed Etienne with a sorrowful gaze. "The fear she would have felt . . . the shame and humiliation—"

"But he let her die with some dignity. You gotta give him that."

"And then he burned down the opera house," Miranda whispered. "He burned down the Rose."

Ashley's eyes misted over. "Both Roses. He destroyed both Roses."

For a long moment, they all seemed lost in their own thoughts. Then Parker spoke up.

"Yeah." Tilting his chair back, he winked at Gage and Etienne. "That's the way to a girl's heart, all right. Give her poison, then burn down her house."

Roo's stare was openly curious. "Tell us the truth, Parker. Are you really just a changeling in human form?"

"Look, *if* I believed all this poison-betrayal crap—which I *don't*—but if I *did*? I'd be looking at your Gray Soldier guy."

"Nathan," Ashley corrected him.

"Whoever. I mean, y'all said yourselves, it all has to be connected, right? So Miss Ellena might have been a spy, but how does that tie in with Nathan's message and him being tortured and shot?"

As a new thought hit, Miranda put down her fork and tapped Parker lightly on the arm. "Parker, what you just said—"

"*Another* brilliant revelation, no doubt." Parker smirked.

"Actually, it was. If Nathan was trying to get a message to Ellena, maybe it was information about the Confederate army. What if *he* was a spy, too?"

"Ellena's accomplice?" Roo arched a quizzical brow.

"If he and Ellena were in this together, then it makes sense. He would have been sending her *lots* of secret messages."

Leaning toward Miranda, Etienne folded his arms on the tabletop. "Travis, he musta been plenty mad, yeah? When he found out Nathan was a spy? And I'm guessing that's when he found out about Ellena, too—when he was torturing Nathan."

"Do you think that's when Nathan got shot?" Ashley groaned and covered her face with her hands. "Do you think Travis killed him after Nathan told him about Ellena?"

Roo's shrug could have been either yes or no. "Talk about betrayal—your assistant *and* your mistress."

"And I bet they were the two people he trusted most in the whole world." Pushing back her plate, Ashley gazed morosely at her burger. "I can't eat any more. This whole thing just gets sadder and sadder."

Miranda's glance was sympathetic. "But I still don't know what Nathan's message is. Or why he's still trying to get it to Ellena."

She'd felt so hopeful while they'd all been talking—so close to solving the mystery, so close to helping Nathan's restless spirit. *But with each step forward, I fall back three.*

By the time they were ready to leave, the rain had tapered off to a saunalike drizzle. The group headed for the truck, Parker and Ashley walking ahead, while the other four took their time.

"You know," Miranda ventured, not sure if it would help or make things more confusing, "I think I've figured out where this whole thing with Nathan started."

She could tell they were intrigued. Repeating the information Aunt Teeta had given her, she told them about her grandfather, the unknown treasure he'd found, and his obsession with it.

"And I think," she said gently to Etienne, "that might have been what Grandpa was talking about that day . . . when he said he should have told you about it but never did."

A muscle clenched in Etienne's jaw. Gage threw him a look, but said nothing.

Pulling another cigarette from her pocket, Roo lit up, turned sideways, and fanned away the smoke. As Etienne reached toward her, she automatically passed the cigarette over to him.

"I believe Grandpa really wanted to help Nathan," Miranda concluded. "And I believe he tried really hard, as hard as he possibly could."

"So we'll keep trying, too," Gage assured her. "We'll figure it out."

Etienne took several long drags on Roo's cigarette. When he handed it back, his expression was more serious than ever.

"Whatever it was Jonas found, he'd have kept it close. Probably in his room somewhere."

"And how does that help me?" Miranda made a futile gesture. "There must be a *million* things in his room."

"But only *one* that belongs to Nathan. And only one person who can find it." Etienne gave her a sidelong glance. "And that's you, *cher*."

27

"Can you come up the back way?" Miranda asked.

Etienne had dropped the others off. Now he and Miranda sat in his truck, parked in the driveway of Hayes House. The stress of the evening had eased since they'd left The Tavern, and she leaned back with her eyes closed while Etienne stared silently out the fogged-up windshield.

"Can you?" she asked again. She still hadn't told him about the attic, about Nathan's unexpected appearance, or about the connection she'd sensed between Nathan and Hayes House. Several times during dinner, she'd wanted to bring it up, but with so many other things to talk over, she'd decided to put it on hold till a later time. *And now's that time.*

"Etienne?"

"We gotta stop meeting like this," he said, poker-faced. "The neighbors, they're starting to talk."

"*You're* the one who started it."

"What, you don't want me to meet your mama?"

"It's not that—"

"I promise she'll like me. Your aunt Teeta, *she* likes me."

"My aunt Teeta *loves* you. She thinks you're wonderful."

"See. What'd I tell you?"

"She also thinks Gage is adorable."

"What can I say? Gage *is* adorable."

Miranda had to laugh. "Look, if we go in the front, they'll both want to fuss over you, and we won't have any privacy, and I can't mention ghosts and weird things in front of them."

"You know, *cher*, I've had a lotta girls talk me into their bedrooms, but this is the first time I've heard *that* excuse."

"This is *not* that kind of invitation. Understand?"

Etienne gave her a solemn stare. He let out a long-suffering sigh. "Okay. Since you twisted my arm—I'll come up the back."

Miranda thought maybe this time he might actually smile. But like all the times before, only a fleeting hint of amusement touched his lips.

"Fifteen minutes," she said, climbing out.

"At least. I gotta park my truck somewhere else. And walk all the way back. And sneak all the way in. Secret rendezvous, you know . . . they take time."

Laughing again, Miranda left him and went inside. To her relief, only Aunt Teeta was up, and she was on her way to bed.

"Your mama was exhausted," Aunt Teeta explained. "Bless her heart, I don't know how she's lasted this long. I told her I'd wait up for you. And I did, and here you are, and now I'm going to tuck myself in. I'll see you in the morning!"

"Aunt Teeta?"

"What, darlin'?"

"Did Mom sleep in her bedroom tonight?"

Aunt Teeta gave a wink. "She sure did. And that's a *real* good sign!"

Gratefully, Miranda hurried up to her room, shocked to find Etienne already waiting for her.

"Hey," he greeted her. "What took you so long?"

"You're impossible." While he stretched out on his side across the end of the bed, she grabbed her favorite pillow and scooted back in her corner against the wall.

"So what's the big mystery?" Etienne focused on her face. "And don't tell me we're gonna be looking through your *grand-père*'s room tonight for that little treasure."

"I think Nathan has some special connection to this house. To the treasure, yes, but also to this house."

Etienne's dark eyes narrowed. "What kinda connection?"

While he listened attentively, she told him about the boardinghouse and barn; she reminded him of the old photograph of Hayes House, of Nathan with the horses, of local families taking in visitors.

"Suppose Nathan took care of Travis's horse and boarded it here. And suppose Ellena stayed here on some of her visits. Maybe this is where the two of them first met. Maybe this was even where they traded information. Probably no one would have suspected them."

Leaning back, Etienne propped himself on his elbows. "So now you gonna be exploring all through the house and all over the yard, trying to come up with clues?"

Miranda couldn't help but smile. "Maybe. I still can't figure out what that stupid watch chain has to do with everything."

"Don't be trying so hard."

Giving a long, languid stretch, he folded his arms beneath his head. His T-shirt had slipped higher, exposing part of his stomach. His jeans had slipped lower, his skin smooth and tan. Miranda looked quickly away.

"Now see?" Etienne scolded. "You're getting yourself all tense, all worked up. And you're never gonna find answers that way. So what'd I tell you?"

"You said . . ." She tried to concentrate. She watched him sit up, move closer.

"You said . . . just surrender to it."

"That's right," he murmured. "That's all you gotta do."

Very slowly, he leaned toward her. He took her face between his hands. His lips were gentle, but his kiss was firm—she melted beneath it as he pressed her tight against his chest. His lips traced a shivery path to her neck and lingered at the base of her throat. His hands slid to her shoulders and down her body, an embrace both relentless and tender—burning where it touched, but never forcing, never intrusive. He whispered to her in his secret language . . . their lips locked in a kiss . . .

"Miranda?" Aunt Teeta called softly.

Miranda's cry was instantly muffled beneath Etienne's lips. Shocked, she stared at him, even as he pulled away from her, snapped off the light, and slipped out of sight beneath the covers. After a second's hesitation, Miranda slid in beside him and yanked the bedspread up to her chin.

"What?" she called back, with what she hoped was convincing grogginess.

Aunt Teeta opened the door, her bathrobe askew, her hair disheveled, and several oversize curlers bobbing on top of her head.

"Oh, darlin', I'm so sorry. I didn't think you'd be asleep yet. You know, I was just thinking—since you and Etienne have been spending so much time together, why don't you invite him over sometime? So your mama can meet him? And ask Gage over, too—he's such a cutie."

Miranda yawned loudly. "That's a great idea, Aunt Teeta. Thanks a lot."

"All right now, hon, you go on back to sleep. Love you."

"Love you, too."

Miranda waited till the door closed. Till Aunt Teeta's footsteps faded down the stairs, till the house was silent once more. She waited a long time.

At last the covers moved, and Etienne, after a thorough look around, threw them back and sat up. He seemed immensely amused.

"Damn, that was close. Your aunt, she woulda skinned me alive if she'd caught me here."

Miranda sank back on the pillows. Her heart was still racing at top speed. She felt excited and happy and breathless, confused and strangely frustrated.

"I think you better leave now," she mumbled.

"Yeah, I think I better."

The kiss he gave her this time was on the cheek and almost brotherly. He jumped from the bed, but paused when he got to the sunporch. As Miranda saw him turn to look back at her, her whole body felt warm.

"What is it?" she asked him, embarrassed now.

But Etienne didn't look embarrassed at all.

"It's good, *cher*." He winked. "And next time, it'll be even better."

28

"WELL, GOOD MORNING, SLEEPYHEAD!" As Miranda shuffled drowsily into the kitchen, Aunt Teeta met her with a big hug. "Your mama already left for work, but look who's decided to grace us with their presence!"

Startled, Miranda saw Gage and Etienne sitting at the table, both with heaping plates of food in front of them. Gage wiped his mouth quickly on a napkin; Etienne watched her over the rim of his coffee cup.

Her mind spun back to last night, cheeks flaming at the memory. *What was I thinking? I should know better! When everything about Etienne Boucher screams GUARANTEED HEARTBREAK—and even though nothing really serious happened—I should definitely know better!*

Halfway standing, Gage pulled out a chair for her. "We thought maybe you'd like a ride to school."

Oh yes . . . and now here was Gage. With that face and that smile and those big brown eyes that just melted her heart whenever she looked at him. And especially since Roo's candid confession— *"He was* amazing*"*—how could a girl *not* imagine other secrets behind the shyness?

Still flustered, Miranda turned and bumped into her aunt, upsetting the coffeepot, splashing the floor, nearly burning her arm in the process. As Gage and Etienne exchanged glances, she had a second of panic. What if Etienne had said something about last night? What if Gage suspected? Did she look guilty?

"Oh, mercy, did you burn yourself?" Aunt Teeta fussed, trying to mop the floor, trying to tend to Miranda.

"I'm sorry, Aunt Teeta. No, I'm okay."

"Here, let me get your breakfast."

"I'm really not hungry."

Ignoring her, Aunt Teeta bustled to the stove. "Gage, honey, I'm *so* glad you came this morning."

"Thanks. It's been a while."

"I used to see you all the time at the office," Aunt Teeta went on. Then, in an aside to Miranda, "His mama and I worked together for years. But she decided to leave and spend more time with her family."

Though Etienne and Gage exchanged glances, neither of them said anything. Miranda wondered if Gage's mom might have quit her job when Etienne's mother got sick.

"So I've had the pleasure of watching these two little rascals grow up." As Aunt Teeta passed the table, she gave Gage's shoulder an affectionate squeeze. "Isn't this Gage just the cutest thing?"

Shaking his head, Gage flushed slightly and tried to concentrate on his scrambled eggs.

"And those dimples," Aunt Teeta teased. "Aren't they just precious?"

Before Gage could ward him off, Etienne leaned over and pinched his cheek. "Just precious. Cute and precious."

"Cut it out," Gage mumbled, lowering his head.

"Miranda, honey, sit down. I wish you'd eat something." Peering out the window, Aunt Teeta gave a shudder. "Y'all be sure and take umbrellas. There's supposed to be a doozy of a storm coming in."

"How much of a doozy?" Etienne asked. "Medium doozy or big doozy?"

Aunt Teeta flapped her dishtowel at him. "*Monster* doozy. Big bad winds, flash-flood rain, and maybe even tornadoes kind of doozy. Miranda, don't you feel well?"

"Just"—Miranda brushed it off—"kind of sick to my stomach, I guess."

"What, darlin', something keep you awake last night?"

Etienne stared at her. Gage stared at her. Aunt Teeta stared at her. Thank God for Gage, who finally seemed to sense her growing distress. Cramming the last bite of sausage into his mouth, he scraped back his chair from the table.

"I'll make sure she eats something later," he promised Aunt Teeta. "Come on, we better go. We're gonna be late."

Miranda threw him a grateful look as the three of them trooped out the door. Still, once they reached Etienne's truck, she couldn't resist.

"You really are cute and precious," she said, touching a fingertip to one of his dimples.

Gage's face went redder. He grabbed her hand and boosted her into the front seat. "See if I come to *your* rescue anymore."

"And I have to agree with Roo and Ashley. You're *especially* cute when you're embarrassed."

"Yeah?" Gage's lips moved against her ear. "Don't tempt me.

I bet you're especially cute when you're embarrassed, too."

Miranda stared at him in surprise. Gage gave her an innocent smile, then climbed in beside her. Etienne seemed completely unaware of their little exchange.

While the boys argued sports scores and statistics, Miranda gazed nervously out at the pewter sky. Thunder rumbled in the distance, and the windshield glistened with the first few sprinklings of rain. As Etienne reached to turn on the wipers, she felt a deep and unexpected chill.

"Listen, Miranda . . . watch . . ."

Surprised, she straightened in her seat. She glanced quickly from Gage to Etienne, but the two of them didn't seem to notice and kept right on talking.

"Watch . . ."

A shiver, even colder now, gnawed at her spine. *Grandpa?* But of course it was him, she recognized his voice—the same tone, the same words she'd heard at the funeral home the night of the visitation. *But why here? Why now?*

"Listen, Miranda . . . watch . . ."

"You okay?" This time Gage looked down at her, half amused, half concerned.

"Somebody walk over your grave?" Etienne teased.

Miranda had heard that old expression many times before—only now it seemed more scary than funny, and she edged slightly nearer to Gage.

Muttering to himself, Etienne bent forward, eyes narrowed on the school ahead and the ominous clouds behind it. There were even more of them now, gray darkening to black, and all of them churning like restless waves.

Gage pointed out a parking space in the student lot. "Did Ashley call you about revising that outline?" he asked Etienne. "She wants to meet at lunch and brainstorm."

"Did you say rainstorm?" Etienne grumbled. "'Cause this one looks like it's gonna be a killer."

"There's tornado warnings," Ashley fretted, pulling a chair up to their table.

The school cafeteria was packed, much noisier and more chaotic than usual. No one was eating outside today because of the rain.

Balancing his tray on one hand, Parker slid into the empty chair next to her. "Hey, don't worry so much. We never have tornadoes around here."

"Well, we *could* have tornadoes around here."

"Ash, when was the last time you heard of a tornado touching down in St. Yvette?"

"What if our house blew away? That would be a really horrible thing!"

"What if your *boyfriend* blew away?" Roo asked mildly. "That would be a really *good* thing."

And then, as everyone suddenly realized the impact of what they were saying, all eyes turned guiltily to Miranda.

"Oh, God, Miranda," Ashley was horrified. "I'm so sorry. I didn't mean . . . I would never—"

"Come on, it was a joke." Forcing a smile, Miranda did her best to brush it off. "Please, don't worry about it."

Neither Gage nor Etienne looked convinced. Miranda stared back at each of them and forced her smile a little more firmly.

"Maybe they'll let us out of school early." Parker sounded hopeful. "Hey, my folks are out of town for a few days—we could all party at my place."

Roo leaned over and lifted the top piece of bread from Gage's sandwich. As Gage watched her, she took out a slice of cheese and a tomato, then put the sandwich back together.

Gage shook his head and resumed eating.

"Full fridge." Parker tried again. "Home theater, swimming pool, and well-stocked bar. Any takers?"

"Yes, the *police* when they come to take you *away*," Roo said.

A clap of thunder violently shook the building. Though the storm had held off so far, Miranda's uneasiness had grown. That feeling of dread in the air—that feeling of grim expectancy. It was like her worst nightmare all over again.

She realized now that Ashley was talking, something about their ghost tour. The others were casually listening, a comment or question or insult tossed out here and there. Laughter and conversation were at full pitch around them. Life at St. Yvette High was going on as usual, and nobody else seemed paticularly bothered by the weather. All Miranda wanted to do was get home to Aunt Teeta's, where she'd be safe. *Well . . . safe from the storm, anyway . . .*

The real downpour began just as Etienne dropped her off after school. Bolting for the door, Miranda got inside and dried off, changed clothes, and fixed herself something to eat. With Mom and Aunt Teeta both at work, the house loomed large and silent around her. Her footsteps echoed over the parquet floors. Thunder shivered the walls and trembled the old foundations.

But she couldn't stop thinking of Ellena Rose.

She'd finally worked up enough courage to take the watch chain from her room, and now, sitting at the kitchen table, Miranda went back over everything she knew—or thought she knew. There was still so much missing. Clues and answers and truths . . .

"Listen, Miranda . . . watch . . ."

Her grandfather's words made her even more restless. *I* have *been listening, I* have *been watching. What am I missing? How do I find it?*

She thought of his treasure. Some small and seemingly insignificant artifact that Jonas Hayes had picked up one day at the Falls and become completely obsessed with. He wouldn't have thrown it away, Aunt Teeta had assured her. And what had Etienne said? *"He'd have kept it close . . ."*

Some connection . . . something important . . . something that Nathan's spirit is connected to . . .

Leaning forward onto the table, Miranda rested her head on folded arms and let her eyes drift shut. She could see Hayes House the way it used to be—the way she imagined it would be—warm and solid and welcoming, with the aroma of home-cooked meals, and a big, roomy barn out back. And he'd be there—*Nathan*—brushing down the horses, when Ellena Rose strolled by. She'd be inquiring about a carriage maybe, but Nathan would be her *real* reason for stopping. *To exchange a whisper. To exchange information.*

Miranda's thoughts flowed. Back through years and seasons and moonlit nights . . . the opera house and the battlefield . . .

"No . . . you're wrong . . ."

"I swear to you . . . for the love of God . . ."

"I'm the one you want. Only me . . . only me."

"Take it . . . the Rose . . . Miss Ellena . . . "

Miranda's head was spinning. Too many images . . . too many scenes . . . all of them painful and heartbreaking. Nathan—rope burns around his wrists . . . cuts from horse-whip lashes; Ellena Rose—a lingering taste of poison on her tongue, and in her throat, her last words choked, her sweet song silenced forever.

"You were my life, Nathan . . . and now you are my death . . ."

"No. Please stop." But Miranda's senses reached out; her mind searched. *You thought Nathan betrayed you . . .*

"I'm the one you want . . . only me . . ."

"Only me."

Tears ran down Miranda's cheeks, and they were Ellena's tears and Nathan's tears. She clutched the braid tightly to her heart.

Why did Nathan betray you, Ellena? How could he have been that selfish? That unfeeling?

Frustrated, Miranda pressed both hands to her forehead. She was here in Aunt Teeta's kitchen, yet it was *another* kitchen, a long-ago farmhouse kitchen. In a house where a beautiful red-haired diva and a handsome stable boy traded secrets and . . .

And kisses . . .

For Miranda could see them now—Nathan and Ellena—alone in the barn at midnight, while Hayes House slept. The way they held each other, clung to each other, in the soft glow of lantern light, as though they were the only two people in the world.

Accomplices . . . and sweethearts.

Slowly, reluctantly, they drew apart. Nathan, handing Ellena his pocket watch . . . Ellena, giving Nathan a watch chain braided from her beautiful red hair . . .

"*Someday,*" Nathan whispered, wiping tears from Ellena's cheeks. *"Someday when this terrible war is over, we won't have to hide like this. We won't have to hide our feelings for each other . . . we'll finally be together."*

"But I'm afraid, Nathan. I'm so afraid! Something bad is going to happen—I can feel *it!"*

"Hush now. Nothing's going to happen, my love. We've been careful; we'll be safe."

"Promise you'll come back to me . . ."

"Yes. Always. I promise."

Very gently Ellena touched the braid in his hand. *"And promise me you'll keep this close to your heart."*

"I swear it. And someday, I'll wear my watch and your chain together. Together, *Ellena. Just like you and me . . ."*

Miranda began to come back to herself.

She could feel the watch chain pressing into her skin—she wanted to hold it close, she wanted to fling it away.

"A fair exchange," Travis Fontaine had said that tragic, deadly night. *"My mercy . . . for your betrayal."*

Through a slow, lingering haze, Miranda stared down at the braid. This beautiful red hair over a hundred years old, yet she could still feel the love, the devotion, the tears in every strand . . .

Ellena's tears . . . Nathan's tears . . . the tears of Travis Fontaine.

Because he's the one, isn't he, Ellena? When Nathan was caught, Travis Fontaine—the other man who loved you so much—saw that watch chain and recognized that watch chain . . .

Because he recognized your hair.

Miranda was quivering. Shaking with fear, with grief, with regret. Shaking with over a century of emotions, the emotions of three people trapped in a pitiless fate.

Oh, Ellena Rose . . . he knew your hair.

Nathan didn't betray you. Even though he was captured, even when he was tortured, he never *betrayed you.*

Miranda's eyelids finally opened. She was sitting at the kitchen table; the hands on the clock had scarcely moved. And instead of the questions that had haunted her, there was only a deep, sad wisdom.

For she knew the rights and the wrongs . . .

The truths and the lies . . .

The betrayed and the betrayer.

"Listen, Miranda . . . watch."

And she knew now what her grandfather had found at the Falls.

29

A HUGE CRASH OF THUNDER BROUGHT HER UP OUT OF her chair. As the lights flickered ominously, Miranda ran for flashlights, laying them out on the table within easy reach. Rain gushed at the windowpanes and pounded on the roof; trees flailed helplessly in the wind. When the front door suddenly burst open, she let out a yell and went running into the hall, convinced the whole front of the house was blowing away.

What she found instead was Etienne, alone in the entryway, shaking off water like a wet dog.

"You!" She let out a sigh of relief while Etienne glanced around the corridor.

"Yeah. Last time I checked, anyhow."

"What are you doing, coming here in this weather? It looks *horrible* out there."

"It *is* horrible out there. But Miss Teeta, she just called me and she was worried, so I figured you might like the company."

"You figured right."

One corner of his mouth twitched. "Yeah, I usually do."

He followed her into the kitchen, then stood dripping in front of the sink. Miranda brought him towels, made a pot of strong coffee, and pulled out Aunt Teeta's latest homemade confection—bread pudding with rum sauce—which she popped into the microwave.

"Great. My favorite." Nodding approval, Etienne continued towel drying his hair.

"Aunt Teeta told me you say that about every single thing she makes."

"And it's true. They're *all* my favorites." Pausing, he shoved his wet hair back from his face and stared at her, eyes narrowed. "Hey, you okay, *cher*?"

"Well"—Miranda drew a deep breath—"I wasn't okay just a few minutes ago. But I think I am now."

"Ah. Is that your way of telling me I'm your hero?"

Miranda couldn't resist. "No. It's my way of telling you that I had a nightmare, but I woke up."

"That's cruel, *cher.* You just stabbed me straight in my heart."

"You'll live."

She watched his lips quirk at the edges, his dark eyes shining with amusement. But then, the amusement began to fade.

"So what *really* happened?" he asked quietly.

She felt silly as her eyes brimmed with sudden tears. She started to turn away from him, but his arms went around her.

"Miranda?"

"Can we just . . . sit down first?"

While Etienne chose a spot at the table, she busied herself with his food, brought him another towel. Anything to distract herself, to keep all the new revelations from crowding in and overwhelming her too fast. Finally Etienne stopped her, took the bread pudding, then gently—but firmly—pushed her down in a chair.

"Whatever it is, you're not gonna get rid of it by running. And I'm always gonna believe you, no matter what."

"I know what really happened now. To Nathan. And Ellena. And Travis Fontaine."

With a look of mild surprise, Etienne pushed his bowl away and leaned toward her. "I'm listening."

"They're all connected, just like we thought. Only the betrayal wasn't just about Travis and Ellena. Ellena thought Nathan betrayed her to Travis. But Nathan didn't. It was the chain and her hair. And the two of them were in love, which made it even worse. And Nathan made a promise to her, but they both died, and they couldn't be together—"

"Whoa, whoa . . ." Etienne's concern had turned to confusion. "Time out. Back up." While Miranda took a deep breath and started over, he retrieved his bowl and ate the bread pudding. He chewed slowly, deep in thought. Then he leaned back in his chair.

"Maybe I should put this another way," he said. "Is there something you *didn't* figure out before I got here?"

"Where the watch is."

"The . . ."

"Watch. That's what Grandpa found at the Falls that day. And what he's been trying to tell me." Miranda's voice tightened. "I think Nathan wants me to take the watch chain to Ellena. And connect it to the watch like they promised."

"A watch. Nathan's watch."

"And I think if I do that, Nathan will be at peace. See, all this time I thought Grandpa was telling me to listen *and* to watch. But he was telling me to listen, because it *was* the watch. So now we have to find it."

"Your *grand-père*," Etienne murmured. "He talked to you?"

"Yes. I heard him. I'm certain of it."

For just the briefest moment, something shimmered in the black depths of Etienne's eyes and softened the chiseled features of his face. "That's good, *cher*," he whispered. "Good for you."

As the two of them continued to talk, the weather continued to worsen. Mom and Aunt Teeta both called to check in—and though neither of them could come home yet, they were grateful Etienne was there. While he went in search of candles, Miranda made another pot of coffee. Refilling his cup, she suddenly had the feeling of being watched, and when she turned around, Etienne was in the doorway, observing her every move.

"I wish you wouldn't look at me like that." Miranda frowned.

"Like what?"

"Like . . . you can see things I don't want you to see."

"Too late."

"Stop." She did her best to sound stern. "Now I know how Gage feels."

"Except for the dimples."

"Right. Except for those."

"Not to worry, *cher*. You got a whole lotta other redeeming qualities."

Picking up a napkin, Miranda tossed it at him. "Drink your coffee."

"Yes, ma'am."

But she could still feel him watching. And when she passed his chair, he caught her and pulled her close.

She stood silently, facing him. She set the coffeepot on the table. Gently she ran her fingers through his thick, dark hair . . . along the angles of his face. She heard his slight intake of breath, felt the sudden tensing of his muscles.

His hands encircled her waist. She gazed down at him, and bent slowly to kiss him . . .

The phone shrilled loudly, jarring them apart. As Miranda hurried to answer it, she could hardly breathe.

"Hello?"

But she couldn't make out the voice on the other end. The voice crying and babbling so fast, words spilling out, making no sense. When she finally heard the name "Etienne," she quickly handed him the receiver.

It was as though he already knew something was wrong. Even before he saw the fear on Miranda's face, even before he took the phone. And then there were only those few short words, those few foreign words he spoke, before jumping up and heading for the door.

Miranda stood frozen with dread. "What is it?"

"Roo's gone. Ashley says she never came home after school."

"What—"

"She's afraid Roo might be at the Falls."

"Now? *Why*?"

"Some argument they got into, something about Parker. And Roo was plenty mad and wouldn't ride with them and said she was gonna walk home so she could think."

"Ashley told me Roo always goes to the Falls when she's upset. But it floods there, doesn't it?"

"That's why I gotta go. *Now.* I'm gonna stop and get Parker."

"What about Gage?"

"Aunt Jules—Gage's mom—just called Ashley's house, looking for him. Ashley told her they were all there studying—she didn't want Aunt Jules to worry." Etienne's expression darkened. "I guess Aunt Jules's van is gone."

"What about Ashley's parents?" Yet as Etienne sighed, Miranda knew what the answer would be. "Let me guess. Ashley told them Roo and Gage are at Gage's house."

"You got it."

"Look, you know Gage must have driven Roo to the Falls. And you know he'll take good care of her."

"Stay here. I'll call as soon as I can."

But Miranda was already grabbing a rain jacket from the front hall closet. "Absolutely not. I'm coming with you."

Before he could say no, she ran after him, out into the storm.

30

"IT'S ALL MY FAULT," ASHLEY SOBBED. "What if she's dead?"

The four of them were squeezed tightly into Etienne's truck. With every shift of the clutch and each turn of the wheel, Etienne's right arm jabbed sharply into Miranda's side, and Ashley bounced back and forth between Miranda's lap and Parker's. The old Chevy truck, way past its prime, rattled and clanked and groaned at every pothole and puddle, but it hugged the roads like glue.

"It's not your fault," Parker reassured Ashley for the dozenth time. "You didn't know what she was planning to do. How could it be your fault?"

"The water always gets so deep at the Falls. The bayou always floods. If she's dead—"

"She's not *dead*." He paused, then mumbled, "I couldn't be that lucky."

"Parker Wilmington, I can't even believe you said—"

"I was *kidding*, Ash. Okay, sorry, bad timing, but I was *kidding*, okay? Roo's fine. And none of this is your fault."

Gulping down a hiccup, Ashley glared at him. "You're right. It's *your* fault."

"*My* fault?"

"You know she caught you drinking in the parking lot!"

"Just a little! I swear, I only had one sip—"

"You're heartless and insensitive, and you hate my sister."

"Christ, Ashley, I *don't* hate your sister—"

"You told her I care more about you than I do about her, and that's not true!"

"I know it's not—and *Roo* knows it's not. It was a joke! I wasn't serious!"

"I'm always defending you, and Roo's always been smarter than me. Roo would *never* get involved with somebody like you."

Parker shot Etienne another helpless glance. "Is that good or bad?"

"I wouldn't be doing any more talking right now, if I were you," Etienne advised him.

"Roo looks out for me. Roo has better sense than I do," Ashley went on miserably. "It's always been that way, ever since we were little. She's always had the brains. And I've always had . . . not the brains."

Etienne's eyes and Parker's eyes met behind Ashley's back.

"Not going there," Etienne mumbled. Then to Ashley, "Don't be worrying about Roo, *cher*. Parker's right—she's gonna be fine."

"Yeah." Parker's tone was equally reassuring. "Gage is with her right this minute."

Miranda could tell Ashley wanted to believe them. But the girl's eyes were still bleary with tears, and her lips were quivering.

"If something happens to Roo, I'll never forgive myself." Sniffling, Ashley stared dejectedly out Parker's window. It was impossible to see anything but gusting rain.

"Nothing's gonna happen to her, *cher*."

"You promise?"

Etienne didn't miss a beat. "Sure, I promise."

As Miranda glanced at his silhouette, she saw that telltale muscle clench in his cheek. His body was rigid. He was clutching the steering wheel so fiercely, his knuckles were white. For the first time, she realized just how worried he actually was—far more worried than he wanted anyone to suspect.

A fresh wave of fear washed over her.

Hunching down inside her jacket, Miranda tried to concentrate on a happy ending. Tried to believe how someday they'd all look back on this and laugh, just another crazy adventure. Outside, the storm shrieked and roared; in here, it was stuffy and hot and damp. She could smell fear and sweat, mud and wet hair and wet clothes, the faint sweetness of Ashley's perfume.

"The road's already flooding." Ashley sounded alarmed. "How long do you think till the bayou—"

"Hours yet," Etienne replied, a little too quickly.

But Miranda's imagination filled in the rest. She braced against Parker as Etienne began swerving more often, more sharply, around broken limbs and downed trees. The wipers were no match for the storm now; the headlights barely penetrated the rain. She couldn't even see the hood of the truck.

"Can't you go faster?" Ashley pleaded.

"Any faster, and *we'll* be the ones needing a rescue." Etienne gripped the wheel even tighter. He hunched his shoulders and took another angry swipe at the windshield.

Miranda leaned in close to his ear. "Don't worry. Gage will be fine, too."

For just a brief instant, Etienne's defenses seemed to crumble. For just a brief instant, she caught a glimpse of emotions—both panic and hope. And then, just as fast, his jaw set in a determined line, and he cast her a smooth, sidelong glance.

"Is that you, smelling like an old cheeseburger?"

Startled, she couldn't help laughing. "That is *not* me—that is something, *somewhere*, in this digustingly dirty truck of yours."

"No, I don't think so. No, I definitely think it's—Hey, that's Aunt Jules's van over there."

"Where?" Leaning across Miranda, Parker squinted out Etienne's window. "Are you sure?"

"As sure as I am that it's stuck in the mud," Etienne grumbled. "And as sure as I am that Gage is gonna be grounded for the rest of his life."

"At least we know they're here." A tiny bit of relief crept into Ashley's voice. "Do you see them anywhere?"

"It doesn't look like they're in the van, but—*Merde!*"

As the brakes slammed and held, the truck skidded deep into water. Parker managed to catch Ashley right before she hit the dashboard.

"Now what?" Parker demanded.

Etienne's tone was as grim as his face. "Well, I guess we know why they got stuck, yeah? No way we can get any farther on this road. The water's too high."

"Is there another way in? Maybe from another direction?"

"Only the bayou."

"What about your boat?"

"That'll take too long, and we can't risk the time." Gunning the engine, Etienne tried backing the truck onto a stretch of higher ground. But when the tires spun uselessly, he shut off the ignition, twisted around, and grabbed two flashlights from behind the seat.

"Take this." Handing one to Parker, Etienne kept the other for himself. "You girls stay here where it's safe."

"Safe!" Ashley wailed. "It's flooded, and we'll float away!"

"You won't float away, Ashley. I swear."

"Hey, we'll take our chances with you," Miranda shot back, scrambling out with Ashley before Etienne could shut his door.

Holding on to one another, the four of them made slow, painstaking progress. What rain gear they wore did little to protect them; within seconds they were all completely soaked. Clutching both Etienne's hand and Ashley's, Miranda stayed alert for alligators and water moccasins and other creepy things that might be escaping to higher ground. She couldn't see into the murky water, couldn't see where to step. She had no sense of direction, no clue where they were headed. *Maybe Ashley and I should have stayed in the truck.*

But Etienne seemed entirely sure of himself. He led them

steadily through the downpour, all of them shouting as loud as they could.

"Roo! Gage!"

"Why aren't they answering?" Ashley looked so pathetic, shivering like a drowned rat. When Miranda stopped to hug her, Parker wrapped both girls in a tight hug of his own.

"Roo!" Etienne kept calling. "Gage!"

A blinding flash of lightning ripped the sky. Miranda caught a split-second glance of what she thought might be the Falls, just ahead of them. She tried to go faster, pulling Ashley along with her.

"Roo! Gage!" Mockingly, the storm flung all their shouts back at them. "Roo! Where are you? It's us! Gage! Come on, y'all—*answer*!"

The four trudged on. As Ashley slipped and jerked Miranda down with her into the water, Parker immediately hauled them both up again.

"They're not here!" Ashley wept. "I know something terrible's happened. I *know* it!"

"No, Ashley, they're okay," Miranda insisted. "I'm sure they've taken shelter somewhere—they just can't hear us, that's all."

But Miranda was just as terrified—totally panicked and trying not to show it. It was like being forced back into the hurricane—the awful tragedy happening all over again—*howling wind . . . drowning rain . . . the house falling in . . . the world falling apart and nobody to help . . .*

Once more she stumbled, then realized that Parker still had a firm grip on her, that he was tucking her inside his jacket, the same way he was tucking Ashley against his other side, shielding them both, steering them both to safety.

"*Roo!*" Parker was hoarse from yelling. "Dammit, are you out here? *Gage!*"

And then . . . miraculously . . . came the faint sound of a voice—thin and weak and frightened, and not so far away . . .

"Here!" it called back. "We're over here!"

"*Roo!*" Ashley screamed. "Oh God, that's *Roo*!"

New strength surged through them as they tried to run, sloshing through mud and muck and water and debris, flashlights slicing the dark.

"I see her!" Etienne called. "Roo! You okay?"

"Yes! But Gage—"

"*Gage!*"

It was the fear in Etienne's voice that pierced Miranda's heart. The stark, raw fear as Etienne shouted his cousin's name and struggled on ahead of them, then suddenly dropped to his knees.

At first Miranda didn't notice anything but the tree. The gigantic tree uprooted and split open on the ground, its massive branches splayed in all directions. But as she got closer, there was movement among the layers and layers of drenched leaves—just a slight movement—and the small, huddled figure of a girl, and the sobs of her desperate pleading.

"Help him! You've got to help him! *Hurry*!"

Scrambling easily over the twisted limbs and foliage, Parker was the next to reach Roo, with Ashley and Miranda right behind him. In shocked silence, the three of them stared at the cuts and bruises on Roo's face and arms, the blood on Roo's clothes . . . but nothing could have prepared them for what they saw next.

"Gage," Roo choked. "He pushed me out of the way. I think . . . I think he's . . ."

Miranda's heart stopped. Gage was sprawled on his back, pinned under one section of the tree. A huge, gnarled branch sloped down across his chest, another had caught his left leg, twisting it behind him at a grotesque angle. Blood had pooled in the wet grass around his head and beneath his shoulders. His eyes were closed. His face was white and still. He looked like some macabre rag doll, tossed carelessly out in the rain.

But almost as wrenching was the sight of Etienne. Etienne kneeling there beside Gage, feeling for a pulse, listening for a heartbeat, his features cold, hard stone.

Miranda didn't realize she'd been holding her breath. Not till Etienne finally glanced up at them, his voice thick with emotion.

"He's breathing. Let's get him outta here."

31

Even then, it took a moment for the terrible reality to sink in. While Roo and Ashley clutched each other, crying. While Parker, grave and stunned, slid his hand along Roo's shoulder, then squatted down on his heels beside Etienne. And while Miranda bent low over Gage, to smooth the hair back from his forehead.

The storm was growing worse. As the five of them struggled frantically to free Gage, the wind blew wilder, the rain fell harder, and the limbs became heavier to move. Several times Gage roused and cried out, temporarily halting the rescue. Miranda doubted he really comprehended much, but she also knew that if his pain had managed to cross the boundaries of unconsciousness, even for a second, then it had to be excruciating.

"Shit!" Parker exploded. "This is taking too damn long!"

Roo glanced at Gage, then at Miranda. Her dark makeup was runny and smeared, her expression shocked and bewildered. "I just wanted to get away, that's all. But he said he was coming with me, that I always think better with him around. I never thought the rain would get this bad. And he's lost so much blood . . . and I couldn't call 911 . . ."

"Right," Parker remembered. "No phone signal out here." Planting his feet wide apart, he balanced himself on the tree's enormous trunk. He ripped off a limb, flung it angrily, then wiped a muddy hand across his brow. "And Etienne's truck is stranded. Which means we can't go for help."

Ashley's fearful eyes swept over Gage. "It's just . . . like Roo said . . . he's lost so much blood."

It was bad enough not knowing the extent of Gage's injuries; it was even worse not being able to reach the ones they could see. The helplessness was unbearable. Miranda felt as if she were watching all the life drain slowly and steadily out of him.

"I've got some tools in the truck." Shrugging out of his jacket, Etienne passed it to Miranda. "Here—try and keep him warm. I'll be right back."

He was off before anyone could stop him. Holding the jacket at arm's length, Miranda wondered what good it could possibly do—like all the rest of their clothes, it was soaked. With Roo and Ashley's help, she managed to work it in beneath the branches, to tuck it around Gage's chest. Gage moaned, his eyelids struggling open. Most of his right arm had escaped serious injury, so Miranda reached down and gently squeezed his fingers. They were slick with blood.

"Look at his eyes." Crouched there with the others, Ashley began rocking slowly back and forth. "He's hurting so much . . . I can't stand it."

Miranda knew exactly what Ashley meant. Gage's big brown eyes, always so soft, so expressive, were now dull with pain, hazy and unfocused. As a muscle flinched in his jaw, the girls crowded even closer, determined to protect him however they could.

"I think he's coming to," Roo mumbled. Stroking his cheek, she leaned in close to listen.

"Cold," Gage whispered.

Up till now, Miranda hadn't really noticed the bluish tinge to his lips. Alarm bells immediately sounded in her brain, but before she could get up, Parker's hand came down on her shoulder.

"Here," he said, "give him this."

With Roo and Ashley looking on in surprise, Miranda accepted the small flask Parker slid from his pocket. She nodded him a grateful smile.

"What happened?" Gage whispered again. "Roo . . . is Roo okay?"

"He doesn't see me," Roo choked, while Ashley and Miranda forced a few sips of whiskey down Gage's throat. Roo took a deep breath, tried to collect herself. "Hey, I'm fine," she told Gage. "And you're fine, too. And everybody's here, and . . . dammit, Gage, why'd you come with me? I told you not to. I *told* you I wanted to be by myself. Why don't you ever listen to anything I say?"

"So . . . cold," he murmured. "Can't . . . feel . . . legs."

"Gage, no. Oh, God."

Miranda glanced over her shoulder. Etienne had waded back from the truck, bringing tools with him. The boys were standing about twenty feet away, locked in grim conversation. Etienne was pointing to the last cumbersome branch that trapped Gage. Parker was nodding, making air measurements with his hands.

This can't be good. As new prickles of fear crept up Miranda's spine, she refocused on Gage.

"He's still saying he's cold," Ashley said.

For the first time Miranda stared at Ashley's pink headband. The girl had pulled it from her hair and was running it tenderly over Gage's face, trying to clean off dirt and blood. How long had Ashley been doing that, Miranda wondered—how long had they all been out here? She didn't even recall *seeing* that headband before—but seeing it now, with Gage's blood all over it, was almost too much for her. She closed her eyes, swallowed hard, tried to concentrate on what Ashley was saying.

"I don't think it's just his legs he can't feel. I'm not sure he can feel *anything*."

Miranda opened her eyes. All this time she'd been holding Gage's hand, squeezing his fingers, getting no response. "It's temporary," she answered, determined to be hopeful. "He's fading in and out right now, and that's good. If he could feel everything—everywhere he's hurt—I'm not sure he could take it."

"Miranda"—Ashley's eyes were wide with fear—"what are we going to do?"

Miranda could only shrug in frustration. As Ashley pressed the headband to Gage's forehead, and Roo continued to stroke Gage's cheek, Etienne and Parker walked over.

"This should do it," Etienne announced. "Now y'all need to hold him down. *Tight*, you understand? 'Cause when we cut this last branch, and it shifts around, he's probably gonna feel it. And it'll hurt like hell."

Roo's stare went slowly from Etienne to Parker. "He's going to die, isn't he."

"And leave you?" Parker snorted. "Not a chance."

And then everything happened so fast. Surreal, like a dream—age-old instincts of love and survival, guiding them, giving them strength. The girls trying to restrain Gage—Parker and Etienne shouting—the crushing branch turning and scraping and tilting, suspended there for mere seconds—just long enough for Gage to be dragged out from under it.

Miranda was distinctly aware of two things.

Gage screaming in agony.

And the world turning red with his blood.

"Quick!"

"Got him!"

"Move!"

As the tree came down again, it hit with an earth-shuddering crash. But Gage was clear of it, and—at least for now—he was still alive.

"Come on—take him to the shelter!"

"The picnic shelter? Are you sure it's safe?"

"It's concrete, and it's raised. What, you got any better ideas?"

Sharp tableaux swept through Miranda's head, imprinting themselves on her brain—bright, piercing snapshots she knew she'd never forget.

The raging storm and the raging emotions. Gage's face twisted in anguish, his broken body, shards of white bone, torn muscles, raw flesh. Gage trying so hard to be brave, trying so hard not to feel, not to cry, even as tears streamed helplessly down his cheeks. And the blessed relief of unconsciousness that followed;

the limp, easy weight of him in their arms; their rushing him to the picnic shelter, laying him down, standing guard—close and watchful and protective—around him.

"Anybody here ever set a broken bone?" As the others regarded him with blank expressions, Etienne pointed to Gage's leg. "Great. Anybody here wanna help me?"

And once again it was as if somehow, instinctively, they all knew what to do. Parker and Etienne tearing off their shirts to stanch the bleeding. Every jacket, every extra bit of clothing commandeered for makeshift blankets and bandages. Caring for Gage, crying for Gage, praying for Gage. When all had been done that *could* be done, only then did everyone finally give in to exhaustion, resolved to wait out the storm.

"Listen," Etienne said. For the last half hour he'd been leaning up against the wall, arms folded across his bare chest, narrowed eyes gauging the flooded woods around them. "I'm gonna try to make it home."

"Now?" Parker gaped at him as though he'd lost his mind. "In *this*?"

"Etienne, that's crazy!" Curled along Gage's side, Ashley raised up in alarm. "There's no way you could get home. Don't even think about it."

Etienne's sigh was tolerant. "Look, it's not that far—"

"I know how far it is," Parker broke in. "But going by truck is one thing. And going by boat is another thing. But trying to swim—"

"It's not that bad yet. I can still make it through if I leave now. And it won't be this deep, the closer I get to the road."

"Roo, say something." Half turning, Ashley appealed to her sister. "He'll listen to you. Tell him not to go."

Roo calmly considered. She'd been sitting cross-legged beside Ashley, with Gage's head cradled in her lap. Her glance flicked from Etienne to Gage, but when she didn't answer, Parker resumed the argument.

"Have you noticed it's very dark out there? Does the word *night* mean anything to you?"

"Nobody knows we're here." Etienne's reply was matter-of-fact. "It's not like they're gonna be sending search parties for us anytime soon."

"At least wait till the rain lets up a little."

"This rain, it could go on for hours." Etienne's mouth settled into a hard line. "And if the water keeps rising . . . I mean . . . Gage needs help."

Throughout the exchange, Miranda kept her thoughts to herself. She didn't want to admit how terrified she was, watching Gage with an increasing sense of dread. His breathing was more ragged now, catching tight in his chest, stabbing deep through his muscles. And even though he was covered with sweat, he'd begun shivering uncontrollably.

At last she stood up. She walked solemnly over to Parker and Etienne. "I think . . . someone needs to go."

As the three of them stared at one another, Etienne pushed away from the wall.

"No." Parker grabbed Etienne's arm. "I'll go."

Surprise crept slowly over Etienne's face. Instinctively, Miranda glanced at Ashley, who seemed oddly frozen.

"Parker—" Ashley began, but Etienne interrupted.

"I know the way better than you do," he said firmly.

"Like I haven't been to your house a million times?" Grinning, Parker shrugged and jerked his chin in Gage's direction. "You got one too sick to go, two too tired to go, and her"—he winked at Miranda—"too damn cute to go. And besides, who's the athlete around here anyway?"

"No, Parker. I—"

"Look." The grin faded from Parker's lips. He moved closer to Etienne, putting his back to Roo and Ashley so they couldn't hear. His voice was soft now, and serious. "You and Gage, you're each other's family. If something happened to you—" He broke off, glanced away, then pulled his eyes back to Etienne. "What would Gage do if something happened to you? Hell, what would *any* of us do if something happened to you?"

Their gazes held steady. Parker swallowed . . . gave a slight nod.

"Let me do this, Etienne. I want to."

Silence fell between them.

A silence louder, wider, deeper than any storm.

It was Ashley who broke it. "Parker, what's happening?"

Almost guiltily, Miranda jumped. She'd been so engrossed in the boys' conversation, she hadn't noticed Ashley approaching. At once Parker and Etienne turned toward Ashley, their expressions somber.

"Parker?" Ashley asked again. But then, as she stared long and hard at the boys, a slow dawn of awareness crept over her. "No, Parker. Please don't be stupid."

Miranda waited for Roo's usual insults. Roo kept silent.

"Hey, I'm up for this." Grin firmly back in place, Parker struck a heroic pose. "Parker Wilmington—explorer, adventurer, and super-swimmer!"

"Parker, you can't go out there—"

"Battling the elements! Wrestling man-eating alligators! Laughing in the face of danger!"

"Parker, I'm serious!" Ashley was close to tears. "It's too far to Etienne's house!"

"Hey, I need the exercise. And the fresh air. And the good news is: I won't even have to worry about dehydration."

But the tears came now, rolling down Ashley's cheeks, while Etienne tactfully moved away and Miranda joined him.

"Please." Slipping her arms around Parker's waist, Ashley leaned into him, peered up at him. "It's too horrible out there. I'm scared."

Parker raised his arms, flexed his muscles. "Fear? Fear is foreign to me!"

"Don't joke about this! I'm really scared something bad will happen. I just *feel* it."

"Ash, nothing bad is going to happen. I'll be careful, okay? I'll be safe."

Miranda suddenly realized she'd been eavesdropping. She hadn't meant to intrude on their private conversation, yet she'd been watching their faces and hearing every word. An eerie chill had settled at the base of her spine. She felt anxious and restless and afraid.

She glanced at Roo. Roo hadn't said anything in such a long

time, just sitting there holding Gage, her head bent over his face. Miranda's heart reached out to Roo, but her own uneasiness persisted. *Something dangerous, something tragic . . .*

Something familiar . . .

Reluctantly she turned her attention to Ashley and Parker. Though Ashley's features were pale and drawn, she seemed composed now, even quietly resigned. Parker was squeezing her in a tight hug.

"You better hurry, Parker Wilmington." Ashley's voice was muffled against his chest. "Promise you'll come back to me."

Parker rolled his eyes. "Yeah, yeah, sure. I promise."

"*Tonight.*"

"Tonight," Parker echoed dutifully.

"Cross your heart."

"Oh, for Christ's sake, Ashley, I said I'd be back, didn't I? Don't I *always* come back? Even when you *don't* want me to?"

Miranda's breath caught in her throat. Fear squeezed in her chest.

It can't be . . . it's impossible . . .

For she knew now why she'd listened so intently to Ashley and Parker, why their conversation had seemed so familiar . . .

Oh, God, no . . .

"Parker," she whispered.

Starting forward, she saw Ashley and Etienne standing at the edge of the shelter. Ashley was shivering, and Etienne's arm was around her shoulders. Miranda tried to call out, to shout a warning, to stop Parker from going, but he'd already dashed into the rain; she could already see the beam of his flashlight growing smaller and dimmer, swallowed by the storm.

Yet his words were still here. They lingered in this dark, frightening, abandoned place—the words he'd spoken to Ashley, and the words Ashley had spoken to him.

Prophetic words and fatal words. Words that tore at Miranda's heart and echoed over and over again in her mind.

The words Nathan and Ellena had spoken . . .

Right before the end.

32

"**Where is he, Miranda?" Ashley whispered.** "What's taking him so long?"

Hours had passed since Parker vanished into the storm. Hours of waiting and worrying and watching hopefully for his return. And though Miranda had kept up a steady show of confidence for Ashley's sake, secretly she was scared to death.

Nathan promised Ellena he'd come back to her . . .

And Ellena never saw him again.

Miranda noticed Ashley's grave expression. She remembered Ashley's fears that something bad would happen . . . and Parker's attempts to reassure her.

Ellena never saw him again.

"Something must have happened." Glancing from Roo to Miranda, Ashley ran her hand lightly over Gage's cheek. "I just have this horrible feeling—"

"Listen to me, *cher*," Etienne broke in. "He's fine. It's just gonna take him some time, that's all. But he'll come rescue us. You'll see."

Miranda could tell how much Ashley wanted to believe him. But as the girl's face began to crumple, Etienne stretched out his arms. "Aw, now, don't cry. Come here to me."

Ashley got up and started toward him, just as Etienne started toward her. He drew her gently against him. And then, while she sobbed quietly, he held her in a strong, solid embrace.

"You're tired, *cher*," Etienne mumbled. "We're all tired; we're all a little scared. It's okay to cry. Just get it all out. We're all gonna be fine. You'll see . . . you'll see . . ."

Miranda also wanted to believe that, though the words of Nathan and Ellena continued to haunt her. She couldn't even share her fears with Etienne, not when he had so much to deal with already.

She couldn't help marveling at him. His calm in the midst of chaos. His detachment holding them together. The way he rested his chin on top of Ashley's head. Patting her back, swaying her ever so gently . . . murmuring comfort and hope. Even though he looked far more strained and exhausted than the rest of them. Even though Gage still lay battered and unconscious, and there was nothing more any of them could do. And even though the storm blew savagely around them, and the black water was creeping over the foundation of the shelter, and inching slowly toward Etienne's feet.

"But Parker *should* be back by now," Roo suddenly murmured to Miranda. "Maybe something really *did* happen."

Miranda threw her an anxious glance. Nodding, Roo fixed a worried gaze on Ashley.

Time crawled endlessly. Minutes stretched to hours, and those hours grew more fearful. The girls kept their vigil around Gage. Etienne continued to stand, his keen eyes watchful for some sign of Parker's return. Miranda could only pray that Gage wouldn't rouse from unconsciousness.

As the night drew on, Parker's absence became almost unbearable. Etienne had started pacing. Roo had scooted closer to her sister, occasionally leaning her head on Ashley's shoulder. Watching Ashley stare so sadly out into the night, Miranda could only imagine what the girl must be thinking. Once again she tried to make positive conversation.

"It's so brave, what Parker's doing." Miranda offered Ashley an encouraging smile.

But Ashley's own smile seemed emotionless. "He should have been there by now. We all know it. People should be rescuing us."

"They'll come, Ash," Roo mumbled.

"He must not have gotten there."

"He did. I'm sure he did."

Ashley took a deep breath. She touched her head against Roo's, then gazed at Miranda.

"I'm not as nice to Parker as I should be."

"How can you even say that?" Miranda was startled. "Parker's crazy about you."

"But I'm mean to him sometimes."

Again Miranda expected Roo to chime in with her usual sarcasm. But again, Roo was uncharacteristically quiet.

"I am," Ashley admitted, almost shamefully. "I *am* mean to him."

"You're *true* to him," Miranda corrected. "And *truthful* to him. I can't think of a better way to love someone."

Just like Nathan and Ellena. Oh please, God, let Parker be okay.

Ashley seemed to find solace in Miranda's words. Lowering her head, she spoke softly to Roo.

"I don't care about Parker more than I care about you."

"I know," Roo said, without looking up. "I just don't want you riding in Parker's car when he's been drinking."

"I know."

"Hey!" Etienne called sharply. "They're here—they're coming!"

Even then, Miranda could hardly believe it. Even then, as she and Roo and Ashley jumped to their feet and saw Etienne signal with the flashlight. To her amazement, other lights were signaling back to them—flashing lights from police cars and ambulances, spinning lights from fire trucks—and there were sirens, and shouts, men running, confusion and chaos—

"*Parker!*" Ashley cried.

He grabbed her into his arms and held her, burying his face in her hair. His sides were heaving, his voice was hoarse. He looked completely drained. "I told you I'd come back."

"Yes—yes—you did. And don't you ever leave me again!"

"How's Gage? Is he—"

"He's alive, but it's bad, Parker; it's much worse. He hasn't woken up, and he's hardly breathing and—"

"It's okay, Ash, they'll take care of him now."

Releasing Ashley, Parker turned to Etienne. A look passed between them . . . a nod . . . a thousand silent words. As emergency teams swarmed around them, Parker spotted Miranda and caught her in a hug.

"God, Parker." Miranda's voice broke. "Are we glad to see you."

"Likewise. And you don't have to call me God. *Saint* Parker's good enough. Where's Roo?"

"Back there with—"

"Gage. Yeah, I see her."

The relief was overwhelming. Miranda had been so terrified, so determined not to cry, so intent on holding it together—at least till she could get home. Now suddenly there were paramedics wrapping her in blankets, examining her cuts and scrapes and bruises, asking her questions, passing her hot chocolate, and she felt so grateful and so relieved and just so glad to be alive . . .

"Oh, Roo," she whispered.

Because all at once she had a straight, clear view of Roo, and the view was heartbreaking. Roo, who was being quickly and efficiently forced out of the way as rescuers honed in on Gage's critical injuries. Roo, who was standing there alone, looking lost and scared and pathetically childlike . . .

"Roo!" Miranda called and started toward her.

But she realized then that the others had noticed, too. Ashley and Parker and Etienne, all of them hurrying in Roo's direction, though it was Parker who reached her first.

"So what'd you do?" he teased gently. "Take bets I wouldn't make it back?"

Despite her best attempt at annoyance, Roo's voice was shaking. "A girl can hope, can't she?"

"Hey, I came back to save you."

"Hey, you came back to spite me."

Parker ruffled her hair. Roo punched him in the abs. While the five of them watched Gage being carried away on a stretcher,

Parker slid his arm around Roo's shoulders. And Roo didn't pull away.

Dangerously close to tears again, Miranda sagged back against the wall and tried to collect herself. In all the commotion, she hadn't even noticed the woman running over to Etienne, but it was quickly apparent that the rest of the group knew her. They crowded in close, everyone talking at once, while the woman listened attentively, scrutinizing each bedraggled appearance, feeling every forehead, stroking every cheek.

"Miranda." Ashley motioned her over. "Come meet Etienne's mom."

She was small and delicate—almost frail in her oversize jacket, floppy wide-brimmed hat, and wading boots that reached up to her knees. She had Etienne's nose and Etienne's hair, and a knowing half-smile that was currently being leveled at her son. Catching his face between her hands, she held Etienne's gaze with her own. Her wide dark eyes caressed and scolded him. His eyes teased back and adored her.

"—want all y'all to get checked out, just in case," Etienne's mom was saying. "Your aunt Jules and uncle Frank will meet us at the hospital. Gage . . . our baby . . ."

Etienne whispered something that seemed to reassure her. She stepped back from him as Ashley touched her arm.

"Miss Nell," Ashley said, pulling Miranda over. "This is Miranda."

Miranda felt the instant appraisal of those coal-black eyes. When Nell Boucher took her hand, Miranda sensed strength, survival, and a heart of immense kindness.

"It's nice to meet you, Mrs. Boucher," she answered shyly.

"Nell," the woman corrected, a dimple showing at each corner of her mouth. She cocked an eyebrow at Etienne. "Okay, I guess you win the bet. She's just as cute as you said she was."

Blushing, Miranda was all too conscious of the others' amused stares. As she had with the rest of them, Miss Nell put one hand to Miranda's cheek and leaned in close.

"I'm glad we're finally meeting," she murmured. "Because I've certainly heard a lot of wonderful things about you."

Miranda was at a loss for words, but Miss Nell didn't seem to mind. Instead, the woman calmly herded the five of them together, then led them out through the storm to safety.

33

"OKAY, Y'ALL," ASHLEY ANNOUNCED. "This is our dress rehearsal. Our last chance to get everything perfect before the big night tomorrow. Any questions? Ideas? Opinions?"

"Yeah, I have an idea." Slumped on the front steps of the Battlefield Inn, Parker choked down a mouthful of cough syrup and tried not to speak above a whisper. "Let's call it off. That would *really* make it perfect. No more ghost tour."

"Walk of the Spirits," Ashley corrected him, irritated. "*Walk of the Spirits*. And we're *not* calling it off. After all this time? All this work?"

"All this suffering?" Roo added. She was perched one step below Parker, and was digging through her pockets for a cigarette. Her face still bore some major bruises from the storm, and a wide gash zigzagged across her forehead, not quite healed. She'd taken great pains to highlight this zigzag with dark, red lipstick.

"You *like* suffering," Parker reminded her. "And, excuse me, but *you're* not the one with pneumonia."

"You don't have pneumonia. You're just jealous because Gage was in worse shape than you, and he got more attention."

"Well, it's *almost* pneumonia. It's turning *into* pneumonia." Tensing, Parker let out a gigantic sneeze. "Shit, I hate this. I feel like my brain's ten times its normal size."

Roo gave him a bland stare. "You know, when people lose a leg or an arm, they think they still feel it, even though it's not really there."

"Will you two behave?" Ashley scolded. "And, Parker, where's that newspaper article your mom was going to give us?"

"Somewhere." Parker thought a moment, then shrugged. "In my car, I think."

"Well, will you please go get it? The sooner we start, the sooner we can all go home."

"She's right." Though unable to hold back a laugh, Miranda came loyally to Ashley's rescue. "Let's just walk it through, and read the script, and make sure we've covered all the basic information. Ashley, what about your costume?"

"I've got the final fitting after I leave here." Ashley's eyes shone with excitement. "Can you believe Mrs. Wilmington went to all that trouble to make it for me?"

"She didn't." Parker scowled. "She got her *dressmaker,* or *designer*, or *whoever* the hell she calls him, to make it for you."

"Parker, that doesn't matter—it was still really nice of your mother to do that."

"You're a southern belle—how could she resist that?"

Ashley shot Miranda a grateful smile. "That was Miranda's idea."

"It made sense," Miranda explained. "A costume sets the mood. It's all about southern history and heritage, so our tour guide should be a southern hostess—hoopskirt and all."

"And I'm the only one who gets to dress up! And I can't wait to wear it! It's like cotton candy!"

Roo arched an eyebrow. "Sticky?"

"No! All pink and fluffy and . . . sweet. I love the way I feel in it."

"I agree," Parker said hoarsely. "I love the way you feel in it, too. And I love the way you feel *out* of it even better."

Roo stared at him. "Wow. You should write greeting cards."

But before he could manage a comeback, Ashley stood on her tiptoes and started waving frantically toward the curb.

"There's Gage and Etienne! Hey, y'all! We weren't sure you were coming tonight! Gage, you are *just* looking better and better!"

Miranda watched the two guys climb from Etienne's truck and start up the sidewalk. Nearly three weeks had passed since that awful night of the storm, and though Gage wasn't fully recovered yet—his left leg was still in a cast—he could hobble unsteadily on crutches. And, Miranda noted, despite his lingering cuts, scrapes, and bruises, his eyes and his smile were just as irresistible as before.

"So we haven't missed anything?" Etienne greeted them. Leaving Gage at the bottom of the steps, he couldn't resist sprinting up and tapping Roo on her forehead. "Hey, love the scar. *Very* Bride of Frankenstein."

Roo looked pleased. Ashley was still focused intently on Gage.

"You're still kind of pale though," she worried, gazing at his face, running her finger along one of his cheekbones. "And your face is still pretty thin."

Gage glanced sideways, trying to avoid the attention. "I'm fine. My leg looks worse than it feels."

"No, it doesn't," Etienne teased him. "You're just being brave."

"No, I'm not. It really doesn't feel that bad."

"Well, at least you can feel *something* now," Parker remarked offhandedly. "The night you got hurt, you couldn't feel much of anything."

"I couldn't?"

"You mean, the girls didn't tell you?" Feigning concern, Parker shook his head. "Well, they had to . . . you know . . . *test* a lot of places on you. Just to see if you *could* still feel."

The flush had already started up Gage's cheeks.

"That's true," Roo agreed. "Of course . . . some places were a lot more fun to test than others."

"A *whole* lot more fun to test than others," Ashley insisted.

Gage's embarrassment reached full blush. Hiding a smile, Ashley pressed her palm to his forehead.

"But you're sure you feel fine now? Because you look a little hot."

"He *is* hot," Roo answered. "Oh. Oh, you meant his temperature."

"Stop," poor Gage mumbled. "I'm fine."

Etienne motioned to Ashley, his expression perfectly serious. "Come on. Y'all know how Gage is—he's suffering in silence 'cause he doesn't want to look weak in front of you women."

"Cut it out," Gage said.

"No, really. We all know you're just being modest."

"Shut up."

Roo fixed Gage with an owlish stare. "You cried when you broke your leg."

"I did not."

"Yes, you did. You cried. You're a crybaby."

The best Parker could offer was a sympathetic shrug. "Sorry, little soldier. You cried."

Gage looked longingly at the truck. Taking pity on him at last, the others stopped teasing and turned their attention back to their project.

In the days since the storm, they'd held many discussions about Nathan and Ellena Rose. Miranda had finally been able to offer them the insights she'd shared with Etienne that day—about the boardinghouse and the secret meetings, Nathan's and Ellena's work as spies and their passionate love, their promise made with the watch and chain, and finally—most important—the tragic truth of the betrayal. Everyone except Parker had been captivated by her story. Everyone except Parker had insisted Hayes House be added to their tour. All of them had speculated as to where Jonas might have put the watch, but none of their guesses had panned out. And though the whereabouts of Nathan's watch remained a mystery, Miranda was still determined to find it and reunite it with the braid of Ellena's hair.

Now, preparing to rehearse their ghostly tour, Miranda was still thinking about her grandpa and the long-ago tragedy he'd passed on to her. She'd hoped to have all the questions answered by now . . . the puzzle pieces together . . . the spirits at peace. *So close . . . but not there yet . . .*

"I wish we could put Nathan and Ellena and Travis on our walk." Ashley sighed. "It just doesn't seem complete without them."

"They're on our walk." Taking Ashley's notebook, Roo calmly pointed to the neatly lettered, neatly organized tour script. "See? Right here. Magnolia Gallery. Opera house fire."

"That's not what I meant. Each of them really, really loved somebody very much. That's what I want people to remember." Ashley put a hand over her heart. "The loves that never die."

"The loves that *made* people die." Parker downed another swig of cough medicine, capped the bottle, then slid it into the back pocket of his jeans. "Sorry, Ash, but that's not the way of the world. If you tell their real stories, people will only remember all the dumb mistakes they made. Like . . . oh, you know . . . torture and murder and arson and treason and—"

"Ah, yes," Roo acknowledged coolly. "Parker Wilmington, the last of the true romantics."

Retrieving her notebook, Ashley hugged it to her chest. Her sigh was more wistful this time. "I know you're right. I mean, we can't ever give away their real secrets. Not on the Walk of the Spirits . . . not to anybody . . . not ever. I mean, Nathan and Ellena and Travis lived and sacrificed and died, protecting those secrets about themselves. If *we* told their secrets, it would be like betraying them all over again."

"Or we could call the tabloids and paparazzi," Parker deadpanned. "They pay big money for secrets and betrayals."

"Parker Wilmington, if I told even *half* your secrets and betrayals, I'd be a very rich woman!"

Even Parker looked amused as the group broke into raucous applause. Looking entirely pleased with herself, Ashley curtsied, then motioned them all toward the Brickway.

"I'm going to be so nervous tomorrow," Ashley confessed, linking her arm through Miranda's. "What if our whole class hates it?"

"Then I'll say I told you so," Parker replied. Roo, Gage, and Etienne had moved several feet ahead to argue something about the script. Hanging back, Parker tried to swallow, but winced at the effort. "Anybody got anything stronger than cough syrup?"

When no one responded, he pointed to his BMW parked along the opposite curb. "You know what? As sad as I know this will make you, ladies, I'm going home and to bed. Alone."

"Parker—"

"Oh, yeah, right—I've got that stupid article in my car. Go on ahead. I'll give it to Miranda."

"Parker, do you really feel that terrible?"

"Christ, Ashley, my throat's like raw hamburger. Is that terrible enough for you believe me?"

The suspicion on Ashley's face turned to guilt, and Miranda felt just as bad. They both knew Parker had gotten sick trying to save them. Maybe he wasn't faking so much after all.

As Ashley caught up to the others, Miranda followed Parker across the street.

Dusk had fallen, and shadows lay deep. While Parker grabbed an envelope from the glove box, Miranda watched Ashley and the others talking beneath a lamppost on the corner . . . heard their muffled laughter and conversation.

"Miranda?" Parker said suddenly.

Startled, Miranda saw him turn around. In the dim light, something in his face caught her attention. Something like bewilderment . . . or even fear . . .

"Parker, what is it?"

He handed her the envelope. After a brief hesitation, he leaned slowly against the side of his car. "Miranda, I just wanted . . . needed to tell you."

"Tell me what"

"Damn. This is . . . really hard."

A spark of worry flared inside her. "Parker, *tell* me. What's wrong?"

"Something happened that night, Miranda." Another short pause before he spoke again. "In the storm."

"What do you mean?"

"When I left y'all there at the shelter, and I tried to get to Etienne's house."

"But you *did* get there. You brought back help, and you saved us."

"I didn't." His voice dropped to a whisper. "I didn't."

"Parker—"

"I mean, I *did.* But not like everybody thinks."

She realized she was shaking. She realized Parker was shaking, too, and there was something unnerving about his stare.

"I got lost," he mumbled. "I got so lost, I didn't have a clue where I was or what direction I was headed. And it was shit-awful scary out there."

As though the memory were too much for him, he sank to the curb and squatted back on his heels.

"The flashlight was like nothing. *Nothing.* And suddenly I just stepped off—tripped—I don't know, the ground just disappeared, and I went down. And I thought, This is it: I'm drowning; I'm going to die."

She gazed at him sympathetically, but he avoided her eyes. His words were tight with emotion. "And then . . . something happened. I . . ."

"Parker?"

"I swear to God, Miranda, there was this light. Like a flashlight, only . . . only *not* a flashlight. More like a lantern, I guess . . . and this . . . I don't know . . . *something* just sort of floated out of the rain, floated right out of the storm toward me. I could feel it on the back of my neck, and on my shoulders—and it grabbed me under my arms and pulled me out."

Parker's hands clenched into fists. He pressed them hard against his temples. "I heard this voice . . . this voice sort of talking, sort of singing. And it sounded . . . like a woman's voice."

"Was the voice familiar? Did you recognize her?"

"No." Adamantly, Parker shook his head. "But she called me Nathan."

34

Miranda went ice cold. As she and Parker locked eyes, time seemed to halt around them.

"And then . . ." Parker drew a ragged breath. "I was totally free. And the lantern sort of . . . *moved* . . . like somebody was swinging it, you know? Waving it in one direction?"

"What happened next?"

"Hell, I ran, swam—both. I was so damn scared, and so damn glad to be alive."

He'd turned his head away. His voice was hollow now, and she had to strain to hear.

"And then it was like I kicked into autopilot or something—I didn't even think about where I was going, I just went straight to Etienne's house. It was like I'd been dreaming, and then I woke up, and I was just *there.* And I found his mom, and she got help—"

Parker's words choked off. For an endless moment neither he nor Miranda spoke.

Then, at last, he looked at her again. Gave a sheepish smile, gave a strained, self-conscious laugh. "So what, am I crazy?"

"No." Reaching out, Miranda firmly took his hand. "No, Parker, you're not. Not at all."

Another laugh, more hoarse this time. He tried to clear

his throat. His nose was running, and his eyes shone with embarrassed tears; he wiped one sleeve angrily across his cheeks. On a sudden impulse, Miranda threw her arms around him.

"What's that for?" Parker asked, both flustered and surprised.

"Just . . ." Miranda pulled back again. She gazed anxiously into his eyes. "Parker . . . you saw it. You saw it was real."

He wanted to forget about it, she could tell. He'd opened himself and shown her his fears, and now he wanted to forget it ever happened. *But you won't forget, Parker. You'll never forget. I've been there. I know.*

"You believe me," she whispered.

"Okay, fine, I believe you."

His stare, always so bold, faltered a little. He tilted his head back and made a frustrated sound in his throat.

"We're not going to be like best girlfriends now, are we?" he accused her. "I mean, you're not going to be squealing at me every time somebody says the word *ghost*, are you?"

"Of course not."

"Because . . . I swear to God, Miranda, if you *ever* tell *anybody*—"

Miranda hugged him tighter. "I won't tell a soul."

"A *soul*? Is that supposed to be funny?"

"I won't tell anyone. I'm just hugging you because you're you."

"Yeah, I get that a lot. Girls want to *love* me, and guys want to *be* me."

Another coughing spasm racked through him. Catching his breath, he shifted away from her, reached wearily for his back pocket, and pulled out the bottle of medicine. Miranda saw him fumble it between his fingers—she heard the sharp clink as it fell and struck the curb.

"Oh shit," Parker muttered. "There goes my fix."

But the bottle hadn't broken. Instead it began to roll slowly into the street, turning over and over . . . over and over—a rhythmic, monotonous sound.

That sound . . .

And Miranda realized she *knew* that sound—or something very like it—it was *familiar*, she'd heard it before . . . *but when? Where?*

"Parker?"

"Yeah?" He'd gotten up now, gone after his bottle of cough syrup. With one smooth motion he scooped it up, unscrewed the top, and took a satisfied gulp.

"Parker, I . . ." *Something . . . I know it's there . . . I want to remember . . .* "I want you to take me home."

Parker froze, the bottle at his lips, poised for another swallow. He shot her a sidelong glance.

"This is so sudden, Miranda. I mean, we hardly know each other, and I *do* have a girlfriend. And there *is*, of course, the issue of my extremely high moral standards. But . . . okay. What the hell. I'll take you home with me."

"Not *your* home. *My* home. Hayes House."

"What? Hayes House? Oh! Sure! Hayes House! Did you think I meant—that I wanted to—hey, I was just kidding!"

The irreverence was there again, the cocky grin back in place. As Miranda climbed into the passenger seat, Parker slid behind the wheel, then gunned the engine to breakneck speed. In less than five minutes they were squealing into the driveway of Hayes House. But even when Parker reached across and shoved open her door, Miranda made no move to get out.

"Let me guess." Parker watched her expectantly. "You really *do* want to go home with me. You were just playing hard to get."

Slowly Miranda shook her head. She gazed down at the envelope in her lap. "I forgot to give this to Ashley."

"Forget it. Why the big rush to get here?"

The sound . . . the rolling sound . . . it's close . . . it's important. "I'm not sure, Parker. There's . . . something—"

"No. Don't tell me. Whatever it is, I don't want to see it, hear it, or go through it ever again."

Getting out of the car, Miranda walked a few steps before turning back to face him. "But aren't you even curious about what happened to you out in the storm? Don't you even want to explore all the—"

"Stop right there. There's lots of things I *want* to explore, and things I most definitely *will* explore. But ghosts aren't one of them. See you later."

She watched him back down the driveway. Within seconds, the BMW had faded from sight, yet the sound—*that sound!*—stayed with her. Parker's bottle of cough syrup rolling out into the street . . . *that rhythmic, monotonous sound . . .*

Why did it seem so familiar? Nagging her and bringing back memories—*except I don't know what the memories are! They're right here, close enough to touch, and deep inside, but I can't reach them!*

Frustrated, she went into the house. Mom and Aunt Teeta had gone out to eat; she was glad to have the whole place to herself. Within seconds she found herself upstairs in her grandpa's room, surrounded by so many things, so many connections to so many worlds . . .

Help me, Grandpa. Nathan . . . Ellena Rose . . . help me.

The room was silent, yet full of echoes. Ghostly whispers from forgotten voices . . . desperate pleas from her grandfather . . . comforting words from Etienne . . .

"Help me, Etienne," she murmured.

"*Whatever it was that Jonas found, he'd have kept it close to him,*" Etienne had insisted.

Especially if it was your last treasure, your last quest, your last responsibility—right, Grandpa?

She walked to the nightstand. Not much had been moved in this room since the death of Jonas Hayes. As her eyes did a sweep of her surroundings, as her hands slid over the nightstand, her mind spun back to that day she'd been in here—*that day I first met Grandpa. He was asleep; I was curious, looking through all his stuff. I touched something, some kind of container, and Grandpa looked at me, and something fell on the floor . . .*

A tin. I remember now.

It rolled under the dresser, and Grandpa spoke to me, and when Etienne came, I forgot about the tin, and I never picked it up again . . .

Her heart raced out of control. She reached under the antique dresser, groped along the hardwood floor. Her fingers closed around a small, round canister.

It rolled when she touched it.

Rocking back on her heels, she pried the round lid from the tin. Her hands were trembling so violently, she could barely lift the old pocket watch from its wrapping of yellowed cloth.

Oh my God . . .

It was as though she held something alive. Something that swelled through her heart and coursed through her veins and burst into a thousand different emotions. Tears flowed down her cheeks, and she touched a fingertip carefully to the tiny spring latch.

The top clicked open. The rusted hinge gave way.

Through shimmering tears, she saw the tiny scrap of paper that fell out into her palm. Very slowly, she began to unfold it, piece by painstaking piece, all too aware of the delicate memories she was holding.

Even after all this time . . .

The delicate memories, and fragile lives, and long-ago brittle promises, all of them crumbling into dust between her fingertips.

Yet the message itself remained.

Six simple words, binding two hearts forever:

Nathan, I love you,

Your Ellena.

35

"What if nobody comes?" Ashley wrung her hands.

"They'll show up," Roo assured her.

"If nobody shows up, it'll be my absolute worst nightmare."

Blowing his nose into a tissue, Parker looked up with bleary eyes. "And if you don't stop talking about it, it'll be *my* absolute worst nightmare."

"Parker Wilmington, how can you say that? For the millionth time, this counts for half our grade. And we can't very well have a Walk of the Spirits if there's nobody to walk with."

Miranda opted for practicality. "Well, we know Miss Dupree and our class will be here. And I know my mom and Aunt Teeta are coming."

"My folks, too," Gage added. "And some of the other kids at school—they said they were interested."

"Yeah. In laughing at us." Flopping into a chair, Parker slid low on his spine. His voice was even hoarser than yesterday, and he winced each time he tried to talk. "Shit, I'll be glad when this is over."

Etienne struggled to keep a straight face. "How come? You scared you might see a real ghost?"

Miranda caught the fierce, accusing glare Parker shot her. But when Parker read the honest bewilderment on her face, he forced a painful laugh. "Right. Good one, Boucher. Real ghosts. Very funny."

The six of them were in the lobby of the Battlefield Inn. While the others scanned last-minute notes and details of the tour script, Ashley was practically wearing out a path in the carpet.

"I'm just so nervous!" Taking the old-fashioned lantern Miranda handed her, she held it high above her head. "Oh, Miranda, carrying this was another wonderful idea of yours! And just look at my dress! Do I look okay?"

Roo gave her sister a bland appraisal. The southern belle gown was an airy, pastel confection of satin and lace and taffeta. "You look . . . pink. Pink and . . . pink. And—"

"Beautiful," Gage broke in. "You look beautiful, Ash."

"So sit yourself down," Etienne ordered. "Before I *hold* you down."

Sticking her tongue out at him, Ashley kept right on pacing, oblivious to her wide hoopskirt sweeping everything in its path—including Gage. Catching himself just in time, Gage backed out of her way and tried to realign his crutches. As Roo slyly tapped his left crutch with the toe of her combat boot, he shot her a warning glance.

"Don't make me teach you a lesson." He sighed.

"As if you could. In the shape you're in."

"Well, in case you've forgotten—you're the reason I'm *in* this shape."

Roo lounged slowly back in her seat. She fixed Gage with a long, unwavering stare. "I told Miranda you and I had sex."

The room went silent.

Everyone froze. And turned. And looked at Gage.

"I—you—what—" A slow, hot blush crept over Gage's cheeks. His eyes widened in disbelief. "Roo—I—you—"

"Gross!" Parker shuddered. "*Way* too much information!"

"*Valuable* information, *cher*." Etienne winked at Roo. "Girls at school, they'll pay a whole lotta money to find out if Gage has any *other* dimples."

While Ashley collapsed in giggles, Miranda tried her best not to laugh. Groaning softly, Gage ducked his head.

"Oh, look!" Ashley let out a sudden squeal. "Look, y'all! I see some people outside! I think they're coming over!"

It was true. After weeks and weeks of painstaking study and planning and rehearsing, opening night was finally here. St. Yvette's first Walk of the Spirits.

"They *are* coming!" Ashley exclaimed. "See, Roo, I knew they'd show up."

Dusk was settling over the Brickway. The air was warm, with a balmy breeze and the skies downy gray. No threat of rain, just a pale sprinkling of stars. Even the Historic District seemed different tonight, Miranda couldn't help thinking. Soft with shadows . . . hushed with secrets . . . sweetly sentimental with memories.

And tonight we'll remember Nathan and Ellena.

Tonight they'll be together again.

She hadn't told the others about finding the watch . . . she hadn't even told Etienne.

She wanted to surprise them.

And she wanted the moment to be just right.

"There's Miss Dupree!" As Parker joined Ashley at the window, the girl bounced eagerly on her tiptoes, using his arm for leverage. "Oh my God—it looks like our whole class is really here."

Parker scowled. "She probably bribed them. She probably told them she'd give them A's on all their projects if they came and walked through ours."

"And there's the principal—and assistant principal—Oh, there's lots of teachers here, too!"

Mildly curious, Roo squeezed in between Ashley and Parker. "Hey, Boucher, there's your mama. And Miss Jules and Mr. Frank. Oh, and Miranda, there's your mom and your aunt Teeta . . . and our folks."

Though no one said it, the absence of the Wilmingtons was painfully obvious. Parker shrugged and turned back from the window. Disappointment settled on the other five faces around him.

"Well," Parker managed a croak. "Better light up your lantern, Miss Ashley. It's showtime."

Ashley stared. Her eyes went saucer-wide, and she clutched her stomach. "I don't think I can go out there, y'all. There's too many people!"

As the others stared back at her, Etienne made a strangling motion with his hands. "Shall I do the honors? Or does *everybody* want a turn?"

He and Parker promptly escorted Ashley out the door. Roo fell into step beside Miranda, with Gage bringing up the rear.

"Just watch her." Roo's tone held mild but sincere admiration. "She's a pro."

Roo was right. As Ashley swept onto the steps, an audible sigh went through the crowd. Ashley dipped and swayed, both sweet and seductive, her voice flowing honey-warm.

"Why, welcome, y'all. Welcome to our Walk of the Spirits."

And so it went. Step by entertaining step along the Brickway, Ashley enticed and enthralled and utterly charmed the tour group. The history and heritage of St. Yvette came magically alive.

"Well," Etienne mumbled to Miranda as they trailed a watchful distance behind the crowd, "they're looking scared at all the right times. And they're laughing at all the right jokes. That's a good sign, yeah?"

"It's better than good," Miranda agreed with him. "It's great. It's unbelievable."

"She threatened them," Parker muttered, jerking his chin toward Miss Dupree. "I knew it! Damn! She bribed them *and* she threatened them."

"No, I don't think so," Miranda said truthfully. "I think it's really the subject matter. It's all so fascinating. And Ashley, of course. She's also fascinating."

"Look at her," Roo pointed out. "Didn't I tell you? She's got every single one of them in the palm of her hand."

Etienne couldn't resist. "You mean right where she's got Parker?"

"Well," Roo shot Parker a look. "Of course, some conquests are much easier than others. Especially with species of primitive brain."

"Is she just talking about Parker?" Etienne raised an eyebrow at Gage. "Or you and me, too?"

The Walk of the Spirits moved on. Through the velvety nightfall, by the eerie glow of lantern light, came haunting and heartbreaking tales. An evil judge and his tortured victims. A kindly doctor, a grave-robbing undertaker, and a mysterious, deadly epidemic. The eternal screams of a child plunging from a nursery window. Curses, spells, and grisly sacrifices; secret voodoo rites. The silent processions and eerie chantings of spectral monks. And finally . . . sorrowfully . . . a ghostly song, the ghostly sobs, from a long-ago opera house.

"As y'all know, this is Magnolia Gallery," Ashley explained. "But what y'all probably *don't* know is that during the war, an opera house stood in this very spot. An opera house with a sad and tragic history. It was called the Rose—for the beautiful red-haired diva who sang there. Her name was Ellena Rose, and whenever she performed, red roses lined the carriageway and spilled from every door and window. Though many men pursued her, Ellena loved only Nathan—a stable boy. But their happiness was not meant to be. One foggy southern morning—and unknown to Ellena—Nathan was mortally wounded. And when the opera house went up in flames that night, Ellena perished in the fire, calling for her sweetheart, who never came."

The tour group was mesmerized. There were gasps, sorrowful murmurs, and muffled tears.

"And sometimes . . ." Pausing dramatically, Ashley raised her lantern. "Sometimes you can hear the soft, sad singing from the opera house. Or see the pale glow of a lantern in the fog. As Ellena Rose searches eternally for her one true love."

Tenderly, Miranda's thoughts reached out. *We'll keep your secrets, Ellena. Your secrets and Nathan's secrets. Forever.*

"Excuse me! Wasn't there something about a watch?" Miranda asked loudly.

Startled, Ashley turned to look at her. Miranda saw the confusion on Ashley's face, her quick, anxious glance at the script. *No, Ashley, it's not written in there—nothing about the watch or the chain.* Etienne was studying Miranda with a shrewd gaze. Gage and Parker exchanged bewildered glances. Roo seemed to be assessing the reactions of everyone else in the crowd.

"Watch?" Ashley echoed, expression totally blank. "You mean . . . like . . . a pocket watch?"

Eagerly, Miranda nodded. "And wasn't there something about a watch chain?"

She had everyone's attention now. All around her, people's faces were tightening with curiosity. Ashley made a helpless gesture to Gage, who was still intent on Miranda. And then, very slowly, Gage began to smile.

"Yes," Miranda said seriously. "I heard this legend once. About Nathan and Ellena exchanging tokens of their love. That Nathan gave her a watch—like this one. And Ellena Rose gave him a chain—a braided chain—like this."

Calmly she pulled both objects from the pockets of her jeans. The tour group seemed intrigued, but her friends gasped out loud.

"Miranda!"

"Oh my God—"

"Where the hell—"

"I don't believe it!"

"You did it, *cher*. I knew you would."

"Just like Nathan and Ellena, the watch and chain are meant to go together," Miranda went on, holding both treasures up so the crowd could see. "One attaches to the other. So they don't get lost."

With her five friends gathered close, Miranda carefully, gently, connected Nathan's watch to the chain of Ellena's hair. Her fingers shook; her heart shed silent tears. And the onlookers, respectfully observing, could only wonder at this fragile, timeless moment they'd just been allowed to share.

May you have happiness, Nathan and Ellena . . .

May you have understanding . . .

May you have peace.

Somehow, Miranda knew they would.

Wiping away tears, Ashley recovered herself and motioned to the crowd. Once more she led them by lantern light through the magical darkness and into the quiet past.

They were nearing Hayes House now. As the group turned off the Brickway and onto the side street, Miranda purposefully lagged behind. Soft lights glowed from the Hayes House veranda and out across the lawn, and it dawned on her that she was smiling again.

I thought I'd never be happy here.

She stopped to gaze up at the windows. And back toward the stone wall that bordered the long-ago battlefield.

"Help us . . . we're lost . . . we want to go home . . ."

"Yes," she whispered. "I'll help you. And I'll listen. And I won't turn you away."

Because, after all, there was time. All the time in the world.

All the time in both our worlds.

Miranda lifted her head into the sweet, southern breeze . . .

And smelled roses.